Shot by Both Sides

SHOT BY BOTH SIDES

A Novel

Meisei Goto,
translated by Tom Gill

COUNTERPOINT · BERKELEY

Copyright © 1973 by Akiko Goto. English Translation © 2008 Thomas P. Gill
All rights reserved under International and Pan-American Copyright Conventions.

Originally published in Japanese by Kawade Shobo Shinsha Publishers, Tokyo.
All rights reserved.

Library of Congress Cataloging-in-Publication Data

Goto, Meisei, 1932–
 [Hasamiuchi. English]
 Shot by both sides : a novel / Meisei Goto ; translated by Tom Gill.
    p. cm.
 "Originally published in Japanese by Kawade Shobo Shinsha Publishers,
Tokyo"—ECIP t.p. verso.
 Selected by the Japanese Literature Publishing Project.
  ISBN–13: 978-1-58243-433-9
  ISBN–10: 1-58243-433-6
  I. Gill, Tom. II. Title.
  PL851.O83H313 2008
  895.6'35—dc22   2008013095

ISBN (10) 1-58243-433-6
ISBN (13) 978-1-58243-433-9

Cover and interior design by Gopa & Ted2, Inc.
Printed in the United States of America

This book has been selected by the Japanese Literature Publishing Project (JLPP), which is run by the Japanese Literature Publishing and Promotion Center (J-Lit Center) on behalf of the Agency for Cultural Affairs of Japan.

COUNTERPOINT
2117 Fourth Street
Suite D
Berkeley, CA 94710

www.counterpointpress.com

Distributed by Publishers Group West

10 9 8 7 6 5 4 3 2 1

Contents

Chapter 1

IT HAPPENED ONE DAY. I suddenly remembered a bird. And not just any old bird—it was the early bird. *The early bird catches the worm.* Or as we say in Japanese, "early rising is threepence to the good." I was standing on a bridge in Ochanomizu. It was early evening. Probably just before six.

It was crowded in front of Ochanomizu station. That narrow strip of gently sloping asphalt was exceedingly restless. Whether you're coming out of the ticket gate or heading into it, it's a place where you can't stop and stand still for a moment. And indeed, nobody does stand still. You're on the go while you buy your newspaper or magazine from the kiosk; you're on the go as you accept leaflets from the various helmeted student radicals.

There's a spot with a row of public telephones, and then a few bus stops and the taxi stand. Of course it's crowded on the bridge as well. All the same, isn't "Ochanomizu" an elegant name for a station? *Ochanomizu*! "Tea water." It's a crossroads for students. I seem to recall that a few years ago the students tried to occupy the whole area around here. They were out to turn the place into a liberated zone—they donned helmets, hid their faces with towels, brought their clubs with them and clashed head-on with the Tokyo Metropolitan Riot Police. But it wasn't long before they had to give the plan up. Turns out it's against the rules to play in the streets. It's a breach of regulations to draw up battle lines in the street. And needless to say, it's even more forbidden to fling homemade explosive devices such as Molotov cocktails. In short the Ochanomizu district, with its exceedingly elegantly named station, did not become a liberated zone. It did, however, continue to be a crossroads for students.

The bridge straddles the railway lines. What's the name of this bridge? Ochanomizu Bridge? Probably. But I wasn't the kind of person to take the trouble to walk from the middle of the bridge where I was standing just to try and confirm the point. It's simply that one fine day it occurred to me that I didn't know the name of the bridge although I was standing right on it.

Suddenly the name "Shirahige Bridge" came to my lips. Azuma Bridge, Komagata Bridge, and was it, er, Genmori Bridge? They're all names from Kafu Nagai's *A Strange Tale from East of the River*, of course. Isaakievsky Bridge. That's the one in Gogol's "The Nose." It's the bridge where Yakovlevich the barber went, after he found the nose of Collegiate Assessor Kovalyov in his bread roll at breakfast, wrapped it in a bit of old cloth, and furtively set out to try and get rid of it. Bridges do need names for sure. When Kafu was sneaking through the alleys and back streets of Tokyo, doing his best to avoid the police on his way to Terajima-machi, it wouldn't be very interesting to say he just crossed "a bridge." Yakovlevich the barber was afraid of being spotted by the police too. After all, what he had surreptitiously wrapped in a rag and hidden in his pocket was nothing more or less than the nose of a collegiate assessor. And I guess the bridge from which he finally managed to chuck that rag-wrapped nose into the Neva River just had to be Isaakievsky Bridge. It wouldn't be too interesting to say "a certain bridge in Saint Petersburg."

It's not just bridges. All those alleys and lanes that Kafu slipped through—deliberately dressed in gardening trousers and old-woman-style wooden sandals, and hatless to conform to the customs of the men who haunted Terajima-machi—they all had names too. However narrow and obscure those alleyways might be, they still had names. At any rate I bet *he* knew them. Even if they really were nameless alleyways, the reader would believe Kafu knew their names. The same with the tale of the barber hiding the rag-wrapped nose in his pocket. What enviable novels! Truth is, I'd love to write all those names of bridges and lanes and alleyways myself. Can't help wishing I could write novels with colorful names like that scattered all over them.

In reality, however, the situation was that I didn't even know the name of the bridge I was standing on. Partly it's because I'm a boy from the boondocks. The boondocks? Yep, leave it at that for the moment. Truth is, my ignorance of bridges doesn't stop with this one. I don't know Shirahige Bridge, Azuma Bridge, Komagata Bridge or Genmori Bridge either. Not that I haven't crossed them—I probably have, without knowing it. Only myself to blame, of course. It all stems from personal reasons. At the same time it's fair to say that Tokyo itself tends to throw me into confusion. In a nutshell, Tokyo has countless bridges without rivers. What on earth would happen if you tried to name all those pedestrian footbridges that have been put up to get you from one side of the road to the other? Of course, someone would turn up who could remember every single one of the names. Someone would try and memorize the whole lot, just to show he could do it. But would Kafu name that kind of bridge in his novels? I just can't picture Kafu crossing a four-lane highway on a pedestrian footbridge en route to the Terajima-machi pleasure district. That is, well, it's obvious really, but I can't write about bridges like Kafu did. Or at any rate I'm not qualified to imitate him. And it's not just the rivers—the whole of Tokyo is covered with countless nameless bridges.

Still—there's no point grumbling about it now. Since you can't very well part the waves of the traffic with your hands and feet, you can't live without crossing these nameless bridges. Of course that's not exactly a new discovery of mine. It's just common sense. And it's no use trying to apply the same logic to lots of different things. Because even if it's true that Tokyo is covered with bridges lacking rivers and names, the bridge I'm actually standing on at the moment surely *does* have some kind of name. It's just that while standing on the bridge I happen to have forgotten the bridge's name. On the other hand, on the bridge I did remember the early bird. So I don't think it would be any great sin if I now decided to call this bridge Early Bird Bridge.

The bus to the university sets out from a stop on this bridge. Actually I got on that bus myself, just once. It was exactly twenty years ago. I got on that bus and set out to take the early bird exam. I never once got on that bus again. Because I didn't need to.

Translate the following Japanese sentence into English:
"Early rising is threepence to the good."

I couldn't write a single word in the answer box. "The early bird catches the worm." A pathetically simple sentence. But you know, gentlemen, life is like that—terribly simple and hard to cheat! Not that anyone's going to say "Yes, sir!" when I say "Gentlemen" . . . The life of a man who just happens to be standing around on a bridge cannot, of course, have anything whatever to do with the lives of you gentlemen of the present age. Because you gentlemen haven't the faintest idea who on earth I might be. Still, if by chance, while passing me by, you gentlemen happened to feel just a fleeting interest in the question of who on earth I might be, it would be because of my overcoat.

Not that it's a particularly eccentric overcoat, one that might catch the eye. In a word, it's a very ordinary overcoat. Though it's just possible it might catch someone's eye as being *too* ordinary. You see, nowadays in our capital city, in Tokyo, the custom of wearing an ordinary overcoat like this has disappeared. I wonder when it can possibly have happened? I can't rightly say. I guess you might get a precise answer if you asked some scholar of fashion, or the head of the clothing department at a department store. The only thing a layman can say is, it came about when respectable buildings started to be equipped with central heating. That, and the fact that you'd drive from building to building in a heated car. Oh, and you might add that every year since Japan lost the war, Tokyo's winters have become warmer. We no longer see the kind of snow that fell that February 26, the day of the military coup. That's the generally accepted view of the matter.

I'm not too well up on what they call the things most people have taken to wearing instead of overcoats these days. It's already been quite a while since those frock coat affairs with hip belts came into fashion—what do you call them, trench coats? I also seem to remember hearing talk of "three-season coats." But both of those were quite a while ago, so I don't suppose they're still in fashion today. And as for the things people wear instead of overcoats nowadays, well—I couldn't put a name to them.

By the way, sorry to bring it up all of a sudden, but what exactly is the connection between cold weather and hemorrhoids? Fortunately I am not afflicted with that particular ailment myself, but there are more than a few men in my circle of acquaintances who do suffer from it. I know of a certain writer of detective novels, handsome enough to appear in television commercials after submitting to the blandishments of a company that manufactures and markets raincoats, and he too suffers from piles. They're the novelist's great enemy. Apparently he even thought of imitating that American writer who shot himself with a hunting rifle, who used to stand up to do his writing, but in the end he had to give it up. You see, he had to write his lines vertically rather than horizontally, and besides, the American author was using a typewriter. There was nothing for it but to sit on a little doughnut-shaped cushion, a shade smaller than a child's swim ring, and I gather he even used to carry it about with him when he went out, until one day he had an operation in which, to use his own words, a thing "about the size of a small pickle jar" was extracted from him. Then there's the head of the labor union at a certain major publishing house . . . and a scholar of French literature, whose languid, elegant hand gesture—brushing away his hair when it falls softly across his face—seems to suit him so well . . . it would appear there's no connection between this ailment and a man's personal appearance. I expect the same goes for the ladies.

Anyway—is there any connection with cold weather? I ask because, as you know, the hero of Gogol's "The Overcoat," Akaky Akakievich Bashmachkin, had hemorrhoids. We're told this was the fault of the climate in that great northern capital, Saint Petersburg. Mind you, Akaky's piles have absolutely no connection with the story of "The Overcoat." Akaky was a Perpetual Titular Officer in a certain government building in Saint Petersburg. Copying documents was his job. Actually it was more than a job. He had a number of favorite letters in the Russian alphabet, and whenever he came across one of them in a document he'd experience a matchless ecstasy. If he ran out of time, he would take the documents home to his apartment and carry on copying until he was satisfied. That was his whole life. Because you see, although Akaky was over fifty, he was still unmarried and living in a cheap apartment.

The only thing that troubled him was his worn-out overcoat. It was no longer up to the job of protecting him from Saint Petersburg's cold winds. The fellows at work laughed at his overcoat, calling it a dressing gown. That was a kind of demotion, like someone being demoted from human to monkey. But what really made Akaky despair was not this demotion suffered at the hands of his work-mates, but Petrovich the tailor's words when he asked him to patch it again. *This overcoat is so worn out that it won't take the needle any-more*—that was Petrovich's announcement.

It turned out, however, that the tailor's announcement brought Akaky an unexpected new dream. Akaky gave up drinking tea in his apartment. It was an economy measure, to save money for a new overcoat. He gave up sending his clothes to the laundry; he gave up lighting his room. If he needed light he would use a corner of the room belonging to the old granny who was his landlady. He'd walk as lightly as possible when out in the street—to avoid wearing out the soles of his shoes. This austere life wasn't a misery for Akaky, how-ever. On the contrary, it gave his life fresh meaning. He spent his days dreaming of the new overcoat, feeling like a bridegroom eagerly counting off the days until he meets his bride.

So it's only natural that when the new overcoat was stolen off him the very day it was finally finished, he lost all hope in life. And that's no exaggeration. His overcoat really was his life, you see. When he arrived at work in his new overcoat, it was as if he'd had his rights restored, just like his coat that had once been demoted to monkey status. But in an instant the overcoat was ripped off him by someone. He followed the advice of his workmates and went to petition an Important Person for assistance. But all he got was a scolding, and he collapsed on the spot. He breathed his last a few days later, in his own apartment. Not long after, a rumor started to spread that Akaky's ghost had been turning up night after night, all over the city. It was haunting Saint Petersburg. The ghost, it was said, would tear the overcoat off the back of any passerby. Among the victims, of course, was the Important Person. But right after he was attacked, the ghost ceased to appear. The Important Person's overcoat, Gogol writes, was evidently a perfect fit for the body of the ghost.

Don't think I'm standing here on Early Bird Bridge to tell some passerby the story of "The Overcoat," however. No, I'm waiting here on this bridge to meet a man called Yamakawa. I arranged to meet him at six o'clock on the bridge. Mind you, the fact I did that doesn't mean I have any connection with the passersby. I'm nothing more than a forty-year-old man wearing an ordinary overcoat. One day, a forty-year-old man in an ordinary overcoat strolls over a bridge. Needless to say, a bridge is something to cross—from this side to that or (as the case may be) from that side to this. But you can't entirely rule out the possibility that the man will suddenly stop somewhere near the middle of the bridge. Why? The man himself doesn't know, of course, but suddenly, around the middle of the bridge, he brings both feet to a halt. I don't think you can state categorically that there's no such person. It would be as if since birth a fellow had thought of nothing but walking around and suddenly thought: human beings can also stop and stand. I too might appear to be such a man. It wouldn't bother me at all if I did.

I don't suppose people will notice my slightly-more-than-usually ordinary overcoat, either. Akaky Akakievich had a cat-fur collar on his dream-like new overcoat. Unfortunately he couldn't afford sable, but from a distance cat fur looks like sable. Of course there's no sable on the collar of my own overcoat. Nor seal skin, or raccoon or cat fur. The color, too, is an extremely subdued, intermediate shade somewhere between grey and blue. But it's made of pretty classy material—pure wool—and although it isn't hand-tailored, it is Made in England.

I'm not the kind of person who makes a fuss about what he wears. My suit, shirt and shoes, in fact all my clothes except the overcoat, are manufactured domestically. My suit's tailor-made, admittedly, but that has nothing to do with aesthetic demands. The upper part of my body is apparently bent to the right. One tailor described it as twisted. He asked me if I ever used a bow and arrow, but I couldn't recall having drawn back a bow hard enough to twist my upper body out of shape. So though the cause of the problem is unclear, if I wear ready-made clothing it looks, apparently, as if someone had hung the clothes on a tilting coat hanger. And it's not just the looks—it *feels* really uncomfortable too. It's not that my right shoulder slopes, in the usual sense of the word. It's not twisted downwards so much as backwards. Or else, my left shoulder's twisted forwards. Either way, there's definitely some twisting there. But I can cope with the shirts and jackets relatively easily. The problem is the trousers. It's extremely difficult for me to walk around in those ready-made trousers with their diagonally stitched pockets. Is it because my legs are short? I'm about five foot five and my shoe size is six-and-a-half. I guess you could say that sounds like a frame created for ready-made clothing. But no—if I try to put on a pair of those ready-made trousers that have virtually no material above the hip, it's sure to bring on walking difficulties. It doesn't feel as if I've just put on a pair of trousers. It's more as if I had something hanging off my waist, and I just can't relax.

So that's why, although I'm not the kind of person who makes a fuss about what he wears, I do insist on having my suits tailor-made. Even so, in the twelve years since I got married, I don't suppose I've bought more than six or seven of them. And I'm still using all six or seven of them. I wonder how many overcoats I've bought? Probably three in the last twelve years. Is that a lot, or just a few? I really couldn't say. Not particularly excessive, I'd guess. But one thing I've always insisted on is that my coats have got to be ordinary overcoats. No trench coats or three-season coats for me, thank you very much. That's why I've always gone for suits made of good strong material that will last for four or five years. Overcoats, overcoats—for me, it's got to be an overcoat every time. Like Akaky's ghost, I've always had a thing about overcoats.

Luckily, my wife hasn't opposed this fussiness of mine. No doubt she reads my yearning after overcoats as a result of my upbringing in the cold climate of North Korea. Not that she's ever said it in so many words—it just suits me to read her feelings that way. And it also suits me to think that even if my reading isn't right on target, it's probably not that far off.

> *This is the northernmost tip of Korea*
> *The Amnokkang River, five hundred miles long*
> *Beyond it, the vast expanse of Southern Manchuria*
> *Freezing cold at thirty below or more*
> *But by mid-April the snow is gone*
> *And in summer the water boils, it's over a hundred degrees.*

Suddenly I found these words coming to my lips, words from "The Song of the Korean Northern Border Patrol." Anyway, it's just as well my wife has never opposed my thing about overcoats. Of course, even if I had met with opposition, I would still have insisted on wearing overcoats—only then I'd have had to dig in my heels and do battle with my wife as well. I wonder when I bought this overcoat I'm wearing right now? Why, it must be three or four years since that day when my wife and I set out for the department store. Of course the two kids came along too. My son's ten years old now and my daughter's five. That's one point where Akaky and I are totally different. When Akaky wanted a new overcoat, he went up the back stairs of the building where Petrovich the tailor lived. The stairs were soaking wet with water dripping from all the washing hung out to dry, and the stink of vodka stung his eyes. The stairs I ascended, by contrast, had a brightly polished brass handrail that seemed to proclaim this staircase as the king of the whole department store. Or maybe I didn't take the stairs at all . . . maybe I used the escalator. Either way, the point is, Akaky was on his own and I was in a family group of four. And, most of all, I didn't have to go so far as to quit tea-drinking in order to pay for my overcoat. It's not as if my wife and kids and I had to sit in darkness at supper time to economize on electricity. Then again, I guess that for some months my wife may have cut a few corners on the dinner budget. But I don't think she ever turned her beady eye on the soles of my shoes in her search for economy measures.

Mind you, although it's lucky that my wife has never objected to my thing about overcoats, one outcome of that is that I've kind of forgotten to tell her the true reason why I have this thing about overcoats. Not that I've been lying to her. I've just forgotten to tell her the truth. I mean, after all, the need never arose. Of course, just because two people are a married couple, that doesn't mean they have to tell each other every single little thing about themselves. At least, that's the view I've taken over twelve years of married life, and it doesn't seem to have caused any problems. Unlike Yamakawa, I've managed to get this far without getting divorced. Yes, that's right—Yamakawa's a divorcé. Not that I'm concerned with the rights and wrongs of divorce at this point. Just stating a fact. Nothing to do with the rights and wrongs of divorce—simply mentioning my own situation as an example of a certain way of thinking about things, not that I've made any particular effort to apply this way of thinking. It would be more accurate to say that no other way of thinking would be possible for a guy like me. Because there are just too many things that I've forgotten to mention, or forgotten to confess to, or whatever.

Besides, I haven't got the kind of philosophy that says you've got to remember every single little thing in the first place. Nor have I got a religious creed that obliges me to issue explanations and confessions even about things I myself have forgotten. And I haven't got a divorce either. So many things I haven't got! Maybe there's something seriously wrong with my whole way of life. But I didn't come to this bridge to conduct some internal debate on whether or not I have some serious problem about that. That's for sure—I didn't come here to sort out that particular issue. And of course I didn't come all the way here just to call up memories of the early bird. No, I'm waiting on this bridge to keep my appointment with Yamakawa. It just so happened that the first thing to float into my mind was the early bird. And that's not all: somehow I even remembered that once upon a time this bridge had been the Bridge of *Golden* Water.

The first time I stood on this bridge, I thought it was called Okanenomizu Bridge—"Golden Water Bridge." That was twenty years ago. The bridge had been used as the model for a bridge in a novel by a rather famous and fashionable novelist that was being serialized in one of the newspapers. The novelist, actually, used the pen name "Lion." I was a pupil at a country high school in Chikuzen, way down in Kyushu, and I happened to be reading this novel as the chapters appeared in the paper. Ridiculously enough, I got it into my head that "Golden Water" was the bridge's real name. What a ridiculous country schoolboy! Mind you, the view from the bridge was just as described in Mr. Lion's story. Was it the east side of the bridge? Or was it the west side? I was such a hick that I literally didn't know my east from my west. But anyway, suppose you're standing with your back to the Japan National Railways Ochanomizu station, facing towards Ochanomizu subway station, looking down from the guardrail on your right at the muddy waters of the river far below. On the right of the river is the platform of the JNR station. Of course in those days we didn't yet have those red subway trains running on the left side of the river. Instead what you could see on the left bank of those muddy waters was a little settlement of scavengers—just as described in Mr. Lion's novel. A salaryman who's living a very comfortable life suddenly takes it into his head to run away from home. In his quest for freedom, he eventually stumbles upon the scavenger settlement under Golden Water Bridge. "I see! That must be the scavenger settlement under Okanenomizu Bridge," I had thought to myself. I'd gazed down at the settlement, with both hands shoved into the pockets of my overcoat. Overcoat? Yes indeed—I was wearing a khaki greatcoat from the old days of the Imperial Infantry. I had been wearing it when I set out from my country town in Chikuzen for the big city of Tokyo. I'd set out for Tokyo to take the Early Bird Exam.

My hair was just beginning to grow out of a crew cut. It would be several months before I could part it, on the left, right, or middle. On top of my head rode the cap of a country high school. Three white lines were sewn into the cap, the top one being thinner than the other two—that was the distinguishing feature. I wore a pair of those studious-looking glasses with perfectly round lenses. The wire arms were wrapped around the backs of my ears. Eventually I caught the bus from Goldwater Bridge and set off to the Early Bird Exam Hall. Early rising is threepence to the good. *Zee aarii baado kachizu za waamu.* The early bird catches the worm. But I could not catch the early bird.

I pulled a cigarette out of the pocket of my greatcoat and put it into my mouth. Then I dropped the spent match over the side of the bridge. There was no longer anything to be seen of the scavenger settlement that Mr. Lion had observed under Golden Water Bridge. But I was just in time to spot the red subway train as it made its fleeting appearance above ground. Probably that direction would be upriver. There's another bridge over there, and the subway train emerges from beneath its concrete girders for a certain fixed time interval. But you can never see the whole train. You can only see three carriages—or maybe four? By the time the head of the train plunges back underground, the tail has yet to emerge above ground. Such was the red subway train that could not yet be seen at the time when I first came to Tokyo to take the Early Bird Exam, wearing my old khaki infantryman's greatcoat.

Chapter 2

WHERE ON EARTH did that greatcoat of mine disappear to? And when exactly did it vanish from my eyes? That's the question that made an early bird of me today.

Do I have to think of a proper-sounding reason for this early rising of mine? Imagine for example that I'm a professional translator of Russian literature and I'm in the middle of translating "The Overcoat" into Japanese for a new complete edition of Gogol. One day, I suddenly remember my own overcoat—my khaki army greatcoat. Where on earth did that coat of mine disappear to? And when exactly did it vanish from my eyes? Early one morning that thought rouses me suddenly from sleep, and I hurry out of the house. Now, that makes a reasonable amount of sense.

Then again, here's another plausible explanation: I'm an exceedingly ordinary salaryman, living in a certain housing complex. Every morning I get on the train and go to work. And one morning in his fortieth year this ordinary salaryman, riding as usual in his packed commuter train, suddenly remembers his old army greatcoat. Where on earth did that old infantryman's greatcoat of mine disappear to? And when exactly did it vanish from my eyes? Suddenly with all the strength I can muster I start shoving my way through the packed crowd of commuters and tumble out of the train at the next station. I dash across the platform and barely beat the closing doors of the train going in the opposite direction. I'm heading away from work, in search of that coat. That makes a lot of sense too. Just the kind of behavior you'd expect from the hero of a novel.

For better or worse, however, I'm not presently engaged in translating "The Overcoat" into Japanese. And although I am a forty-year-old man, and I do indeed live in a corner of a housing complex, I am not a salaryman who has to get on a commuter train every morning. So I suppose you might say I'm not really cut out to be the hero of a proper novel. Then again, I'm not alone. People of rather obscure origin can be found around all of us, I'm sure. There's probably someone like that in your own vicinity. You don't know his occupation, his age, his family circumstances, or his monthly income. A man like that may well sit next to you every day. He might be smoking a cigarette right there on the railway platform, or noisily slurping noodles at the station snack bar. Or he might be sitting next to you in the movie theater getting offended about some western-style pornography. Come to that, what about all those people you brush past on the footbridges every day? Out of all of them, how many do you actually know anything about? And how many of *them* know anything about *you*? Tokyo isn't your firm. It isn't your university. And of course, it isn't your regular bar. At the same time, that's no bad thing.

I am not a salaryman who gets up early every morning. Night after night I sit glued all night to my desk. There in a corner of my four-room apartment in a five-story building, it's as if I were keeping some kind of vigil. Not that anyone's asked me to keep the vigil all night long. It's just my style. And no, I'm not a Russian-Japanese translator working on a new version of Gogol's "The Overcoat." Even so, in the twenty years since I came up to Tokyo from Chikuzen in that old coat, that khaki infantryman's greatcoat, I've just kept thinking coat, coat, coat. Come what may, I've always wanted to write my own "Overcoat"—even if it's just an imitation. In short, I am what I am. I—myself, in the true sense of the word.

Still and all, I just can't remember what happened to that coat of mine. Or else I've forgotten even to think about where that missing coat might be. What on earth *have* I been thinking about all this time? True, I've stayed alive this whole time, so I must have thought about things. That's probably why I forgot to think about where the coat was. A huge contradiction. But there you go—I couldn't keep on living just thinking coat, coat, coat all the time. It's obvious, really, but contradictions are what have kept me alive.

Anyway—suddenly one fine day I woke up early. No need for further explanation. It's not just me—anyone can have a day like that sometimes. One day something suddenly happens, not necessarily anything any of us has planned as part of their daily schedule. Nor anything we've been looking forward to, or dreaming of, or trembling anxiously in anticipation of. One day, something just suddenly happens. That means we don't know what's going to happen. Matter of fact, as long as we're alive, anything can happen. We can't rule out a thing. And as for *why* that thing happens—well, that's even more unknowable.

The one thing I can state clearly is that my coat was not stolen by anyone. Not so in the case of Akaky Akakievich, who when robbed of his brand-new coat set out first for a police box near the scene of the crime, where he saw a light dimly gleaming. A single constable was standing there, as if propped up against his halberd. He advised Akaky to go see the Police Inspector the following day. Returning dejectedly to his lodgings, he was told by his landlady that he'd get nowhere with the Police Inspector; he should instead go straight to the District Police Superintendent. The next morning Akaky rose early and went to see the District Police Superintendent, only to be told that he was still asleep. He went again at ten, but was told the same thing. There was nothing for it but to go again at eleven. This time he was told that the District Police Superintendent was out. Even then Akaky persisted. On his fourth visit he finally managed to see the District Police Superintendent. This time he went at lunchtime. But the result was almost the same as if he hadn't been granted an interview at all. The District Police Superintendent didn't show much interest in the stolen overcoat—instead, he wanted to know about Akaky's nighttime morals: Hadn't he dropped in at some house of ill repute? In the end Akaky wasted the whole day. It was the first time in his entire life he'd missed a day of work. The following day, on the advice of one of his colleagues in the government department where he worked, he went to appeal directly to a certain Important Person. And that's when he got told off for being impertinent and collapsed on the spot . . . Now, in my case, where was the best place to go?

Obviously it wasn't the police station. An Important Person? No, that had nothing to do with it either. I got up from my futon and put my smoking jacket on, over my pajamas. Then I went to the four-and-a-half-mat room next door, picked up the pack of cigarettes from the desktop, pulled one out and put it in my mouth. I had second thoughts, though, catching sight of the overflowing ashtray on my desk, and put it back in the pack. My vigil the previous night had lasted until 3 a.m. With all the cigarettes I'd smoked, my throat probably resembled a soot-caked chimney. Somehow I had to avoid the first thing going through my throat and straight into my empty stomach being one more stream of tobacco smoke. Even a single cup of water would do. I left my four-and-a-half-mat room and went into the dining room.

There in the dining room having breakfast with my wife were my fifth grader son and my daughter, who was still in kindergarten. It was that time of day.

"Oh!"

"Good morning!"

"Good morning, Daddy!"

That's how my wife, son and daughter greeted me.

"Good morning," I replied.

They were watching the breakfast show on TV. The time shown at the bottom of the screen was 7:36. The TV sat on top of the dish cupboard. I sat down in a chair right in front of it. That's my regular place at table. It's to stop the children from getting too worked up about TV programs during meals.

"What time does school start these days, I wonder?"

"Half past eight, Daddy," said my son.

"And kindergarten?"

"Nine o'clock!"

It was the first time I'd sat down to have breakfast with the kids for a very long time. But we couldn't eat together. There was nothing for me to eat, you see. My wife and children have bread for breakfast. I hardly ever eat bread. And I was way off schedule. When I'm on the night shift, I don't have breakfast until eleven at the very earliest, and sometimes I don't have it until 2 p.m. I sneaked some toast off my daughter's plate and had a mouthful.

"Well . . . aren't you going back to bed, then?"

"No, I can wait until after the kids have left."

"I thought I heard you making an appointment with someone last night."

"That would be Yamakawa. But it's not until six."

"Daddy, do you ever go somewhere this early in the morning?"

"Uh-huh."

"Where?"

"Somewhere good."

"A department store?"

"Don't be silly!" put in my son. "Daddy wouldn't go someplace like a department store."

"And what time are you going out?"

"Well let's see. I think I'll leave at nine."

So saying, I picked up the newspaper and went to the toilet. It was the first time in ages I'd read the morning paper like that. How long had it been? A month? Probably longer, actually. Recently I'd been having my vigils every night, and I'd almost stopped reading the morning paper. Instead I'd ask my wife to tell me the highlights after I got up and was eating my first meal. Had there been any weird incidents or not? I'd ask her. Had some "important person" died, or not? I had got into these really lazy habits. Wars, murders, child kidnappings, riots, plane crashes, student protests, sex crimes etc.: had there been any big incidents along those lines, I'd ask my wife, and only if there had would I bother to look at the newspaper myself . . . and then only the relevant page.

This lazy habit was partly the fault of my eyes. Why are newspaper articles laid out that way? I can't understand people who read the newspaper at the same time as eating a meal. Someone must have invented that layout, I suppose, but it's terribly tiring on the eyes. Is my astigmatism getting worse? Or is it because I'm overdoing my nocturnal vigils? Or is it because I've turned forty? I should have my eyes tested. Not today, though.

I sat down on the white horseshoe-shaped toilet seat and started leafing through the newspaper. No major incidents, it seemed, but of course there were a number of faces of "important people" on the front page. And there was a piece about this Japanese soldier who'd gone into hiding in the jungle on Guam at the end of the war and survived there all by himself for twenty-eight years. His popularity still showed no sign of waning, apparently. He'd already started a tailoring business in Nagoya. I was sure he made overcoats too—of course he did. Surprisingly, the story this time was that he was going to get married. What an amazing guy. When he first came back he said he wanted to write his memoirs about living in the jungle and being ready for the next big war. Had he finished, I wondered? If he'd managed that, he ought to have a worldwide bestseller on his hands—bigger than *Robinson Crusoe*. Yet it seemed he was going to get married before finishing his memoirs. Bit of a shame, wasn't it? Marriage would probably take the edge off the memoirs. Or maybe the publishers saw it the other way round: maybe they wanted the miracle man's sexual experiences included in the memoirs.

OK, I was going to leave the house at nine and go—where? The Missing Persons section of the newspaper caught the corner of my eye. Approach the newspaper? I imagined an article about my missing coat in the Missing Persons section. But what about the photo? My own mug shot? Meaningless. A photo of me in my old infantry-man's uniform—now that would mean something. Mentally I started drafting a text to place in the Missing Persons section.

"I am searching for the pre-war infantryman's greatcoat pictured in this photograph. Would the person who bought this coat or in any other way acquired it around 1952 or '53 please get in touch. Reward for any information, whether or not the item itself still exists. Telephone number . . . Akaki."

Something like that. Funnily enough, my name, Akaki, although it's a perfectly ordinary Japanese name, happens to be almost the same as the Russian name, Akaky. Although Akaky Akakievich himself never went to the newspaper office. It was Collegiate Assessor Kovalyov who did that, the one who lost his nose. But when he tried to place an ad in the paper appealing for information on his missing nose, they teased him about looking for someone with a funny name like *Nose,* and he was sent home in great despondency. Apparently even in those days newspapers in Saint Petersburg had certain standards. And if I tried something similar with my great coat? Just then it occurred to me I didn't have a single photograph of myself wearing the greatcoat. In fact, I didn't have any photographs at all of myself from that year, the year after I failed the Early Bird Exam, the year I spent studying for a second chance to get into university—with or without greatcoat.

From March 1952 until May 1953, a period of just over a year, I lived in a town in Saitama prefecture that has a slightly odd name— *Warabi*, which happens to mean "bracken" in Japanese. I think it may have acquired city status by now, but in those days it was just Warabi town, in North Adachi County. A lot of muddy gutters ran through the town, so there were also a lot of mosquitoes. It was a very forlorn little town, a former staging post on the old Nakasendo highway. I had spent six years going through junior and senior high school at Chikuzen, an out-of-the-way town in the countryside of Kyushu, but Warabi felt even more out of the way. Even so, I did not go back to Chikuzen after my failure on the Early Bird Exam. Well I did go back for the summer holidays, but only for a couple of weeks. I wonder why? I'm sure there are reasons, but I can't seem to remember them right now since the faces of two women suddenly come floating into my mind's eye.

One of them is the landlady of the place where I lodged in Warabi. The other is the lady who ran the pawnshop about a hundred yards from there. I guess both were over sixty? Still, to me those faces had an impact like the face of the sacred monk Kobo Daishi appearing to me on the eve of a meandering pilgrimage. I noisily folded up the newspaper. And, as if the train along the Keihin-Tohoku line had already reached Warabi, I rose from the horseshoe-shaped toilet seat and burst out of the toilet door.

That was how I decided on my destination: the first stop on my pilgrimage in search of the lost coat.

"Any incidents?" My wife asked the question I usually asked myself.

"Oh yes! Yes indeed."

"That old goat getting hitched?"

"What?" My wife caught me off guard there. For a moment I thought she'd said *that old coat getting stitched*.

"You know, Mr. Yokoi. He's going to get married, right?"

"The old soldier they found on Guam?" My daughter, still watching TV, joined the conversation. Apparently my son had already left for school.

I would have to hurry too. I got dressed in great haste. I couldn't shave in my smoking jacket. I washed my face and had a shave in great haste. Then I had my breakfast in great haste.

"Meeting someone?"

"Nope, on my own."

"You're in quite a fluster."

"Well I've got to finish my pilgrimage by six."

"Pilgrimage?"

"Er, sort of. I've got to go see some places."

"That's a little unusual, isn't it?"

"It's been twenty years, you know."

"Well—the weather's supposed to be fine today, and a spot of exercise will do you good."

Did I talk about anything else with my wife, I wonder? I may have discussed dinner arrangements. I wouldn't need dinner. My wife knew about Yamakawa—though only from his late-night phone calls. Actually he'd bothered us with some very late-night calls a number of times. Of course he was drunk. You couldn't call him a very suitable person for an evening rendezvous. That's probably what she was thinking. We always had a lengthy chat about Yamakawa whenever I went out to see him. About how he'd been getting along recently, what with being divorced and all that. I always made a big joke out of Yamakawa and his carryings-on. In conversations between my wife and me, he always played Pierrot. It was a kind of excuse for me, a price I was willing to pay. Because when I went out with Yamakawa, it was a sure bet that I wouldn't be home before dawn. Right then, however, I had no time. I didn't even say anything more about the "pilgrimage." If I got too leisurely, I might end up stumbling back into the maze again. It wouldn't do to lose sight of Kobo Daishi's face leading me on. The things I took with me on my pilgrimage were very simple—a small memo pad, stuffed into my pocket, and a single ballpoint pen.

I left the house. As I headed for the bus stop to catch the bus that went round the housing complex I heard a voice calling me from behind.

"Daddeeeee!"

Without even noticing it, I had overtaken my daughter, who was on her way to kindergarten with two or three other children.

From the housing complex station I headed down first to Kita-Senju on the Tobu line. Traveling around Saitama prefecture is exceedingly inconvenient. It's probably got something to do with the old highways from the Edo era. I live in a mammoth housing complex with about seven thousand households. It used to be an area of rice paddies on the outskirts of Soka, a staging post on the old highway leading north to Nikko and beyond. *Spring departing: birds cry, and tears appear in the eyes of the fish.* When Basho set out on foot from Kita-Senju on the Narrow Road to the North, with "the thought of seven thousand miles lying before me," Soka was the first place he stopped. Now, however, a mammoth housing complex has arisen from the paddy fields, and the Tobu line has acquired a new station especially for it. Nowadays the Tobu line connects to the Hibiya subway line, so you can go directly to Ueno, Ginza, Roppongi and all the way to Meguro. On the other hand, if you want to go to some other town in Saitama, such as Urawa, Kawaguchi or Warabi, you first have to go south into Tokyo and then back out north on some other line. Of course, there are buses—but only about one an hour. Soka was a staging post on the old Nikko highway, while Warabi was a staging post on the old Nakasendo highway; but as I say, getting from one to the other is a mighty awkward business. I guess this system where all roads lead to Tokyo was kind of convenient in the old days, when Tokyo was still called Edo and the daimyo had to travel there from their regional strongholds and spend every other year at court with the shogun. Anyway, the fact remains that to this day the quickest way to travel between these two towns in Saitama is to go all the way down to Tokyo's Ueno station and then back out on the Keihin-Tohoku line.

I couldn't get a seat on the train going down to Ueno. The morning commuter rush hour wasn't quite over yet. I must have left home a little before the 9 a.m. departure I'd planned. I got on the first Tobu line train that arrived—it had yellow cars with a red line along the side. The ones that carry on into the subway line have silver cars. A lot of the cars with the red lines have been replaced with new stock lately, but sometimes there'll be one of the old kind on the train that has a toilet at one end. The silver carriages are more comfortable to ride in. But for a pilgrimage from Soka to Warabi, maybe the old-style cars with the red line are more appropriate . . . though it means an extra change of trains at Kita-Senju.

At Kita-Senju, the silver subway train was waiting to depart from the other side of the platform. This one was almost empty, and I could even feel the car rock slightly as I got into it. Anyway, I was still thinking about the two old staging-post towns. When I first came up to the Tokyo area from Chikuzen, the first place I stayed was Warabi, on the old Nakasendo highway. And now, twenty years later, I was living in Soka, on the old Nikko highway. Did fate have a hand in my journey between the two? Not that it had been a direct journey—not at all. The route that ran from the Nakasendo highway to the Nikko highway had more bends in it than the Yamanote loop line. It had been ten years since I started living in the mammoth housing complex that had arisen like some colossal mirage out of the rice paddies on the outskirts of Soka. Just a little while after the birth of our son, who is now ten, we happened to get lucky—our name came up in the public housing lottery for the Soka complex. In other words, we drifted there by chance. We had been putting our names down for pretty much every new public housing project in the Tokyo area— central Tokyo, outer Tokyo, and nearby prefectures: Kanagawa, Chiba and Saitama. We weren't particularly hoping to live in Soka. We had no particular reason to hope for such a thing.

It was a bit like *Gulliver's Travels*. Certainly Gulliver was a man with a powerful curiosity. His thirst for knowledge included linguistics, literature, history and any other field of study related to as-yet-unknown aspects of human life—but he wasn't an explorer. He was a doctor, and fairly impecunious. He got on a ship because he needed to make a living. To make a living, he left his wife and children behind and boarded the *Antelope* as ship's doctor. Of course the *Antelope* never planned to sail to Lilliput. When it set sail from Bristol, on September 5, 1699, under the command of Captain William Prichard, it was headed for the East Indies. Nevertheless, Gulliver wound up among the little people of Lilliput. Originally he never planned to be an explorer, to go there. It's so much like real life. He didn't sally bravely forth from home, in search of these amazing little people. No, on the contrary: he was washed ashore unconscious, and the Lilliputians found *him*. He didn't choose his encounter with the little guys. He just happened to bump into them, perfect strangers, totally unexpectedly, after being washed ashore, on their land. Housing complexes are just like that.

Sitting in the almost empty silver train, I pulled the little memo pad out of my coat pocket. On the first page, I wrote "March 1952–

May 1953, Warabi town, Saitama prefecture." What sort of circuitous path had I traveled from Warabi to my present abode at Soka? I gave an involuntary little sigh. I was no Basho, but like him I felt as if I had seven thousand miles stretching before me. I turned to the next page of the memo pad, and sketched there a little map of the Tokyo area railway network. First the Yamanote loop line. Then, at a tangent to the right, the Keihin-Tohoku line. The Chuo line, shooting right through the middle of the Yamanote line. The Akabane line, going north from Ikebukuro to Akabane. And running east from Akihabara towards Chiba—the Sobu line.

These were all JNR lines, but I still needed to draw in some of the private lines. The Ikegami line, from Gotanda to Kamata. The Seibu Shinjuku line, and the Seibu Ikebukuro line. And then the lines I was using now—the Hibiya subway line and the Tobu line.

Then I started writing in the names of the stations on the lines, and the dates I'd lived near them. By the time the silver train reached Ueno, I had completed the record of my travels, as follows:

- Keihin-Tohoku line: Warabi (Mar '52–May '53)

- Akabane line: Itabashi (June '53, ca. 1 mo. Behind Takinokawa Post Office. 2nd floor)

- Seibu Shinjuku line: Saginomiya (July '53, ca. 1 mo. Walk through wheat fields)

- Chuo line: Yotsuya (Aug '53, ca. 3 mos. Nr. Yotsuya Tax Office)

- Yamanote line: Takadanobaba (Nov. '53, ca. 1 yr. First behind Waseda Shochiku Cinema, then in house next to fishmongers nr. Suwa Shrine)

- Chuo line: Ogikubo (Oct/Nov '54, ca. 1/2 yr. Left at Ogikubo 1st precinct bus stop, 2nd floor, 2.5-mat room?)

- Ikegami line: Yukigaya Otsuka (Apr/May '55, ca. 1 yr. Nr Yukigaya Theatre)

- Chuo line: Nishi-Ogikubo (Mar/Apr '56, ca. 1/2 yr. Halfway between Nishi-Ogikubo and Ogikubo)

- Yamanote line: Takadanobaba (ca. Oct '56–Mar '57. Over rotary at Totsuka 2nd precinct, 1st left, 1st right, alley)

- Keihin-Tohoku line: Oji (Mar '58, ca. 2 mos. Quite long walk below Asukayama Park)

- Sobu line: Shin-Koiwa (May '58, ca. 1/2 yr. Right at east exit shopping street, left at new road, next right. Nr. Arakawa Embankment —?)

- Ikegami line: Ebara-Nakanobu (ca. end of '58 to Sep '60. Behind Enzan elem. school)

- Seibu Ikebukuro line: Shiina-machi (Sep '60, ca. 1 yr)

- Chuo line: Higashi-Nakano (Oct '61–Dec '62).

- Tobu line (Hibiya subway line): present housing complex (Dec '62–?)

Phew! My first attempt to put pen to paper was nothing like Basho's opening haiku on his way north. For goodness' sake, how many places had I lived in? I started putting little numbers in rings next to each location, starting with one. My present dwelling in the housing complex turned out to be number fifteen. This was the tortuous ten-year journey that had taken me from Warabi staging post to Soka staging post. It was a maze I'd been wandering through after I arrived at the great metropolis from that little country town in Chikuzen, down in Kyushu. It was the record of a wandering pilgrimage, like Kobo Daishi's journey through the eighty-eight stations on

Shikoku Island. It was the time and space I'd been living in. It was a trail I'd left, like snails do.

In that single page of my little memo pad, inscribed with a simple ballpoint pen, I could glimpse countless human faces. The faces of all those men and women crowded together between the station names, like the ties laid together on the rail lines I'd drawn between the stations. Right now, though, I didn't want to look at them. Men and women were staring at me out of the darkness of the maze, but for now I had to stop up their mouths. My own mouth too, which wanted so much to start talking to them. Because I knew that if by some remote chance I happened to open my mouth and start talking to one of them, in the end the faces, packed together now like ties on the rails between the station names, would awake, rise up as one, and run amok through my memories, immediately smashing my plans to smithereens.

That is why I made no annotation whatsoever on my diagram, save for place names and dates. I omitted all personal names, including wife and children of course. One day, of course, I will surely want to make a really thorough pilgrimage to all the places written in the memo pad. And when that time comes, I will no doubt resume my acquaintance with all the men and women packed between the station names like railway ties. One day, with this map as a guide, I will surely start a tour through the maze of my memories. And it will be a tour of hell at the same time, a meandering journey through memory hell, from the first to the fifteenth station. When, I wonder, will that happen? I haven't the faintest idea. After all, I haven't even reached Ueno yet. I hadn't even made it to the first station.

Anyway, my present concern was that coat. Where and when on earth did I allow that khaki infantryman's greatcoat to disappear from sight? This was the sudden moment of doubt that had woken me up so early this morning. And I had got on the train. Anyway, I had to go to Warabi. To Warabi as fast as I could. I closed the little memo pad and put it back in my coat pocket. The train stopped. Ueno at last.

Chapter 3

AT UENO I changed to the Keihin-Tohoku line. There was plenty of space on the train. When I first came up to the Tokyo area from my little country town in Chikuzen, all those years ago, the first train I got on also ran on the Keihin-Tohoku line. It was on a certain day in March, twenty years ago, and the train was pretty crowded. Could have been the evening rush hour. In those days it took about twenty-four hours to get from Kyushu to Tokyo on the express sleeper. I was hanging on to a leather strap, dressed in my stiff-collared school uniform with a wartime infantryman's khaki greatcoat on top of that. From my left hand dangled a large, brown shoulder bag. I wasn't wearing the cap with the white lines though. That symbol of a boy from the boondocks, with its three white lines so earnestly sewn into it, had been tucked away in the shoulder bag.

Besides the shoulder bag, I had with me one other item of luggage: a little bundle of Kyushu souvenirs. Wrapped in an old-fashioned cloth kerchief were four boxes. They contained *meika hiyoko, tsuru no ko manju, niwaka senbei* and *bontan-zuke*—sweet little chick-shaped cakes; sweet, sticky-soft white buns with centers like crane eggs; hard oblong crackers with sad faces on them; and pickled pomelo (a sort of grapefruit). Now, however, the package was dangling from the hand of Koga, who had come to meet me on the platform of Tokyo station. He'd come right up to me as I got out of the express sleeper from Kyushu, and said "*Osu!!*" He wasn't wearing an overcoat. He had no socks on his feet—just wooden sandals. His fists were lightly clenched and his style of greeting was straight out of karate school. His hair was a mess. He had rather high cheekbones, and I could see a small scar on the left one. His eyes weren't black, but distinctively auburn.

I couldn't actually tell you whether he had a typical Kyushu physique. I have a feeling the cheekbones were a little on the high side. But his surname, Koga, was Kyushu through and through. Within Kyushu, it's especially common in Fukuoka and Saga prefectures. Those could well be the only two prefectures in all Japan where you find that surname. There were lots of Kogas at middle school and high school in Chikuzen, where I spent six years. Every class was bound to have one or two. There were some Kogas among the teachers too. You could definitely say that Koga is one of those uniquely Kyushu surnames. And in the neatly wrapped bundle now dangling from Koga's hand were the sweets I'd brought with me, which were also representative of Kyushu—gifts for the folks once we got to Warabi, of course.

My destination was the house where Koga's older brother lived with his wife. They had rented a cottage on the grounds of somebody's house. Of course I had only been told about this—I didn't know Koga the elder myself. Actually I'd only just made the acquaintance of Koga the younger, there on the platform of Tokyo station. We weren't related. It was "Uncle Azuma," a relative on my mother's side, who'd arranged for me to stay at Big Koga's house. "Uncle Azuma" was not really my uncle. I think he was some kind of cousin of my mother's. His surname was the same as her maiden name, so I doubt they were such distant cousins, but to this day I don't know exactly what their connection is. We just called him "Uncle Azuma" because he was the proprietor of a restaurant called the Azuma.

As for Koga's older brother, he's a civil servant in some ministry now, but then, when he had just come back from military service at the end of the war, he became a political activist out in the provinces, like so many others. He wasn't in the Communist Party. Apparently he was an extremely moderate democrat. You could say Koga's big brother was actually a pretty rare bird. This was a time when everyone seemed to be joining the Communists—the barrel maker's son back from the kamikaze squadrons, the sandal maker's daughter who got to play ping-pong at the national athletics tournament, the clam vendor's son back from basic training, the tobacconists' pretty daughters . . . each and every one of them became good party members. Maybe it had something to do with his education—Koga's big brother had been to Takushoku University, in Tokyo, which was known both for martial arts and nationalism.

My big brother also read *Red Flag,* the Communist Party newspaper. He was three years older than I. The oldest son of the town hall treasurer used to come slouching down the street in his wooden sandals, delivering *Red Flag.* He was two or three years older than my brother. He wore glasses with thick black frames and his long hair was swept straight back. In summer he delivered the newspaper in his running vest—still with the wooden sandals, though—and he'd be sucking on a popsicle that was virtually down to the stick. Of course we knew each other by sight. He'd spent a year at art school in Tokyo, apparently, but his health broke down and he'd had to come home. His little sister was in the same grade as I at high school.

The part of town where I lived was known as "Officers' Town" during the war. About seven miles away was Tachiarai Airbase and Anti-Aircraft Artillery Unit, and the families of officers working there apparently lived mostly in our neighborhood. I say "apparently" because I arrived there only after we lost the war—a year after, when I was repatriated from North Korea. We went to live in the house where my mother's sister and mother (my grandmother) were living with their families. Of course they had changed the name of the neighborhood. The families of the officers had already left. After the war, a lot of high school teachers lived there. There were teachers all around us—three who taught Japanese literature and classical Chinese, and others who taught physics, biology, English, arts and crafts, even calligraphy. The teacher next door taught history and geography. The uncle who'd been my mother's older brother had already died, but he'd also been a teacher—he'd taught physics and math at the same prefectural middle school that my brother and I later graduated from. My aunt was yet another teacher, of Japanese and Chinese, at the prefectural girls' high school.

This onetime officers' town was now a quiet residential district of the little country town in Chikuzen. Though we had to share a house with my aunt's family, it was still too good for the likes of us, mere evacuees from North Korea that we were. It had a redbrick front gate and six-foot-wide corridors on either side of the dwelling space, with verandahs and a garden that, though small, could still be used to grow vegetables. It was only a minute from school, too, if you ran. It was a rented house, actually, owned by an elderly couple who had come back from Brazil or Hawaii or somewhere.

Just once, invited by my brother and a Kyushu University student who'd been at middle school with him, I actually attended a Communist Party study meeting at a local community center. We read the *Communist Manifesto*. I quit after that one time. I was invited to a record concert too, but I didn't go. The only dancehall in town was a tiny single-story wooden building. The couple who ran the place were also apparently party members; record concerts were held once a month at this dancehall. My big brother seemed to have the hots for the sandal maker's daughter, the former ping-pong star. The student from Kyushu University seemed to have a thing going with the tobacconist's daughter. What about the barrel maker's son back from the kamikaze squadrons? What about the clam vendor's son back from basic training? What about the treasurer's son who delivered *Red Flag*? It wasn't so much the *Communist Manifesto* that I found offputting—it was the lascivious atmosphere at the study meeting. Jealousy? Maybe that was it. The fact is I admired the colonel's daughter, who also lived in Officers' Town, like me, and I would flush bright red every time the two of us passed in the street, but there wasn't a thing I could do about it. Her family was the only one left from the days the neighborhood really was an officers' town. A wooden signboard up at the entrance to her house, on the right side as you faced the vestibule, read: "Family of the late Infantry Colonel XXXX." She was in my grade at school.

Incidentally, it seemed that Big Koga's political activities involved helping out at the campaign offices of a certain candidate he was supporting in elections for the local assembly. That was how he ended up hanging around the Azuma restaurant. Uncle Azuma was big in local politics—in fact, he ran successfully against his hated enemy in the catering business, the master of the Suisenkaku restaurant, and was elected mayor. He ran with the official backing of the Socialist Party, mainly to show his opposition to his rival, since the master of the Suisenkaku was backed by the Liberal Party. I can't imagine there was any deeper reason than that—though come to think of it, his fair complexion, short stature and something about the juxtaposition between his glasses and moustache did make him look a little like the leader of the Socialist Party at the time, a politician nicknamed "Old Slowpoke."

Electioneering was paid work, so I got together a couple of my schoolmates and we set out to help with the campaign. I'm pretty sure I was in my first year of high school at the time. Campaign headquarters were located in a big liquor store in the town's main street. The daughter of the establishment was a celebrated beauty;

she did actually resemble some actress or other. This was already after coeducation came in, so she went to my school, a year ahead of me, and she played on the basketball team. For some reason a lot of good-looking girls played on the basketball team. The sight of them in shorts was erotic. These girls had just taken off their pantaloons! That's how dazzling the effect was. The liquor store owner's daughter wore a one-piece dress at election campaign HQ and briskly served up drinks and snacks. Of course there was no way this was going to get me any closer to her. With my two schoolmates, I'd sometimes run away from the campaign truck and go climbing up to Maruyama Park, beyond the school, still clutching the megaphone. Once there, we'd throw ourselves down for a rest in the square in front of the war memorial.

In those days, Koga's big brother was probably going in and out of election HQ as well. This would have been before he became a civil servant in a certain government ministry. The two of us had never been introduced. His name came up only about three months before I set off for Tokyo. I was planning to go there without telling Uncle Azuma. If I could get accepted by the university's law faculty, he wouldn't mind looking after my living expenses in Tokyo, he apparently told my mother. That was just after I started my third year in high school. No doubt he figured if I could graduate from law school, I could probably become a prefectural assemblyman or a lawyer. That's how highly I was regarded among my relatives. It seems he even had it in mind to adopt me if things went well. Uncle Azuma had only one child, a daughter. True, he'd adopted her husband into the family, but his daughter and adopted son-in-law had failed to produce any children. The whole law school concept was quickly nipped in the bud—by none other than cheeky me. Call it an excess of youthful indiscretion. And that's why I planned to keep quiet about my plan to go up to Tokyo, though in reality, things didn't work out that way.

That's how, in brief, Big Koga and I got to know about each other. And it was for those reasons as well that, when I arrived in Tokyo for the first time in my life, the first train I got on at Tokyo station was not on the Yamanote line, nor the Chuo line, but the Keihin-Tohoku line.

"I hear your old man was in the army, *shenpai*." That's how Little Koga opened the conversation, the bundle of cakes dangling from his hand. He meant *senpai*, a term you use to address your seniors, even though he was really the same age as my big brother. He just had this habit of calling everybody *shenpai* with that thick Chikuzen accent. I hadn't heard a thing about Little Koga. The first I got to know about him was from the man himself, right there in the train. He told me he was lodging with his older brother and his older brother's wife, while attending Koryo University—a school I had never heard of. For his part, he knew nothing about Uncle Azuma. On his way through one of the old-style middle schools he'd applied to some kind of correspondence school connected with the navy, and he'd wound up working on a ship. After the war ended he carried on as a seaman on fishing vessels, freighters etc., but then, just the year before, he'd taken an examination and got into university. His big brother, who'd been to Takushoku University, recommended that he try for Koryo, which, I now learned, for the first time, was actually the same institution, renamed after the war. General MacArthur banned the old name, which literally meant *Colonial University,* so they changed to the elegant new one, which literally meant *Crimson Imperial Tomb University.* Koga of course asked me which school I was applying to. Tokyo University of Foreign Studies, I blurted out, the old school of foreign languages where Futabatei Shimei had studied Russian long ago. But he didn't seem to know it. So our conversation about universities soon came to a halt.

Apparently the custom of calling everybody *senpai* came from the karate club at Koryo. The standard greeting between them was *osu!* That bothered me hardly at all, but I did feel a bit uncomfortable being called *shenpai*. Why? Probably because he couldn't pronounce it right; *Chikuzen*, likewise, became *Chikujen* for him. Being born in northern Korea and living in an environment where colonial Japanese was spoken until I reached the first year of middle school, I had never acquired the *Chikujen* accent. Of course after six years at middle and high school I had almost perfectly mastered Chikuzen dialect. I could fight in it, or talk dirty in it, but I just couldn't bring myself to pronounce *s* like *sh* or *z* like *j*. That's why it bothered me to be called *shenpai* by Little Koga. I was a country boy from Chikuzen and I couldn't even speak with a Chikujen accent.

"My dad wasn't a career soldier," I replied.

"But he was killed in the war, right?"

"He died of a disease he got on the front. According to the official report."

"What rank was he?"

"First infantry lieutenant."

"Did he go to military academy?"

"No, he was a one-year volunteer."

"Ah, a one-year volunteer."

"He was an only son, so he just served a year and went home a second lieutenant and carried on his business, but then something happened and he was called up to serve again, as first lieutenant."

"I see—one of those officers who got promoted just before the war ended."

At that moment, an old infantryman's greatcoat floated into my field of vision. I was surprised. I glanced to the left and right of my leather strap, but I couldn't see anyone else on the train wearing a coat like that. The old infantryman's greatcoat that had suddenly caught my attention was my own. I wondered if that's why Little Koga had brought up the topic of my father in the first place.

"This is a very crowded train," I remarked, still thinking about the coat.

"That's because there's speedboat and bicycle racing today."

"These people are speedboat and bicycle gamblers?"

"A whole bunch will get out at Kawaguchi—they're the speedboat fans. The ones that stay on till Omiya are the bicycle crowd."

Come to think of it, I do seem to recall that an awful lot of passengers were clutching sports tabloids. But in that case, it must mean that after all, it couldn't have been early evening when I arrived in Tokyo twenty years ago, as I'd imagined.

"What's your brother doing these days, *shenpai*?" asked Little Koga.

"He's working at an American army camp."

"Oh. The one at Itatsuki?"

"No, Kashii."

"Oh. The one at Kashii, eh."

After a brief pause, he came out with this: "*Shenpai*, you think the money your brother sends will be enough?"

"Hmm . . ."

Actually I had no idea. Of course at the time I didn't know about the outcome of the Early Bird Exam. It just somehow floated into my head that I was bound to pass. I had a foolish, excessive trust in the accuracy of the tests they used in those days to assess students' suitability for higher education. My score had been good enough to get me through the initial screening. Mysteriously enough, despite my fond belief that I was going to pass, I had given no thought at all to what would happen after that. Did I think I was going to carry on attending high school a one-minute run from Officers' Town? Of course not! Yet when I was actually asked about it, I couldn't come up with a convincing answer.

To be fair, I had taken the effort to ask one of my senpais, who had got into Waseda University, about the cost of living and lodging in Tokyo. A room with two meals a day was about five or six thousand yen a month, he said. Mind you, that was for a shared room. If you wanted a room of your own you were looking at another one or two thousand yen. If you didn't have the money for the room-and-board option, the next step down was to rent a three-mat room and save as much money as possible on meals. There were various ways of doing that—using the university canteen, going to cheap restaurants where you bought meal coupons in advance, or simply cooking for yourself. The cheapest meal in town was a plain bowl of noodles at the university canteen—thirteen yen. The usual student scholarship was two thousand yen a month, and if you could land a special scholarship you got three thousand. If you were going to a private university you'd have to spend nearly all your scholarship money on fees, but if you got into a national university the fees were only five hundred yen a month, so if you got a three thousand–yen scholarship you'd have enough left over to pay your room rent. And if you stayed in a student dorm, it would be cheaper still. And of course you could get various part-time jobs. The student from Waseda was too busy as an activist to hold a part-time job himself, but if you went to the university co-op, or the Student Support Association in Kudan, they would set you up with a part-time job or a room. Some families would take you on as a home tutor and give you dinner as part of the deal. And of course I could go and eat at his place now and again. If it was just for a few days in the month, he'd see me right. Anyway—I wouldn't starve.

That was pretty much what my senpai from Waseda told me. The activism he was involved in was called Zengakuren, or something like that. Anyway, if his comments were anything to go by, I could probably make enough money to avoid starvation so long as I *didn't* get involved in that kind of activism. Other than that, I thought I'd just go and see how things turned out.

I passed on to my mother and big brother what the senpai had told me.

"Who told ya that?" asked my brother.

I mentioned the senpai's name. He'd been a year behind my brother in the old middle school.

"What's he doin' there?"

"Doin' French studies at Waseda." I answered in the same Chikuzen dialect he used. I didn't mention the student activism.

"Huh. Who still bothers with fancy literature these days?"

"Well anyhow," said my mother, "take a good look with your own eyes, and tell us what you see."

"Now look here kid," said my brother "Got any idea how much the Yanks pay me?"

"Uh, nope."

"Didn' think so. Maybe it's better you don' trouble yourself with difficult stuff, what you think, Ma?"

"Well he's only got himself to blame if he gets into hot water, turnin' down Uncle Zuma off the bat like he did."

It was true—that did seem a foolish youthful whim. At the time I had already read Gogol's "The Overcoat." I believe I read it in the cheap paperback edition from Shunyodo. The pages were made of that really coarse paper. I didn't yet know anything about Gogol's early years. It was around the time he set out from the Ukrainian provinces to seek his fortune in Saint Petersburg, the Russian capital.

In August 1828, when Gogol was nineteen, he graduated from the seven-year grammar school in Nezhin. He went back home for a short spell, but in December he set out for Saint Petersburg with his friend Danilevsky, burning with hope that he might realize his cherished dream of becoming a judge.

In 1829, when he turned twenty, he made tremendous efforts to secure a post as a government official, but they came to nothing. He placed his final hopes in an epic poem he had written back in his Nezhin days, about idyllic country life in Germany, entitled *Hans Küchelgarten*. He published it under the pen name "V. Alov," but the reviews were terrible. Disillusioned and disheartened, he went traveling in northern Germany, returning to Russia in September. In November, Bulgarin managed to fix him up with a low-ranking position in the Ministry of Interior.

Of course I'm not Gogol. I have no *Overcoat* in me, no *Nose*, no *Diary of a Madman*, no *Nevsky Prospect*, no *Government Inspector*, no *Dead Souls*. Probably the only respect in which I can hope to catch up with Gogol is lifespan—he died at forty-two and I'll reach that age in a couple more years. Still and all, to think that his reason for traveling to the capital was to become a *judge*! Of course, this all happened well over a hundred years ago. And in Russia. I know all that and more—yet still and all, I can't help feeling a keen interest in the detailed chronology of Gogol's career.

He was born in the village of Bol'shiye Sorochintsy, Mirgorod county, Poltava prefecture, Ukraine, on March 20, 1809, the sixth year of the Bunka era here in Japan (all dates are according to the old Russian calendar; March 20 corresponds to April 1 in the new calendar). He was the first son of Vasily Afanasevich, a petty landlord, member of the gentry, and retired first lieutenant; and Maria Ivanovna, his wife.

In 1818 (at age nine), he entered Poltava county elementary school, along with his younger brother, Ivan. In summer of the following year, his brother suddenly died of a fever—a terrible shock for Gogol.

In 1821 (at age twelve) he entered the newly established Nezhin grammar school. While there, he developed a keen interest in literature and drama, started a student magazine that was passed around among his schoolmates, and performed in amateur dramatics.

In 1825 (at age sixteen) he lost his father Vasily to illness.

Do I perceive some connection between my own situation and that of Gogol so many years ago? The death of his father, a retired first lieutenant? His ambition to become a judge? "If you go to study law, I'll take care of your living expenses in Tokyo." Did Gogol also have someone like Uncle Azuma in his life? Of course, his situation must have been totally different from mine. His family were petty landowners in the village of Bol'shiye Sorochintsy, Mirgorod county, Poltava prefecture, Ukraine. They probably had fifty or sixty serfs working on their estate.

His father's death meant something different to him as well. As for his father having been a first lieutenant, like mine—well, that was an absolute coincidence, a transparent ploy that wouldn't fool a child. Above all, let's not forget this all happened well over a hundred years ago—and in Russia, to boot. Even so, the fact I didn't know about Gogol's ambition to become a judge is no small matter. After all, it was my admiration of Gogol, a Russian who lived over a hundred years ago, that twenty years ago made me set out for Tokyo from the little country town in Chikuzen.

To me, Gogol wasn't just some Russian guy who lived over a hundred years ago. And he wasn't just a "great writer" of nineteenth–century Russia. Nor the "mother of Russian literature" nor the "founder of realism." You might say he was my fate. By which I mean that twenty years ago when I set out for Tokyo from the little country town of Chikuzen I felt that I *was* him, in 1828, graduating from Nezhin Grammar School and setting out for Saint Petersburg. Except for one vital thing I didn't know.

I didn't know that Gogol longed to become a judge. What if I'd known that twenty years ago? Of course it's no more than a naïve speculation. However, I believe I probably would have accepted Uncle Azuma's proposition. Mind you, even if some such stroke of fate *had* led me to enroll at the Law Faculty, I don't suppose I would have become a lawyer. I doubt I'd have become a prefectural assemblyman either. No, I probably couldn't have become either of those things. Reason being—I went up to Tokyo out of admiration for a man who went to the capital in hopes of becoming a judge, but was unable to fulfill his dream.

At five foot five, I found the old infantryman's greatcoat a bit too big for me. When did I first set eyes on that khaki greatcoat? Probably it was the day before I set out for Tokyo to take the Early Bird Exam. It was then that I also knew I would wear this coat on my journey to the capital.

The first time I tried it on, my mother burst out laughing: the hemline and sleeves were dangling all over the place.

"Looks like a ghost in an overcoat."

My brother, lying there with his head propped up on his elbow, gave a cynical laugh. For his sake, I didn't just chuck the ghost-like overcoat onto the tatami floor. My brother was a sentry at the US military camp at Kashii. A sentry is a kind of human clock. A human being who keeps awake right through the night. That day, I guess he'd just come back from the night shift. His jeep-colored, standard-issue uniform, the kind used by anyone working for the occupying army, hung on the wall in the six-mat room. On the breast pocket flap was a tin badge. On it, in English, was written: *Civilian Guard*. I guess that meant he was a private security officer, not a soldier. But what on earth was my brother supposed to be guarding? The American families living inside the army camp? Or the pan-pan girls who swarmed around the camp? I had hardly ever heard my brother talk about his work as a security guard. Maybe he talked to Mother about it. Did civilian guards get to wear helmets when they were on duty? Did they get to carry a truncheon, or something? He never brought home a truncheon or helmet, at any rate. Still, when my big brother left what was once the Officers' Town for work, he wore the jeep-colored uniform of a civilian guard in the US military.

"I'd say we need to take the hem up two and a half inches, and the sleeves? Let's see, just two inches."

Mother didn't use any ruler or tape measure—just her eyes. At last I took off the ghostly overcoat. Which of the two coats—the old khaki infantryman's greatcoat or the jeep-colored US civilian guard uniform hanging on the wall—was more appropriate for the one-time Officers' Town? Both were surely the kind of thing you'd expect to find in a house somewhere in a defeated nation.

"Any Japanese who fit this coat would be one with a good frame— for a Japanese," said mother, taking out her wooden ruler now to check the adjustments.

"You should be happy—didn't ya always wanna be a soldier when you were a kid?" said my brother, still lounging around on the floor. What he said was true. It was a suitable overcoat for a guy like me who'd wanted to be a soldier since he was a kid. I couldn't think of a single thing to say in reply.

"Didya forget the toy sword ya took that time?"

The incident my brother brought up suddenly is now forty years in the past. I wasn't even a year old. Or maybe it was something that happened while my first birthday was being celebrated? Various items were lined up on the tatami mats in front of the family altar: an abacus, a ruler, an ink stone, an exercise book, a picture book, a harmonica, a crayon, a triangle, a pencil case, a toy trumpet, a drum, a colored ball, a tank, a car, a steam train, a cannon, a sword. There may have been even more things lying there. There may well have been a little china saké bottle and a cup.

I was there, cradled on my great-grandfather's lap. Behind my great-grandfather sat my grandmother and my father and mother. It was probably the custom for other relatives to come and join this innocent little ceremony. Great-uncles, great-aunts, uncles, aunts, various cousins. From above the altar, yet more faces looked down from photographs. My grandfather, my great-grandmother and "honorable photographs of their majesties the Emperor and Empress." Observed by the massed ranks of family and friends, which item would I grab? This was a fortune-telling game adults liked to play: they'd watch the one-year-old child crawling over the tatami, and divine his future from the item he first picked up in his right hand. It wasn't just a matter of aptitude or career. If the kid grabbed the saké flask, or the cup, for instance, I expect it meant he was going to be a heavy drinker. Anyway—I grabbed the toy sword.

I wonder where my brother was at the time? From what angle did he see me crawl out from between my great-grandfather's knees and pick up the toy sword? Of course I can't remember. And that's not the only thing I can't remember, of course; I haven't the slightest intention of claiming I can recall all this stuff from when I was one year old. My memories are not of the birthday fortune-telling game itself—they're memories of the dozens and dozens of times I've been told about it: *The toy sword ya took that time.*

> *I love soldiers and when I grow up*
> *I'll have medals on my chest and a sword at my side*
> *I'll get on my horse and say "giddy up, let's ride!"*

"Yes . . . your father used to talk about it a lot. 'That youngster'd make a real fine soldier. Not like Kazuo—he's light on his feet and he's got a voice that carries: "a good voice for givin' orders." He was always goin' on about that, your father."

Saying that, my mother finished sewing up the hem of the khaki greatcoat. Kazuo was my big brother; the youngster was me. My brother had worn glasses since third grade. Maybe it was genetic, since he and my mother were both terribly shortsighted. He couldn't do more than five or six chin-ups on the bar. I could do fifteen, easy, twenty if I did a monkey, meaning I ended up all red-faced and openmouthed like a monkey. Actually I was good at climbing trees too. I would jump from roof to roof along the storehouses in the back garden. I had absolutely no use for ladders. In short: I was cut out to be a soldier.

As things turned out, my brother had reached the fourth year of middle school by the time we lost the war, and he never entered any kind of military academy. His eyesight was so bad the whole thing was out of the question. I do remember hearing some talk about him going to accounting school, but he never took the exam. Being the kind of guy he was, I don't think my brother ever felt very comfortable in middle school. But I too had a humiliating experience at school. The way I saw it, going to accounting school to be an army paymaster simply didn't count as a military career. That I survived to my present age of forty I probably owe to my mother, who stopped me from taking the entrance exam for military school.

In April of the year Japan lost the war, I entered Wonsan Middle School in northern Korea. I can sum up life there with these words: we were wet weather students. On good days, we'd be grubbing up pine roots to eat; we only studied when it rained. That year, the entrance exam for the military school was in August. The exam was to be held at divisional headquarters in Ranam. Several boys in my class—class three in the first year—wanted to take the exam. I was one of them, of course, but my mother wouldn't let me. Once he was called up, my father had gone to the command center in Daegu. He'd been made a liaison officer, which apparently meant he had to move around a lot. Mother had written to him, but hadn't yet received a reply, and not being able to contact him was the reason my mother gave as grounds for not letting me take the exam. By the time of next year's exam she'd certainly be able to contact him—just wait a year, she told me.

I didn't know my mother's true feelings on the matter. To this very day I still don't quite know. But by the time my class pals set off to take the exam, Ranam had already ceased to be the kind of place where people worried about schools and exams and the like. It was around the time the Soviet Union came into the war. I don't know exactly what the state of battle was, but every day refugees were pouring in from Ranam and Cheongjin, heading south on desperately overcrowded freight trains, people stuffed into every boxcar and clinging to every flatbed. Right up to August 15, I had no idea what became of my class pals. I have less than no idea what became of them after that.

Mother saved me from the jaws of death. Even if I hadn't been killed at Ranam, I'd certainly have been separated from my family in northern Korea after we lost the war.

The reason I wanted to go to the military school was clear and simple: if I was going to be a soldier anyway, at least I wanted a higher rank than my father. Not that I was unhappy with my father's position as infantry reserve first lieutenant. No, it was just that, being the son of an honorable first lieutenant, I ought to go to the military academy and become a senior field officer. My older brother, by making no effort to do any such thing, was betraying his ancestry. What kind of a son of a first lieutenant was that? As an officer's son, he should be ashamed of the way he lived, I figured. Ridiculously enough, I even had a fantasy where, as a colonel who'd just graduated from military academy, I turned toward my father, the one-year volunteer reserve first lieutenant, stood stiffly to attention, and gave him a crisp salute.

"Isn't this a military officer's coat, Mom?"

"Well now I don' really know . . ."

"Dad's had two rows of breast buttons, didn't it?"

"Was that so . . . ?"

Where on earth had my mother got hold of this coat? It wasn't secondhand. The khaki coat may not have been made for a military officer, but it was spanking new. Still, I asked no more about it. If I did, something was sure to happen. Anyway, my mother had already forgotten the difference between the coat my father wore as an officer and the one he'd worn as a rank-and-file soldier. She probably couldn't give a damn about that kind of distinction anyway. It was perfectly natural for her since she always thought that way.

"That was a real nice piece of cloth they used," my mother said. "What a waste. That stupid war . . . stole all the people . . . stole all the stuff."

Mother had taken up the hem of the coat. Now this private's greatcoat was a perfect fit for me—all five foot five of me. I gazed upon it in silence. A mysterious feeling came over me, hard to describe. Apparently my brother sensed it. Still lying there with his head propped up on his elbow, he shoved his jaw in the direction of the American civilian guard uniform hanging on the wall.

"If you don' like that coat, how 'bout tryin' thisun?"

What my brother probably wanted to say was: "Still thinking about Dad? Hurry up and forget him! What's the big deal about Dad?"

Chapter 4

ONCE THE TRAIN leaves Akabane, you cross the iron bridge over the Arakawa River and get to Kawaguchi. Twenty years ago, the next station after that was Warabi. These days, however, West Kawaguchi station is sandwiched in between. I suppose the sprawling suburbs have merged together. I do recall that the stretch of the Keihin-Tohoku line from Kawaguchi to Warabi was long. I have a feeling it took over four minutes.

Warabi station had changed too. In a word, it was bigger. Going up the stairs from the platform was a lady who seemed the very model of a salaryman's wife, leading a little girl by the hand. Probably married to a man who had not the slightest connection with the soil of Warabi. Where was she born, I wonder? And where did she grow up? Of course there was no reason I should know. But now she was living in Warabi. Probably to do with her husband's work. Living in a public housing complex? A company dormitory perhaps? A rented house? Or had they bought some cheap and cheerful place? Well, one thing was for sure: the reason they'd built that new station at West Kawaguchi was the dramatic increase in families like hers. That is, Warabi station had turned into a housing complex station pretty much like the one where I lived.

The square in front of the station had changed too. Buildings had gone up to the left and right of the entrance to the shopping street in front of the station. When I arrived at this station for the first time in my life, with Little Koga, it was the kind of place where you wouldn't be surprised to see tricycle taxis parked in front. In those days the station toilet was outside. Next to it were a number of old wooden buildings, little workshops belonging to Oki Electric. Or were they warehouses? There was no sign of Oki Electric now. What had been built there in its place? Not entirely clear. All I could tell was that Oki Electric was gone. The entire area was so utterly changed that you couldn't even tell for sure where the site of the former Oki Electric might have been.

One corner, on the right of the entrance to the shopping street, used to be a jumbled little street of cheap bars. A drinking street? More like a drinking alley. It wasn't even big enough to be called a lane. In the year after I failed the Early Bird Exam, I used to go drinking there now and again. Sometimes I went there with Little Koga. We'd drink second-rate saké or shochu or Torys, the cheapest brand of whisky. I have a feeling that one time I got into a bit of trouble in that drinking alley. But I can't seem to bring to mind exactly what happened. A quarrel with another customer? A dispute over the bill? Something to do with a woman? There seem to have been some dodgy women in that alley. Those tiny little bars had room for only four or five customers, and if two or more of them were women you could be pretty sure they were the shady type. Was it that kind of trouble? I just can't recall. But one thing *is* for sure: I went to that drinking alley several times wearing that greatcoat.

I wonder if the trouble had something to do with the coat? Some drunken customer picked a fight with me while I was wearing it? Or maybe I was short of cash to pay the bill and had the coat taken off me in lieu of money. There might have been some sort of disagreement about the value of the coat on that occasion. I can't put my hand on my heart and swear that no such thing ever happened in that alley. For a start it's exactly the kind of thing that could so easily happen, and besides, I often used to take the coat to the pawnshop with my own hands. Yes indeed—the Nakamura Pawnshop, about a hundred yards from my lodgings. So I knew how much money you could get for the coat. If there'd been a dispute, it would probably have been because one of the women in the alley refused to recognize the worth of the coat if taken to the pawnshop.

I started walking along the station shopping street, in the direction of the old Nakasendo highway. Not that it didn't occur to me to have a quick peek at the old drinking alley first. But a quick look from the outside showed there were buildings all over the area. Had the drinking alley gone underground, beneath the buildings? Or maybe the buildings were just a façade, and if you went round the back you'd find those shady little bars, still there, just the same as before. Maybe I should just pop round the back for a quick look? But hang on—it was still just ten in the morning. More to the point, I first had to visit the place I was lodging twenty years ago. That was my primary objective. The first place of worship on my pilgrimage. I hadn't gone to the trouble of getting up extra early this morning and coming all the way to Warabi just for a spot of sightseeing at the ruins of a station-side drinking alley from twenty years ago.

I just happened to have this little flashback in front of the station, that's all. A feeling that there'd been some kind of trouble there. Of course it was no big deal. I'd say the fact that I couldn't even remember what had happened was proof of that. Suppose, for instance, somebody had snatched the coat off my back in the darkness of that drinking alley, well—that's the kind of thing you'd remember, even if you didn't want to remember it.

All very different from the case of Akaky Akakievich. His overcoat was brand new. It had cat fur on the collar. He had it stolen off him on his way home from a party at the assistant head clerk's house. The party had been called in the name of celebrating Akaky's new coat. Actually the guys at the office had originally said Akaky himself should throw a coat-celebration party, but that was just malicious teasing—they knew perfectly well he could do no such thing. Then the assistant head clerk had invited all the staff to his place instead of Akaky's, but in fact it wasn't really a party in Akaky's honor at all—the day just happened to be the assistant head clerk's name-day.

Probably the only common factor between Akaky as he set out for home from the assistant chief clerk's house and me when I left the drinking alley in front of Warabi station twenty years ago was that we'd both ingested a fair amount of alcohol. Akaky had been treated to vegetable salad, cold slices of veal, meat pasties and *pirozhki* at the party, and he'd also drunk two glasses of champagne. His mates made him drink against his will. Fact of the matter is, he was drunk. After all, this was a man who until recently thought twice before having a cup of tea, never mind glasses of champagne. And he wasn't the kind of Russian who drank vodka instead of tea. No mystery if a couple of glasses of champagne were enough to get him drunk. As proof of that, he very nearly gave chase to a woman who happened to pass him in the street.

Incidentally, I wonder how many glasses of shochu I had drunk that night twenty years ago in the drinking alley in front of Warabi station? Let's suppose for the sake of argument that I'd gone one drink over the recommended three. Probably my degree of drunkenness would have been about the same as that of Akaky after his two glasses of champagne. Did some woman happen to pass in front of me that time, I wonder? Or not? Well, if she *did* happen to pass in front of me, I expect I'd have done the same as Akaky and suddenly started to run after her. Because I can't imagine that the person who emerged from the little drinking alley in front of Warabi station twenty years ago having drunk four glasses of shochu was a happier human being than Akaky. No, I cannot possibly believe that. No way.

Why? Well, why think of the reasons after all these years? I was a person who'd come from the countryside of Chikuzen. A person who'd made a mess of the Early Bird Exam. I was that sort of person, and I was drunk on four glasses of shochu. Late one night, wearing an old khaki infantryman's greatcoat, I suddenly went off in pursuit of some woman I didn't know who happened to pass in front of me. What more do you need by way of a reason? Nothing, I'd say. I started following the woman. It really was a long, long road, that station shopping street. Almost dead straight, too. The shops on either side of the road were already closed, of course. I guess the distance between me and the woman was—what?—about thirty yards. I expect she'd just got off the last train. She had the collar of her overcoat turned up. Couldn't quite make out the color of it, though. Gradually the woman's form came floating up clearly in front of me as it came under a streetlight. Shoulder bag hanging there. Little by little her form once again became hard to make out. I suppose the distance from one streetlight to the next would be about a hundred yards? The woman approached another streetlight. By the looks of it, both hands were in the pockets of her overcoat. The woman didn't look back. Nor change pace. The distance between her and me did not change. Where on earth was she going? Was she going to head straight out to the Nakasendo highway? Just then, she approached another streetlight. She was wearing a beret! A student, maybe? Or a waitress? Or a student doing a part-time job as a waitress? Or could she be a woman like the one that Piskaryov followed in "Nevsky Prospect"? Surely not!

Piskaryov was a poor, unknown painter in Saint Petersburg. The woman who passed him one evening on Nevsky Prospect was a brunette. He suddenly started following her. Because "he wanted to see where this lovely being dwelt, who seemed to have flown down from heaven right onto Nevsky Prospect, and would surely fly off again no one knew where."

Piskaryov's heart was on the verge of bursting. Everything in front of his eyes was turning misty, and heaven and earth seemed all but ready to collapse.

"The sidewalk rushed under him, carriages with galloping horses seemed motionless, the bridge was stretched out and breaking on its arch, the house stood roof down, the sentry box came tumbling to meet him, and the sentry's halberd, along with the golden words of a shop sign and its painted scissors, seemed to flash right on his eyelashes."

The brunette eventually disappeared into a four-story building. He went running up the stairs after her. But it turned out to be a house of prostitution. Piskaryov ran home to his apartment in a state of shock. He became an opium addict—in his hallucinations, the brunette would appear as his chaste and virtuous wife. He started painting nudes to pay for the opium he bought from a Persian dealer. Eventually opium destroyed his brain. Piskaryov cut his throat with a pallet knife and died.

I was now the Piskaryov of Warabi. It happened when one of the streetlights lit up her beret. No, that's not right. It wasn't that I was the Piskaryov of Warabi; it was that she was the brunette of Warabi. That's how I wanted it: she was not to be a student, or a waitress, or a student doing a part-time job as a waitress—I wanted her to be the brunette who plunged Piskaryov into despair. At all costs, that's what I wanted her to be. That way would leave me with some hope. Worse—if she wouldn't be that way for me, I would have no hope.

At that moment, the woman suddenly stopped. On that long, long, dead-straight shopping street, there was just one place where a road led off to the right. It was almost exactly halfway from the station to the old Nakasendo highway. The road that led off to the right went through the grounds of Warabi Shrine, and when you emerged on the other side and crossed a muddy little stream, you arrived at the back entrance of my lodgings. In terms of distance it was probably something of a shortcut. But the back entrance was locked around nightfall. For that matter, at this time of night I'd probably have to clamber over the gate even at the front entrance. Anyhow, if she was going to turn off here, I too would of course turn off. I was no Piskaryov. I wouldn't run away like he did. The place where she stopped was under the streetlight, right there on the corner where the shortcut turned off. I wondered if she looked like Yoko san . . . or not. Yoko san was the only prostitute I knew at the time. She was a prostitute who lived a couple of miles from my little home town in the Chikuzen countryside. She was also the only woman I'd ever known. Therefore there was no need for me to run away like Piskaryov. Far from running away, I was all ready to go running towards the woman. That was because the woman under the streetlight suddenly turned and looked back. But just then, as I was about to dash towards her, somebody's hand grabbed the shoulder of my coat and pulled me back. At the same time a whistle sounded shrilly in my ear.

"Can't you see the traffic lights!?"

Quite unexpectedly, I was stopped in my tracks. It was a traffic policeman in a white helmet who had pulled me back with a sharp tug on the shoulder of my coat. No doubt he was the one who had blown the whistle, too. Now I understood the situation. The lights were indeed red. Cars were driving along from left and right, passing each other in front of the lights. In a situation like this anybody would have pulled me back, even if they weren't a policeman.

"I'm awfully sorry." Instead of hanging my head I scratched my hair in embarrassment. "But excuse me—is this the Nakasendo highway?"

"Nakasendo?"

"Yes . . ."

"Look, where are you going anyway?"

"Well actually, I . . ."

"No . . ."

"What?"

"This is the bypass, you know."

"Oh really? Sorry, I'm visiting for the first time in twenty years, you see."

"For detailed route information, kindly inquire at the police box."

"So, would I hit the Nakasendo highway if I continued straight this way?"

"Hit?"

The policeman in the white helmet inclined his head quizzically. I inclined my head too, and kept it inclined as I crossed the bypass. The lights had changed, you see, and it wouldn't do to talk with him any longer. There was of course no bypass there twenty years ago. The road from the station to the Nakasendo highway was a long, straight road that was crossed by no other road. It just slammed into the Nakasendo highway at right angles and ended there—a perfect T. It didn't cross the highway. It didn't cut through it either.

Or then again, maybe the bypass I'd just crossed *was* the Nakasendo highway? Still with my head tilted in doubt, I carried on walking. But it turned out that the bypass really was a newly constructed road. A little later I got to the place where the road to the grounds of Warabi Shrine turned off the main road. It was the place where the woman I'd been following that night twenty years ago, after leaving that drinking alley in front of the station, had suddenly stopped and turned.

Of course there was no reason whatever to suppose that the woman with the coat with the upturned collar and the beret might still be there. Was she a student? Was she a waitress? Or was she the same sort of woman as the brunette whom Piskaryov had followed on Nevsky Prospect? I prayed that the woman with the coat with the upturned collar and the beret might be a brunettish woman. But in the end, her true form remained obscured. It is the truth that she not only stopped under the streetlight, but suddenly turned to look back at me. I instinctively made to rush to her, but just about managed to stop myself, instead reaching into my coat pocket to produce a cigarette. Then, just like a B-movie actor playing the part of a man who has put a cigarette to his lips but cannot seem to find his matches, I went up to her with my hands fidgeting in my coat pockets.

It truly was a terrible performance. But as far as I knew, it was a kind of signal. It was also a sort of challenge.

"Excuse me, sir, do you have a light?" Brunettes often use that kind of line, but this time I'd be the one asking. If only the woman in the coat with the upturned collar and the beret was of the "brunette" variety, she would understand my drift immediately. The skillfulness or otherwise of the performance would be beside the point.

"Can't you sound a little more convincing than that?" No, surely I wouldn't get that kind of answer. And indeed, I didn't. Of course I took care. I did my best not to be like a stereotypical B-movie actor. The only reason I'm talking to you in the middle of the night like this, young lady, is because I wish to borrow a light for my cigarette. The light is not some kind of signal or cue, but simply my objective. Needless to say, it is not some kind of challenge. I am, as you may observe, in a state of alcoholic intoxication. And I have no intention of concealing that fact. That's right—I've had a few drinks. Yeah, yeah . . . and all on my own, pathetically enough. And at this piss-hole in front of the station where I don't know anybody. Yeah, it's the pits. Laughable really. Up all night, drowning my sorrows because I messed up on the Early Bird Exam. But maybe we're both strangers here. I tell you—I know the names of quite a few foreign countries outside Japan, but I'd never heard of Warabi before I came here. What's it mean? Bracken? Fern? Whatever. Thing is, I'm a complete stranger in this town—Bracken, Fern, Bean Sprout, whatever it's called. Nobody knows me, and of course, I don't know anybody. I have no proof of identity. I'm not in high school and I'm not at college. I don't even go to a crammer. I'm not an office worker and I'm not a factory hand. I'm not a live-in newspaper delivery boy and I'm not a pachinko parlor attendant. The women in the bars around the station that I sometimes go to—well, they don't know the name of the elementary school I went to, or the junior high school, or the senior high school. Since I'm in a town I'd never even heard of, you could say that's only natural. In short, I am a complete nobody, from a town that no one has ever heard of. Still and all, the lady at the pawnshop has a good line. What do you think she calls me? *Sonny.* "But sonny," she says. "All right then sonny." That really gets to me somehow. Whenever the lady at the pawnshop calls me sonny, I can't help thinking that that's really what I am—just another sonny boy. Mind you, there's a particular lilt to the way she says *sonny* . . . Lilt? Or maybe accent? Maybe it's a way of saying things they have in this old staging post on the Nakasendo highway. Anyhow, that *sonny* is a mysterious *sonny*. And I am no more than that mysterious *sonny*. A *sonny* who couldn't be anything other than that mysterious *sonny*. Oh and by the way—I'm drunk. But that's not why I came up to you and stopped and started talking to you when you suddenly stopped and looked at me just now. No, it's not because I'm drunk—I just want a light for my cigarette.

"By the way, what time is it now?" asked the woman in the coat with the turned-up collar and the beret.

I had just finished lighting my cigarette.

"Thank you very much."

I made as if to return to her the matches that she had opened the flap of her shoulder bag in order to take out and give me.

"Er, would you like a cigarette yourself?"

"Me?"

"How about one for yourself?"

The woman silently shook her head.

"Don't like Hikaris?"

The woman shook her head silently again. I put the box of *Hikari* cigarettes in my coat pocket along with the matches.

"I don't like smoking in the cold," she said.

"Ah—your matches!" I took out the woman's matches that I'd inadvertently put in my pocket. "Thanks."

"It's all right—keep them. I've got others."

"Oh, really?" Glancing at the matchbox, I noticed Beethoven's face on the label. *Classics and Coffee—L'Ambre.* I turned the matchbox over. Beethoven was only on one side.

"You're welcome to it. What time was it again?" Those were the woman's last words.

"Hmm . . . what time *could* it be, I wonder?" As I replied, I pinched Beethoven's face between thumb and fingertip. Then I slowly exhaled cigarette smoke. "It was eleven when I left that bar . . ."

Just then, the woman wearing the coat with the turned-up collar and the beret started walking away. Another sudden event. The direction she chose was also surprising. She didn't take the shortcut that turned off on the right, nor did she continue towards the Nakasendo highway; instead, she started walking in the direction of Warabi station. She was going back the way she came. Was she planning to look at the station clock?

"Hey, hey!" I called out to her from behind. She glanced back briefly. Then she took her left hand out of her coat pocket and appeared to glance at a wrist watch.

So ended that incident of twenty years ago. The distance between me and the beret gradually widened, of course. Eventually I could no longer even hear the sound of her footsteps anymore. That was probably because I myself had started to walk again. Ah, the click-clack of wooden sandals as folks stride along the highway! Of course, I wasn't wearing wooden sandals. But it was the kind of night when the clack of wooden sandals made that kind of frozen reverberation. I no longer met anybody as I walked along. I wasn't following any-one. I didn't even come across a dog. I continued straight on, just like that, until I hit the Nakasendo highway and turned right. I passed Warabi Post Office, I passed the Nakamura Pawnshop. Of course it was totally dark behind the latticed doors. If it were daytime, you'd be able to see a single big zelkova tree coming up on the right about here. The liquor store owner's zelkova. It was an old liquor store, with the name of a brand of saké displayed in a big frame. Between the liquor store and the two-story tea shop was another old wooden gate. I stopped in front of that gate. The gate was shut. First I gave a little push. But I gave that up at once, and tried giving it a light knock with my right fist. But I gave that up at once too. Eleven o'clock was the curfew for this gate. If I overdid the knocking, the tea seller liv-ing next door to the left would wake up. It was a retail tea shop. The tea seller wasn't my landlord. The two-story house with the tea shop was rented. The family that lived on the ground floor and ran the tea shop and the family that rented the upstairs floor were both ten-ants. The landlord lived in the main house, behind this gate. And it was in the main house that I rented a little three-mat room, my own little nest.

Unless I got through this gate, I could not return to my nest. Were the Koga brothers already asleep? They might possibly still be awake.

The Koga brothers were renting an outbuilding next to the white-washed storehouse that stood just to the right of the main house. It had a couple of tatami rooms—three mats and four-and-a-half mats, a dirt-floor kitchen, and a small room with floorboards; Little Koga, the Takushoku University student, lived in the floorboard room. But all this was behind the gate. Maybe if I pounded on the gate with all my might and called out for Little Koga, he would appear and greet me with a friendly *osu!* The only thing was, the teaseller's family next door would wake up first. Actually, I'd already had a complaint from them, via the landlord, for that very thing. So it was no good knocking at the gate. "A monk knocking at the gate under the moon," as the old Chinese poem had it, wasn't an option here. In that case the monk in the moonlight had to push upon the gate. But the way things had been decreed, after eleven the gate wouldn't open even if you pushed it. So it was no good either pushing or knocking.

Of course, I wasn't a monk. And if neither pushing nor knocking would work for me, it was permissible to step back and have a little think. So, first I took off the old infantryman's coat and slung it onto the roof of the gate. Then I found a foothold in the wall on the liquor store side of the gate, opposite from the tea store, scrambled up the side of the gate, and succeeded in getting safely over. That showed what you could do with the elbow power of a man capable of fifteen chin-ups.

Was the moon shining down on the gate as I climbed over it that night? Or not? I couldn't say for sure. Because as soon as I'd dropped down on the other side of the gate, I pulled down the old infantry-man's coat from where I'd slung it onto the roof of the gate, cocooned myself in it from head to toe, tiptoed past the Koga brothers' out-building, and sneaked into my three-mat nest. I really didn't have the leisure to gaze up at the cold moon.

One thing I am sure of, though, is that my coat came through the escapade unscathed. The true nature of the woman in the beret who stopped under the streetlight and looked back at me remains unclear. But I was not totally in the dark about her. Even I could figure out that the thing the woman with the coat with the upturned collar was after was a wristwatch rather than my coat. Was she, in fact, a "brunette"? Of course, I couldn't say for sure. But if that was in fact the case, she had valued my khaki overcoat less than a wristwatch. If I'd had a wristwatch on me, then she'd have figured that even if worse came to worst and I didn't have a penny on me, at least she wouldn't make a loss on the deal. Or did the woman with the beret take one look at me and make a rapid calculation that her own value as a "brunette" was equal to that of my old infantryman's greatcoat *plus* a wristwatch? Was that why she immediately turned on her heel the moment she knew I didn't have a wristwatch? Surely not!

But even supposing that *was* the case, it would have been a decision made entirely on her own. Maybe the reason she turned back towards Warabi station in such a great hurry was that she was looking for an overcoat more appropriate to her own value as a "brunette." One might surmise that she'd gone back to the drinking alley near the station to try and get herself followed by some other man wandering drunkenly out of the place in a different overcoat. What sort of overcoat was she hankering after, I wonder? Sable? Beaver? Would she have been satisfied with a coat with a cat-fur collar that, from a distance, looked like sable? Of course I had no idea, since what she'd have been after was an overcoat she judged to be a suitable match for her own worth.

Say whatever you like, you have to admit that in that beret she was a pretty classy overcoat thief. Not like the robbers who attacked Akaky Akakievich. The two of them just came right up out of the dark, stripped the coat off his back and made off with it. "He suddenly saw two men with moustaches right in front of him, although it was too dark to make them out exactly. His eyes misted over and his heart started pounding. 'Aha, that's *my* overcoat all right,' one of them said in a voice like thunder, grabbing him by the collar. Akaky Akakievich was about to shout for help, but the other man stuck a fist the size of the clerk's head right in his face and said: 'Wanna call out? Go right ahead!' All Akaky Akakievich knew was that they pulled his coat off and kicked him in the knee, he fell back in the snow and after that he knew nothing more."

Even if by some remote chance my overcoat had ended up in the hands of that woman with the coat with the turned-up collar and the beret that night twenty years ago, I surely would not have had as terrifying an experience as Akaky. I'm not just talking about myself either. The same would apply to any other man who had had his overcoat stripped off him by that woman in the beret. Anyway, most important—no harm befell my coat. Nor my wristwatch—since that night my wristwatch was safe and sound in the vaults of the Naka-mura Pawnshop.

This alone did not make everything clear, however. A certain night twenty years ago—but *which* night? Could I put a date to it? That was the thing. Because that way at least I would know that the coat was still safely in my possession at that point in time.

- Keihin-Tohoku line: Warabi (Mar '52–May '53)

Of course I wasn't wearing the coat *throughout* that period. Let's start by considering 1952. I recall with certainty the wind off the Kanto Plain that was blowing on me for the first time in my life when I went up to Tokyo to take the Early Bird Exam in March, and that it was decidedly cold. It was a yellowish early spring wind, with sand mixed in it. After taking the Early Bird Exam, I went on a Hato Bus tour of Tokyo. Then I went to the Imperial Theatre to take in a musical starring the great "Enoken." Was it *The Imitation Murasaki and the Rustic Genji*? I rather think it was something like that. Who was the leading lady? Fubuki Koshiji? Shizuko Kasagi? I'm not quite clear on that point, but I do remember one thing—she wore a gorgeous twelve-layer kimono, and when she whirled round to show you the rear view, there was nothing there but a butterfly G-string! Yes, it was that sort of musical, with a fancy wardrobe. Why did I go to the Imperial Theatre, though? I really don't know anymore. Probably I was invited by that classmate of mine who got into Waseda University. Or maybe the idea came from another classmate who joined the Maritime Self-Defense Force. Either way, the three of us definitely went out together to see *The Imitation Murasaki and the Rustic Genji*. The three of us had been classmates for six straight years in that country town in Chikuzen, right through junior and senior high school.

But now then, you ask: Was I wearing the old khaki infantryman's greatcoat when I walked up the crimson-carpeted stairs of the Imperial Theatre, or not? That's a tricky one. Speaking in terms of the time of year, I certainly should have been wearing it. The coldness of that March Kanto wind, blowing on me for the first time in my life! In my memory of the sandy yellow early spring breeze, that's how it was. But the coldness of that night twenty years ago with the woman with the beret did not have the feel of a March breeze to it. No sir— it had to be midwinter. Midwinter, sometime between March 1952 and May 1953.

"Which means . . ." I spoke the calculations out loud. ". . . at least until sometime in December 1952, or January to February 1953 . . ." the old infantryman's greatcoat was still in my possession.

Still and all, what a boringly long, straight road, it was this single road leading out from Warabi station to the junction with the old Nakasendo highway! Actually this may be something that applies generally to staging posts on the old highways. In the Meiji era they laid down the track for the railways, but often, apparently, a long way away from the old highways. It's a bit like that in Soka too. Admittedly Soka is served by a private line rather than JNR, but there's a similar straight road, with shopping streets on either side, leading out from the station to meet the old Nikko highway. Of course you couldn't possibly compare it to the road from Warabi station to the old Nakasendo highway for sheer length. It couldn't be more than a quarter the length, if that. The Warabi road was in a whole different league. I wonder if someone who used to live there had particularly incurred the wrath of the Meiji government, so much that the railway line had deliberately been laid a really long way off, condemning the old highway to history as the new era got under way? It had been utterly ruined. The road I was walking along was the sort of road that provoked this sort of thought. It got to a point where I was hallucinating that I'd been forced to walk along this road non-stop for the last twenty years.

Hey-ho! I gave an involuntary sigh. Then I lit a cigarette, turned right onto the Nakasendo highway, and set off walking in the direction of Warabi Post Office, which was in fact the direction of the Nakamura Pawnshop.

Chapter 5

A FAMILY CAR was parked in front of the gate of the Ishida family's house. Could it be the son's car? Or a car belonging to the man who ran the liquor store next door? Twenty years ago, the son and heir of the Ishida family had been in his second year at Urawa senior high school. What on earth might have become of him twenty years on? He was the oldest and the only son of the family. He had a couple of little sisters, one at junior high and one at elementary school. His name was Ei'ichi. Then there was Takako, and—what was the name of the youngest girl? Dad had died in the war. Granddad had been village or town headman or something. But twenty years ago he was already gone. Grandma was still alive and well, though—a dignified white-haired old lady, well suited to the role of village headman's wife. Maybe village headman's rather than town headman's wife. The mother of the house was always wearing baggy work pantaloons. Well I don't suppose she wore them all year round, of course, but in my image of her twenty years ago she is wearing those pantaloons.

The Ishida family was, in short, a long-standing pillar of the Warabi community. I daresay they were landowners. And that's probably why they came down in the world after the war ended. Twenty years ago, no one in the Ishida family worked. The mother of the household wore those work pantaloons as her ordinary housewife's and widow's wear, not because she was working in the fields or whatever.

On the grounds stood an old bungalow that at some time in the past seemed to have been a little workshop with spinning looms. They had carried out some renovations and there was a family living in it. Then there was Big Koga living with his wife in the outbuilding next to the whitewashed storehouse, and Little Koga rooming there as well. The two-story house next to the entrance gate had the tea - vendor's family living on the ground floor and another family renting the upstairs floor. And then, in a three-mat room in a corner of the main house, there was me. That completes the list of tenants paying rent to the Ishida family twenty years ago. My room rent was eight hundred yen a month. How much, I wonder, were the fees at Urawa Senior High School?

It was a black car, the one parked in front of the gate. I am awfully ignorant about car makes, but this was not, in any case, a shiny new one. It didn't look like a foreign car either. I could see some kind of cuddly stuffed animal toy in the backseat. Maybe that was what made me think it was a family car. I imagined the figure of the Ishidas' only son with his wife and kids sitting in the back, gripping the steering wheel. By now he would be a man of thirty-seven or thirty-eight. Oy, Ei-chan! It *was* "Ei-chan" we used to call you, right? By the way, remember that overcoat I used to wear in those days? That's right—the old khaki infantryman's greatcoat.

If he was a salaryman these days, however, you wouldn't expect him to be home at this time of day. And there was probably an eighty or ninety percent chance that he'd gone to university and become a salaryman. He'd been a diligent high school boy, with a shaven head. Maybe he'd even got into Tokyo University and become a high-ranking official in some ministry. You couldn't rule it out. As the only man of the Ishida household, he'd been in a position where he really had to make something of himself. He was the lone star of hope for the Ishida family—a respected old lineage that had come down in the world. Then again, I wondered if the Ishida family still lived behind that gate anyway? Truth to tell, this doubt was not one that came to me suddenly. This very doubt was what had stopped me from buying some Soka *senbei*, the rock-hard rice crackers that are the local specialty, as a calling-present for the Ishidas when I set out from Soka this morning. Anyway, it was time to go through that gate! Or then again, maybe I should be making inquiries at the tea store first?

I went round to the other side of the car. The front entrance to the Ishidas' compound was just as I recalled it—a little latticed door under the main gate. But they weren't selling tea at the little house to the left of the gate. I suddenly fell under the spell of a childish fancy. What if I quit the apartment in the mammoth condominium on the outskirts of Soka, and came and rented this little two-story wooden house instead? And how about getting my wife to run a little store selling tea on the ground floor?

"Excuse me," I called out through the door. There was no reply. I felt relieved, since I was on the verge of forgetting why I was calling out to the space behind the front door in the first place. Of course I hadn't come visiting Warabi in hopes of finding suitable premises near the old Nakasendo highway to open a tea store. But what made me so hesitant? My objective was to track down the whereabouts of my old coat—nothing more and nothing less! I threw away my childish daydream about the tea store. This time I went straight round the black car and put my foot right through the gate. But just as I got through the gate, I stopped in my tracks, because I was about to bump right into a young housewife with plastic sandals on her feet. Apparently she had emerged from the side entrance of the two-story house.

"Oh, sorry, please do excuse me." My apology was almost a conditioned reflex, and I actually got more flustered as I looked at the housewife's face. "Ah, um."

"What?"

"Er, Takako san?" Then, hurriedly, I took back my words. I'd got it wrong, evidently. "Oh please—I'm sorry, do excuse me."

Apparently, though, the young housewife was not the type who was abnormally wary of strangers. Without turning a gaze on me that might seem to be inspecting my appearance too closely, she silently made as if to go out through the gate. That meant it would have been all right for me to carry on into the grounds of the house. There, I could have checked the appearance of the Ishida residence twenty years on with my own eyes. But something—maybe the fact that somehow the whole garden seemed so different from what I recalled—made me stop the young housewife and ask her another question. Had I perhaps come through the wrong gate?

"Er, actually," I asked her in a voice that really had lost all confidence. "In there, there used to be . . ."

"What?"

"It would be about twenty years ago . . ."

"You mean the Ishidas?"

"Ah, so you *are* Mrs. Ishida?"

"What?"

"I mean, about the Ishidas' house there . . ."

"If it's the Ishidas you're looking for, they live in the two-story house behind this house on the left."

"Two stories?"

"Go right through to the back of the compound and you'll see their name on the house."

It was about thirty minutes after that when I met Mrs. Ishida for the first time in twenty years. Of course it wouldn't have taken thirty minutes to just walk straight there. When she had finished answering my inquiries, the young housewife with the plastic sandals started walking towards the gate, then stopped almost at once. That was because I'd started walking out behind her. It felt as if she were standing there waiting for me to say something. She probably thought I was going to ask her something else. But I just gave her a little nod and walked out of the Ishidas' gate ahead of her. There was nothing else for me to ask her.

Fruit? Or cakes? I was wondering about a calling-gift for the Ishidas. In the end I went to the rice-cracker shop. There was a rice-cracker shop just to the left of the two-story house that used to have the tea store in it. I can remember when it opened. The shop was launched exactly twenty years ago. The Ishidas did not have very good feelings about this shop. Probably the reason was, the owner had bought the property from the Ishidas and then redone the interior to turn it into a rice-cracker shop. Twenty years ago, the Ishidas would much have preferred to hang on to that house, even if they had had to rent it out, but some overwhelming circumstance had forced them to sell it.

In the rice-cracker shop, I was obliged to wait for quite a while. Would it have been twenty minutes? At first I was standing up, but after a while I sat myself down on a little stool and lit up a cigarette. That's when I remembered about the shop opening twenty years ago. Was this the time of day when they baked the fresh rice crackers in the little factory out the back? There was just one little old lady looking after the shop. There were only two customers in front of me. But it took her twenty minutes to serve just those two customers. I began to feel a little annoyed. I'd made a big effort to get up early today—was it right that my hard-won time was being wasted in a rice-cracker shop? Maybe it was my own irritation that made me recall the grudge that the Ishidas held against this shop when it had opened twenty years ago.

However, I don't seem to have felt any contradiction in taking a box of those begrudged rice crackers to the Ishidas as a calling-gift. Far from it —all I was thinking about was how to get my hands on that box of rice crackers as soon as possible so I could carry it round to the Ishidas' place. I didn't have the leisure to calmly sit there observing the old lady's old-fashioned movements as she slowly counted out the rice crackers, neatly packed them into a cardboard box, put on the lid, wrapped it in fancy paper and then carefully tied it up with a flat ribbon in the pattern of a cross.

Then again, why did I have to be in such a hurry, I wondered? After all, had I not already confirmed that the Ishidas' house was still there, on the plot furthest from the gate? And it was still a few minutes before eleven in the morning. Even assuming I would leave the Ishidas' place before lunchtime, I still had a good hour in hand. And if that turned out to be insufficient time, I could always leave and come back after lunch. I took the neatly arranged box of assorted rice-cracker nuggets, so carefully wrapped and cross-ribboned by the old lady in the rice-cracker shop, and this time I strode without hesitation through the gate that led to the Ishidas' house.

Things certainly had changed in the grounds of the Ishida residence. The first thing I noticed was that the whole place felt as if it had got more narrow and cramped. What had changed, and how? It seemed that absolutely everything had changed. However, I plucked up the courage to ignore each and every one of the changes in the compound, and headed straight to the plot at the back. Because otherwise all the time in the world could have passed and I still would not have made it to the Ishidas' front door.

The Ishida residence was a two-story building, just as the young housewife in plastic sandals had said. Well, fair enough. One wouldn't be that amazed to find that they'd made some changes to that old wooden bungalow in the course of twenty years. However, what did give me pause for thought was the intercom they'd had fixed to the side of the front entrance. Of course I have nothing against intercoms *per se*. It was just that I couldn't imagine how to introduce myself when I addressed that small, square microphone.

"Excuse me." And then, "My name is Akaki . . ." I would state my name. The tricky bit was what to say after that.

"As a matter of fact, I am the Akaki who rented a room in your house twenty years ago." Yes, but then they'd want to know why that should concern them. Was the man who'd lodged with them twenty years ago now some kind of salesman?

These intercoms certainly are handy little devices: they sow consternation in the hearts of visitors who don't want to reveal their true identity. Visitors can be differentiated by this device. *I can't get through to you using this device. Please just show me your face. I'd be able to make myself understood if you could just see me. We could definitely communicate with each other!* But you wouldn't get through that way. You'd have to persuade a person you couldn't see. If you couldn't get through that way, that would be the end of the matter. Because you can't make someone open her front door against her will.

"Err . . ." I said, and slightly adjusted my hair. This was turning out to be even harder than a telephone answering machine. Maybe because it was so hard to give my name. Who am I and where am I from? Akaki from Soka? That wasn't going to cut any ice.

"Er, is the lady of the house at home by any chance? It's Akaki, the man who was introduced to you twenty years ago by the Koga brothers who used to rent your outbuilding . . ."

It would appear that Mrs. Ishida was out. The house had one of those outside wooden walkways, and near the front-left corner (as you faced the main entrance), there was a child's swing that someone had assembled from a kit. There was a tricycle too. Maybe Mrs. Ishida was no longer around? Certainly the Ishida residence had assumed a more youthful appearance, with its two stories and its intercom. Could it be that the silvery-haired grandmother who'd been married to the village headman, and the mother who used pantaloons for everyday wear, had already both passed away? If that was so, who would be left in the household who knew me and the Koga brothers?

"Err . . ." For a third time I put my mouth close to the intercom: "Umm, where is the firstborn of the family, Ei'ichi, working these days, I wonder? Or . . . no, if Ei'ichi san isn't there, perhaps I could talk to Takako san . . ."

If that didn't work, I might as well just pack it in. Having made myself so clear, I suddenly felt as if I'd regained a great warmth and generosity of heart. I stepped back from the intercom and walked down the concrete steps in front of the entrance. And then I had a look at the Ishidas' garden for the first time in twenty years.

The first thing I noticed missing was the well. Twenty years ago, right in the middle of the Ishidas' garden, there'd been a well with a pump, under a tin roof. Summer or winter, people would wash their clothes and their faces under that tin roof. The same for the Koga brothers. But then, the next thing I noticed missing was the outbuilding where the Koga brothers used to live, next to the whitewashed storehouse. Now that it was gone, you could see the main storehouse it had stood in front of. The storehouse looked unsteady and isolated on its own like that, like a building that had survived a fire. The side wall was the brownish color of a dirty old person's skin. Twenty years ago, that wall had been hidden from view. All you could see in those days was the front of the storehouse, with its thick iron door, because the Kogas' outbuilding had been built so close to the left wall of the storehouse that it was almost touching.

Why, then, did the garden as a whole feel smaller and more cramped than twenty years ago? No doubt because a low fence had been put up where the well and pump used to be, and a house was standing on the other side of it. Maybe Takako san had got married and they'd built it for her? Or was it another property for renting out? It had a nice, blue-tiled roof that gave it an exceedingly at-home kind of atmosphere. I wonder how much it would cost to rent a room at the Ishida residence these days? But surely this new two-story house wouldn't have the kind of pokey little three-mat room I used to rent twenty years ago. Was it a chambermaid's room? It could have been that, or possibly a manservant's quarters. You went through the gate, and there was this old paved pathway, laid alongside the earthen wall that marked the boundary with the liquor store next door. The pathway led straight to the warehouse. If you turned left, you'd walk past the Koga brothers' outbuilding and reach the broad walkway that ran around the outside of the L-shaped main residence. To the right of the walkway was a latticed doorway. But the entrance to my little three-mat nest was neither via the walkway nor through the latticed door. I used to go in and out through another door, which you reached by making a little left turn at the corner of the walkway, turning right along the side of the main residence, and then continuing right to the back of the house on the west side. It opened and closed horizontally, just like storm shutters do. There was a dirt-floor area about one mat in size before you went up a step to the room itself, which had three edgeless tatami mats laid out in a row.

This three-mat room was untouched by sunlight all year round. After all, it was the most westerly room of a large, L-shaped wooden bungalow. There were several other rooms jumbled together to the east of the room, and on the west side there was a latticed window, through which you could glimpse a workshop belonging to a small iron foundry. The foundry was run by the family that had moved into the former loom shop and turned it into a dwelling. Apparently they were making stuff out of scrap iron. From morning onwards, the sound of that scrap iron being turned into stuff came clearly to my ear. After all, the factory was only two or three yards away.

What all this meant was that the path that turned left at the corner of the wooden walkway, then turned right along the side of the main residence and finally reached the entrance to this three-mat room, was like an alleyway running through the garden of the Ishidas' house. As a matter of fact there was moss growing on the ground outside the latticed window. But this path, so like an alleyway through the garden, was a sort of private road to me. When I came home after the 11 p.m. curfew and climbed over the gate, I was able to make my way along that path unobserved and sneak into my three-mat nest. Though I should mention that if I needed to take a leak I had to get it done before climbing over the gate. If I happened to forget that little matter when climbing over the gate, I would have to quickly relieve myself somewhere between the gate and the storehouse, aiming in the direction of the earthen wall. You see, the toilet I was supposed to use was a good old-fashioned traditional Japanese ladies' toilet. Probably it was installed for the use of some serving girl who used to have the same three-mat room I was now occupying. You only had to open a single sliding door to get from the three-mat room to the main residence, arriving first in a four-and-a-half-mat room that was basically used as a kind of storeroom. It stank of damp old cloth. The ladies' toilet had been built adjoining that room, and one evening I happened to relieve myself there in a standing position, only to meet with an extremely embarrassing scolding from the silver-haired grandmother the following day.

"Mr. Akaki, that toilet is designed to be used in the squatting position!"

Could that have been the very day after I met the woman with the beret? Or not? Possibly it had been long before that. Either way, it must have been after one of those nights when I missed the curfew, clambered over the gate and sneaked into the three-mat room. And I must have been drunk. Having to clamber over the front gate was a direct consequence of drinking a lot of booze and missing the curfew. I knew of no other way to kill time until past eleven o'clock.

Another thing I couldn't do sober, of course, was going to the far side of the river. The far side of the river? Yes indeed, I mean the far side of Ryogoku Bridge. When on earth did I get into the habit of crossing that bridge on my own? I couldn't tell you offhand. But I'm certain that on one occasion I came back from the far side of the river on the last train and clambered over the front gate. Was I wearing the coat that night too, I wonder? That detail eludes me. Maybe the coat was in the safekeeping of the Nakamuras when I set out that night? Either way, one thing I can say for sure is that this happened some time after the night with the beret woman—because the night I met the beret woman, the only prostitute I had known was Yoko san.

"Mr. Akaki, that toilet is designed to be used in the squatting position!"

No, surely not! Surely I could not have got that scolding the day after I got back from the far side of the river and clambered over the gate. Still, it makes me wonder who on earth it could have been who taught me about the location of Kameido Third Precinct, on the far side of the river? Could I have read about it in Kafu's *Strange Tale from East of the River*? Or did I hear about it from Little Koga?

"Hello there . . ."

At that moment I heard a woman's voice calling me from behind. I turned around and there was a woman standing in the open doorway of the Ishida residence. My self-introduction, made over the intercom, had finally got through. I put an embarrassed hand to my hair, bowed and made a couple of steps in her direction.

"Please do excuse me for dropping in so very suddenly like this."

I came to a halt, poised with just one foot on the concrete step in front of the porch. I slightly adjusted my grip on the rice crackers in the box with the cross-tied ribbon. But the face of the woman who had opened the front door and called to me was that of a perfect stranger.

"Well, then . . ."

"Er, excuse me, but which Akaki san might you be?"

"Ah, well, as I mentioned over this intercom, I'm actually someone who used to be a tenant here at the Ishida residence—admittedly some twenty years ago."

"Tenant?"

"Ah, well, I say that, but really I was just lodging here. Renting a room."

"Oh. Well, I'm afraid I haven't really heard anything about that, you see."

"Excuse me, but I was wondering about the lady of the house . . ."

"Meaning what?"

"Er, the mother, that is, Ei'ichi san's mother."

"Mother, you say?"

"Yes, that's right. As I said, the, er, lady of the house."

Mrs. Ishida, I learned, was out. But I still had hope, because I had established that she was still well.

"Excuse me, but would you happen to be the wife of Ei'ichi san?"

"Yes, I am Takako, what of it?"

"Takako san?"

"But forgive me if I sound rude—I have no acquaintance by the name of Akaki."

"What?"

"Just now, on the intercom, you mentioned Ei'ichi san and Takako san, which was why I opened the door."

"Ah yes, well, what with it being twenty years, and visiting totally out of the blue and all that, I was worrying about how to explain myself, so I sort of mentioned a few things that might have stayed in your memory."

"That's as may be, but I'm afraid I wouldn't have seen any need to open the door if you hadn't mentioned the name 'Takako.'"

At some point in this conversation I had withdrawn the one foot I had placed on the doorstep. However, needless to say, we had been talking somewhat at cross-purposes in the course of the exchange. An exceedingly commonplace, not to say utterly banal, misunderstanding had arisen. This was a different Takako. The Ishidas' eldest daughter, a junior high school pupil twenty years ago, was a Takako; and their son and heir, Ei'ichi, had married a woman who was also a Takako, but a different Takako, and I had just met her for the first time, twenty years after I last set eyes on the other Takako. The misunderstanding soon became apparent. Because Mrs. Ishida herself, who had apparently been out and about in the neighborhood, came home. She arrived just as I was on the point of handing the cross-ribboned box of rice crackers to the new Takako. I had just decided that it might well be counterproductive to continue the exchange any further, and was preparing to beat at least a temporary retreat from the scene.

Of course, even if my old landlady had not got back home at that precise moment, a minor misunderstanding like that of the two Takakos would probably have become apparent. Not only was it such a *small* misunderstanding, it was also no more than a commonplace, banal misunderstanding. It was a trick that would barely deceive a child. But the reason I have to make such a fuss over that misunderstanding is that it was all thanks to it that I was able to meet my old landlady. If that woman hadn't happened to be another Takako san, my gabbled introduction over the intercom would never have got through to her. The reason the front door was opened was that she was another Takako san. And if the front door hadn't been opened, I would have had to emerge from the gate of the Ishida family compound still clutching the cross-ribboned box of rice crackers.

What a commonplace, banal, chance coincidence! And yet sometimes it can happen that a chance coincidence that commonplace and banal can be the saving of a forty-year-old man who is the height of discretion. You can't entirely rule it out. Indeed, I myself was saved. Thanks to that coincidence I was able to achieve my objective of meeting Mrs. Ishida. Not that all would have been irredeemably lost had it not been for this commonplace, banal coincidence. The meaning of my early-bird start to the day would not have been rendered totally meaningless in an instant. True enough, I was saved by one coincidence. And I have duly emphasized the coincidence as well worth emphasizing, but that is not to say I'm trying to explain the whole thing as caused by a coincidence. My forty-year life hadn't gone quite that smoothly, I'll have you know. I wasn't that lucky a person.

If the coincidence of the two Takakos had not happened, I would presumably have emerged from the Ishidas' gate, futilely enough, still clutching the box of rice crackers intended as a calling-gift. And one may surmise that the rice crackers, still in their cross-shaped ribbons so carefully tied by the old lady in the rice-cracker shop, would then have been carried to the Nakamura Pawnshop. Because if I couldn't get to meet my old landlady at the Ishida residence, there could be no other candidate but the Nakamuras as the next stop on my pilgrimage in search of the overcoat. So even if that commonplace, banal coincidence had never happened, my early-bird start to the day would not have been rendered instantly meaningless. Still, one has to admit that something changed. At the very least the presence or absence of that coincidence surely changed the order of events on that particular day. And I don't think the fate of the rice crackers in their pretty cross-ribboned box was the only thing that changed.

Chapter 6

"WELL I NEVER! If it isn't Mr. Akaki!"

I heard the voice of my old landlady who had just come back from somewhere.

"Well! So, then, really, after all!" Takako san responded. I found myself sandwiched between the two of them just below the doorstep. Mrs. Ishida wasn't wearing pantaloons. I bowed to my old landlady for the first time in twenty years. Then I greeted her in a manner appropriate to meeting someone for the first time in twenty years. However, I have to admit that putting it into words, naturally enough, made it sound exceedingly ordinary.

White hairs were noticeable on the head of my old landlady. Not as noticeable, though, as they'd been in the case of the old lady, the wife of the village headman. Of course, her face wasn't like the old lady's either. She had slightly deep-set eyes, high cheekbones, and dark eyebrows. The tension had dissolved from the widow's face of twenty years ago, leaving it looking more kindly. No feeling of a former village headman's wife either. Was she just about sixty? The old grandmother had had more of a roundish face, if you like: wide, clear eyes and double-folded eyelids, and a small mouth. When I knew her, twenty years ago, the elegance of her youthful years had changed to a stately dignity. But when I looked at the face of my former landlady, I actually forgot all about the old lady.

"Well, Mr. Akaki, do come on in!"

I remembered that "do come on in" of hers. It had a rising inflection. Still the same high-pitched voice, too.

"What a splendid drawing room, Mrs. Ishida!"

Indeed, the drawing room had a complete set of Western-style furnishings. The table, the deep, soft armchairs, were still new. They'd probably been bought as a set three or four years ago. There was a piano, too. Also a model of a Western-style motorized sailing ship that reminded me of H.E. Bates's short story, "The Ship." There were a couple of oil paintings as well. It was, in short, a drawing room where you saw no sign of extreme interests or ideas. No memorial items—no trophies with red and white ribbons for golf or mah jongg, say. I daresay the only son of the Ishidas was the kind of person whose daily life didn't involve that kind of thing.

In the drawing room, I asked what had become of the Ishida family in the twenty years since. The first thing I learned was that the old grandmother had died some five years before, at the age of seventy-eight. But I didn't burn any incense in her honor at the family altar. Mrs. Ishida didn't suggest it.

"The year after Grandma passed away, we knocked down that old house."

"Really."

"Although really Ei'ichi wanted to keep the old house, so at first we were thinking about having it repaired. We had all sorts of estimates, and in the end it seemed that it would cost more to fix it than to build a new house."

Her son had indeed gone on from Urawa Senior High to the Law Faculty at Tokyo University. He needed just one extra year of study, and got in at the second attempt. After graduating, he didn't become a government official, choosing instead to work for a large oil firm that had a famous company baseball team playing in the metropolitan league. He'd already been a salaryman for a dozen years or more. His wife was the Takako san I had just been talking with. They had three children, two at elementary school (third grade and first grade), and a four-year-old.

"Hello!"

A little girl, who looked about four, came into the drawing room with her mother and greeted me.

"Well, hello!"

"Excuse me," said her mother. "I really was awfully rude just now."

"Not at all—it was all my fault for showing up out of the blue like that. I'm the one who should apologize."

"No, no . . . but you see, I'd never heard anything about you," said Takako san, excusing herself. Then she spoke to her four-year-old daughter.

"That's right, you see—Papa never told Mama anything about this nice man."

That was probably the truth of the matter. I wonder if some other tenant lived in that three-mat room at the back of the west wing after I left? Maybe somebody did rent it. But probably by the time Takako san arrived at the Ishida residence it was just being used as a store-room. Or possibly as a study room for the youngest daughter? Either way, it had nothing to do with Takako san. Takako san was a person with no need to know me.

"So, whereabouts in the house?"

"Aha . . ."

I gave a vague little laugh in the direction of Mrs. Ishida. Would it be better for me to answer? Takako san's question might have been intended for Mrs. Ishida.

"Well, I was studying for a second try at getting into college at the time, you see—"I thought I might as well give some kind of answer.

"Yes, Akaki san, I wonder how far back we should go," said Mrs. Ishida.

"College?"

Takako san continued to display interest in my life as a lodger at the Ishidas. Maybe it was because we were a similar age. Would she be about the same age as her husband? I guessed she was two or three years younger than me.

"Yes, you see I'm from Fukuoka originally, from the country."

"Hmm, yes, this all happened twenty years ago."

"Yep, I've grown a lot older myself, Mrs. Ishida. But you've hardly changed."

"Oh Mr. Akaki, you *are* gallant."

"Where are you from, if I may ask, Takako san?"

"You're asking about my hometown?"

"Yes . . ."

"Well I'm from Chichibu as a matter of fact."

"Oh really? To be honest, I was a bit confused with there being another Takako san here. Although actually that mix-up turned out to be a blessing in disguise."

It seemed that Takako san's interest in my lodger's life at the Ishidas' was still not exhausted. Because from there, the conversation moved on to the other Takako—the Ishidas' eldest daughter. Apparently she had married the eldest son of the family that had been renting the second floor of the tea store to the left of the front gate.

"Akaki san, do you remember him?"

"Yeah, I think I did see him a few times, though I never spoke with him. In those days he'd have been a college student, wouldn't he?"

"That's right—in those days he was at the Engineering Faculty of Metropolitan University. He went to night school there for five years, you know, and then he went off to France and did some kind of research on highway construction."

"Is that so? I remember thinking at the time that he was a very serious-minded character."

"Yes . . . Ei'ichi had a few French lessons with him, actually."

"I see, so that's how it was."

Takako was now living in Tokyo, and her younger sister in Yokohama. Each of them had two children. And that about wraps it up for the news I learned of the Ishida clan, there in the drawing room. Then it was my turn to be asked a few questions. Briefly I summarized the last twenty years. College, ten years at a company, marriage, children, the housing estate in Soka, quitting work, and the present. But I fear my replies were exceedingly rambling and vague. At any rate, my account had no chance of matching that of the Ishidas' son, or their first daughter's husband, for clarity and brightness. After all, I was the kind of man who would visit his old lodgings of twenty years before in broad daylight when it wasn't even a Sunday.

"So, have you already been living in Soka for ten years, Akaki san?"

"Yep, Soka—where the rice crackers come from."

So saying, I helped myself to one of the Soka rice crackers in the dish placed upon the drawing room table. Mrs. Ishida started laughing, as though she found something amusing.

"That close, eh? Funny old world, isn't it?"

"Yes indeed, Mrs. Ishida. I sometimes get this really strong feeling that it's a funny old world. After all, when I left Kyushu for the first time in my life, I ended up here in Warabi. And now, twenty years down the line, the place I've been living in these last ten years is Soka—in the very same prefecture of Saitama!"

"So," asked Takako san, "is this your very first visit to Warabi since then?"

"Yep, it's really been twenty years. Though I have been to Urawa a few times, for business at the prefectural hall and so on."

"OK then, what brings you here today, I wonder?"

"Well, it's not exactly a matter of business as such, just something I sort of suddenly remembered. Usually I'm still in bed at this time in the morning, or only just up, but today I just suddenly woke up early."

"Yes, Akaki san here was always a night owl, just like our Ei'ichi. That Koga san was an early bird, though."

"Koga san?"

Takako san didn't know about the Koga brothers, either.

"He was an acquaintance from my hometown, who rented the outbuilding that used to be next to the storehouse."

"Oh really? My husband never said anything about that, you see."

I glanced back at Mrs. Ishida. She had just broken one of the hard little Soka rice crackers with both hands, and was on the point of putting one of the little pieces in her mouth. Maybe she was just remembering about Little Koga and his early-bird lifestyle. What got Little Koga up early in the morning when he was a student at Takushoku University was his karate practice.

The space where Little Koga practiced karate was roughly in the middle of the triangular piece of ground bordered by the front gate of the Ishida compound, the whitewashed storehouse, and the well with its tin roof. He had driven a wooden board into the ground there, a foot wide and a little over a yard high, and tied two or three layers of thick straw rope around it. What time did that early bird rise from his nest, I wonder? Big Koga, who was a public official, always left for work at 7:40. That meant breakfast must have been just after seven. For me too, of course. I would go over to the outbuilding where Koga senior and his wife lived, and eat with them. How much did I pay for my meals, I wonder? I can't quite seem to remember right now, but anyway, Little Koga's karate practice always lasted thirty minutes before breakfast.

I often watched him practice. I could hear the battle cries he emitted from my three-mat room. I was often woken up by those battle cries, because I'd hear water hitting the straw ropes tied round the practice board. Then he'd strike the ropes with his right fist. Five times, ten times, fifteen times! Aftrer that he'd go with the left fist. Five times, ten times, fifteen times! Little Koga had blood smeared over his fists.

"Good morning to you!" I would call out to him from the area round the well.

"*Osu!*"

So saying, Little Koga would draw in his chin and take a deep breath. Having done the punches, next he'd practice his chops—fifteen each again, with the left and right hands. Then the kicks—barefoot of course. Shouting out his battle cries, he'd aim toe-kicks at the wet ropes. Then he'd turn his foot sideways and give it some kicks with his instep. Finally he would face the yard-high practice board, say "*Osu!*" and bow respectfully.

That would be the end of karate practice for Takushoku University student Koga. Takushoku? Yes indeed. Although the name was still banished Little Koga still had *Takudai*, short for Takushoku, on the right lapel of his karate suit. On the left lapel was his name, *Koga*, in the same black ink.

He didn't encourage me to take up karate. Why not, I wonder?

"Won't you give it a try, *shenpai*?" On just one occasion did he say that to me. As I recall, it was when I went to see the "Koryo Festival" at his university, now officially named Koryo University since its old colonial name had been purged, which stood on a hill near Myogadani. What month was it, I wonder? I went along with Koga senior. It was a Sunday, presumably, or a public holiday. I can't remember much of what I saw there. But I do recall the sight of the karate practice room, looking like some kind of stable, in one corner of the sports ground. What made me associate it with a stable, I wonder? I don't really know. Was there a smell? No, I don't think so. It was a room like a freshly built log hut, with karate suits hanging on the wall and seven or eight members of the club sitting cross-legged on the floor. Among them I saw Little Koga's face.

"*Osu!*" Big Koga called out, while peeking into the room.

"*Osu!*" The voices of the seven or eight people in the room came back as one. Big Koga looked round at me and grinned. Little Koga stood up and came out from the room.

"Won't you give it a try, *shenpai*?"

That was probably when he said it to me. I think I remained silent, or maybe I gave some kind of noncommittal grunt. It was Big Koga who replied to Little Koga's invitation, in dialect.

"*Bakarashika, chi!*"

At which point, Big Koga gave me another grin.

"*Bakarashika, chi?*"

This time it was Little Koga saying exactly the same thing. Then he just stood there, nodding to himself thoughtfully two or three times.

After that I still watched Little Koga's morning karate practice quite often. But he never encouraged me to have a go at karate. Could it have been because of that "*Bakarashika, chi!*" from Big Koga?

"*Bakarashika, chi!*" is, needless to say, Kyushu dialect. Among the regional varieties, it is particularly associated with the Chikuzen dialect. It's very difficult to translate into standard Japanese. Not so much difficult as virtually impossible, actually. The problem is the final "*chi!*" *Bakarashika* is not much different from a standard Japanese *bakarashii*, meaning *stupid* or *silly*. The *chi!* adds emphasis, first of all. But that's just the simplest of its functions. The *chi!* also suggests that the statement it accompanies is an impersonal truth, accepted by the masses. In other words, a self-evident truth. Something *so* self-evident that it's ridiculous even to state it. Then again, the *chi!* has a double nuance: the person using it is both making a bit of a clown of himself and showing a certain contempt for the other fellow. The grin Big Koga gave me was probably a way of conveying the same double nuance by facial expression.

It's not that I won't be satisfied until I've carried out the most exhaustively nitpicking grammatical analysis of this one Chikuzen expression, or translated it as closely as possible to standard speech . . . but I do think it would not be an entirely meaningless exercise to see if we can get this *chi!* as close as possible to standard speech: "What an idiot! Nobody (in this democratic world we now inhabit) takes karate seriously anymore! (Except for you, little brother! Eh, Akaki?)"

This isn't a perfect translation. But it's also fair to say it's not a mistranslation. As a free translation, I think it's worth about 85 percent. Big Koga had been a student at Takushoku University during the war years. Little Koga was a member of the karate club at the postwar, post-defeat Takushoku, a university whose very name was still proscribed. The hill on which "Koryo" University stood made bleak viewing: the brownish school buildings on top of the hill seemed themselves to be tilting. However, my soul did not feel particularly stable, either.

"*Bakarashika, chi!*" With this richly nuanced Chikuzen phrase, Big Koga had expressed on my behalf my own views on karate. Needless to say, Big Koga meant well. But I was someone to whom my own older brother, a sentry employed by the occupying army, had spoken the following words: *You should be happy—didn't ya always wanna be a soldier when you were a kid?*

And I was also a person who had been told the following: *Don't forget the toy sword ya took that time.*

There was probably no mistake about it: the reason Little Koga didn't encourage me to take up karate was that *"Bakarashika, chi!"* He was the same age as my older brother who worked as a sentry at the American army camp at Kashii. My brother was a reader of *Red Flag*. Little Koga was a member of the Takushoku University karate club. And I was neither of those. I was just a country boy from a little town in Chikuzen who'd once hoped to go to military school, who'd come up to Tokyo wearing an old khaki infantryman's greatcoat. A person who'd failed the Early Bird Exam, who was neither a student nor a salaryman—not a factory hand, not a pachinko parlor attendant, not a paper boy living in a dormitory. So what on earth *was* I? Truth to tell I was just, in the words of the mistress of the Nakamura Pawnshop, a single, exceedingly ambiguous, "sonny."

"What do you think of Koga san's karate?" One morning twenty years ago, by the side of the well in the garden, the Ishidas' only son asked me that question. He was wearing the black trousers of his school uniform and had a little towel hanging out of his pocket. He was a high school boy who looked good in wooden sandals. I guess he had big feet. Then again, wooden sandals don't suit people with high insteps. I guess he was a couple of inches taller than me, and about an inch taller than Little Koga.

"Hmm, what can I say?"

I looked at Little Koga punching away at the wet straw rope. I was standing next to the Ishidas' son by the side of the well. We were watching the karate practice together.

"Has Koga san got his black belt yet?"

"Well, I imagine he hasn't got quite that far yet."

"I had a go at it myself the other day."

"Did you, Ei-chan?"

"Yeah. One evening. Just a little bit, you know, to see what it was like."

"And how was it?"

"Painful." He made a fist of his right hand and looked at the top row of knuckles.

"Yeah, it *would* be painful."

"How about you, Akaki san?"

"Of course I've given it a try."

"And how was it for you?"

"Didn't hurt at all."

"Why not, then?"

"Heh, heh, heh, heh . . . why do you think?"

"You've done karate before, somewhere?"

"No, not at all. Koga san's the first person I've ever seen doing karate the proper way."

That was probably true. The only karate I'd seen before observing Little Koga was done by street performers smashing tiles for show. They didn't wear proper karate suits; they wore flashy samurai trousers. They had long hair and sweat bands. They would gradually pile up more and more tiles to smash with their bare hands: first three, then five, then seven. They were street vendors, so of course they were selling stuff. Chinese herbal remedies? Acupuncture manuals with diagrams showing pressure points? Or some kind of almanac? Put on the spot, I couldn't remember, just like that, what they were selling. Sometimes instead of using roof tiles they'd pile up two or three red bricks on the ground. I saw that done several times at the square in Asakusa, on your right as you face the statue of Kannon. But where was I the first time I saw the tile-smashing, I wonder? Would it have been in the grounds of Suga Shrine, in that country town in Chikuzen? Or would it have been in that square in front of Anchoji Temple, where they have markets on festival days? Either way, it was some kind of karate. Did they start off like Little Koga? Did they work hard at their practice, punching and kicking at a straw rope tied round a wooden board that was a foot wide and a little more than a yard high?

Or did street performers have some kind of training school, especially for street performers? No, that seemed unlikely. Surely they didn't first take up karate with the intention of becoming street performers. They probably had no more intention of doing that than Little Koga did. Surely the karate club at Takushoku University was no training school for street performers. But in that case, what *was* Little Koga's objective in taking up karate? Japanese spirit? Anti-Communism? Smash democracy!? Or was there something else, totally different? I had never asked Little Koga about that.

"All right then, why?"

The first son and heir of the Ishidas addressed me again.

"What?"

"Why didn't it hurt when you did karate?"

"Ah, that! Well, I'll tell you."

I took up the stance for delivering a karate punch, self-taught from copying others.

"Well, I didn't actually hit the board."

"But you did have a go?"

"Yes. I pretended to hit it, but I stopped my fist before it hit the board."

"Oh . . . I have a feeling there might be some sense in that, but I don't quite follow."

"It's all right, Ei-chan, there's really nothing in it worth thinking about deeply."

"Oh . . ."

The only son of the Ishidas cocked his head to one side and crossed his arms.

"OK, Ei-chan, let me ask *you* a question. Why do you think Koga san practices karate in the first place?"

"Why . . . ? Well, it's just a sport, isn't it?"

"I see . . . sport, eh."

Now it was my turn to fold my arms. That, undeniably, was a clever answer. Simple and clear. So unlike myself. Why couldn't I be simple and clear? Some problem in the brain? Actually that could be it. Because truth to tell, karate and sports were two things I just couldn't put together in my head. Karate was violence. At the same time, though it was an exceedingly contradictory thought, karate was also a thing of the spirit. Violence or spirit, that's what it was. The kind of violence and spirit forbidden by the textbook democracy of the new-style senior high schools. Boxing was OK. It was one of the official disciplines at the senior high school section of the annual National Athletics Meet. But kendo and judo were out. Back in the 1950s, they were still banished from the new-style senior high schools. What about karate? I wasn't absolutely sure, but in my mind it was the same kind of spiritual violence or violent spirit, and therefore banished by the textbook democracy of the new-style senior high schools.

What was the objective of Little Koga's karate practice? I clung to these foolish doubts for the reason I just gave. I couldn't give a simple and clear answer like that of the honor student from Urawa Senior High School. But no, it was definitely not loyalty to the textbook democracy of the new-style senior high schools that stopped my fist just before it hit the board with the straw rope around it. It was a mystery to me. What a mysterious figure I cut, caught between my big brother reading *Red Flag* and working as a sentry at a military camp run by the occupying army, and Little Koga, the same age as my brother and a member of the Takushoku University karate club. That mystery came to me every time I squared up to the karate board, as I repeatedly did, poised to strike in that copied karate pose, and stopped my fist five inches short of the board. I was caught in the crossfire between:

You should be happy—didn't ya always wanna be a soldier when you were a kid?

and

"Bakarashika, chi!"

What a ridiculous karate punch! That ridiculousness had nothing to do with the firstborn son of the Ishidas. Would there have been any way, I wonder, of conveying that ridiculousness to this honor student of Urawa Senior High, I wonder?

"That sport's too tough for me," said the only son and heir of the Ishidas, his arms still folded.

"Yeah, Koga san may actually have the right kind of physique for karate."

I thought of Little Koga's fist—cocked back like a chicken leg, is the way I put it. It was true: karate, as a discipline banished by the textbook democracy of the new-style senior high schools, seemed an appropriate sport for "Takushoku University," itself still proscribed.

After that, of course, I met the only son of the Ishida family on many more mornings by the well side. He'd be standing there in his school trousers, arms folded, towel dangling from his pocket, watching Little Koga's karate practice. One person I never once met at the well side, however, was the Metropolitan University student who would later marry the Ishidas' oldest daughter, Takako. You see, even though he lived in the two-story house to the left of the front gate, he never used the well for washing his face. He never came to watch Little Koga's karate practice either. Possibly that future master of engineering and future husband of the Ishidas' eldest daughter despised karate. It's only natural there should be such people. Probably, one may surmise, the only reason Little Koga's early-bird karate practice wasn't banished from the Ishida residence was that the old grandmother had become a little hard of hearing. Otherwise there would naturally have been complaints about Little Koga's battle cries, one

assumes. And one other reason Little Koga's early-bird karate practice wasn't banned was that all the people in the Ishida family were
early birds themselves.

"I wonder what that Koga san is up to these days," said Mrs.
Ishida.

"Hmm, as a matter of fact I was just thinking about him myself."

"You don't know either, then, Akaki san?"

"I'm afraid not. I haven't heard anything of him since we parted
ways here."

My life with the Koga brothers in the grounds of the Ishida residence had lasted exactly one year. From March 1952 to March 1953.
Then Big Koga got transferred to the Fukuoka bureau. When that
happened, Little Koga also left the Ishida residence. Apparently he
was going to live in a dormitory at Takushoku University. I myself
left the Ishida residence a couple of months later. During those two
months no one was living in the outbuilding.

"I wonder what sort of job he's got?"

"I wonder."

Frankly, I couldn't guess. Did he finally graduate from Takushoku
University? Is he still doing karate? Of course I don't know. But
if I could suddenly meet Little Koga now, I'd want to ask him not
about karate, but about that coat. I wonder if Little Koga remembers that old infantryman's greatcoat? Of course, he should remember it. Because I'd taken him with me on occasion to the Nakamura
Pawnshop before heading off to the drinking alley in front of Warabi
station, where I'd exchange the coat for one pawn ticket and eight
one-hundred-yen notes. Yes indeed: the price of my coat at the
Nakamura Pawnshop was the same as a month's rent on the three-
mat room in the westernmost corner of the Ishida residence.

"Takako san, it's a little early for lunch, but shall we order some
noodles or something?"

Mrs. Ishida invited me to stay for lunch. I turned the offer down, however, instead rising from my chair in the drawing room. "No, I really must be on my way, Mrs. Ishida."

"Oh, that's a shame."

"No really—I will come again, if I may, and this time I'll ring up properly to let you know in advance. I'd love to see Ei'ichi again, so I'll come when he's off work next time, and I'll be sure to telephone."

"You should do that. I'm sure Ei'ichi would like to see you again too. It really was a bit sudden today."

"I really am sorry to have barged in on you all of a sudden. And I'm so glad to have found that everyone's well. You know, until I caught sight of you today, after I got off the train at Warabi station, all the time I was walking here, I was thinking somehow or other that there might be nobody here anymore, you see."

"Oh, Akaki san, that could never be. We'd have nowhere to go if we left Warabi, after all."

"Ah."

"Although I'm already of an age where there'd be nothing wrong with you thinking that I might have already died, Akaki san."

"No, no Mrs. Ishida, the thought never crossed my mind!"

I turned to address the old lady as she started laughing: "Because if you weren't here, there'd be no meaning at all in my coming out to Warabi."

"Well it's awfully kind of you to say so . . ."

"No, really. Actually what happened today was that I suddenly started thinking about that coat again, and that made me feel I just had to see you, Mrs. Ishida."

"What?"

Mrs. Ishida had risen from her chair, but now she sat down again. I too somehow returned to a seated position. Or was it perhaps I who first sat down again? It didn't really matter, however. Because the issue I had raised was not the kind of thing you just could stand around chatting about anyway.

"Mrs. Ishida, do you remember the coat I had in those days?"

"Koto?"

"No, coat. Besides your good self, Mrs. Ishida, I have no one I can ask about that coat."

"It's very kind of you to say so, Akaki san . . ."

"Well, actually . . ." I checked to make sure that Takako san had left the drawing room before continuing. "Sorry, but it was a little bit difficult to talk about it in front of that Takako san. After all, it's a subject that has absolutely nothing at all to do with the Takako san of twenty years ago."

"Yes, it really is most mysterious, isn't it. Twenty years ago I had no idea that Takako would become Ei'ichi's bride . . . I didn't even know where she was, or what she looked like or anything at all, you know."

"Yes, indeed, absolutely, me too, I never thought for even a moment that twenty years later I'd be seeing my old landlady again to ask about that coat. And that's why I'd really like to ask what you can remember about it."

Mrs. Ishida's memory, however, revived in a most unexpected way. For somehow she had misheard my inquiry about the coat and thought I was asking about some old friend of mine.

"Now you mention it, Akaki san, I *do* seem to recall that there was somebody who used to come and visit you now and again."

"What?"

"He even stayed the night a few times in that little room of yours, didn't he?"

"Oh yes . . . now let me see . . ." However, it was not the struggle to remember this friend's name that plunged me into thought. The only person who ever came to see me in that three-mat room at the

Ishida residence was Kuga. The third son of the monk who ran the Zen temple in the little country town in Chikuzen, he'd been in my year all through the six years of junior and senior high school.

No, what plunged me into thought was Mrs. Ishida's misunderstanding, a misunderstanding that had suddenly brought to mind my memories of Kuga.

"Was that friend of yours also studying to retake his college entrance exams?"

"That's right, that's right!"

Impulsively I overstressed my reply. The old lady's answer had brought a moment of despair. But at the same time it had brought me a totally unexpected new source of hope . . . in the person, needless to say, of the long-forgotten Kuga. Why had I forgotten about him? If it's a mystery you want, there's a real one for you.

"Well, good heavens, what a windfall! Although actually, it wasn't Kuga that I came to ask you about today."

"Koga san?"

"No, not Koga, Kuga."

"So . . . this friend of yours, Kuga san, you've lost track of him like Koga san, have you?"

"No, actually—it's my coat that I've lost track of. Although—"

"Koto? That's a very strange name, I must say. Though I've heard of people called Goto . . ."

"Er, no no, this coat I'm talking about isn't a person, it's the overcoat I used to wear twenty years ago. The soldier's coat I was wearing when I first came to your house twenty years ago. It was khaki, the kind of greatcoat they used to have in the Japanese infantry a long time ago. But . . ."

"Oh I *see*! All this time you've been talking about your *overcoat*, right?"

"That's right, that's right, it was actually that overcoat, greatcoat sort of thing that I wanted to ask you about today, Mrs. Ishida. I suddenly started wondering where on earth that old overcoat, or rather that old greatcoat, had got to, and when it disappeared."

"*Your* coat, Akaki san?"

"Yeah."

"You mean to say that at some point you lost that overcoat?"

"That is correct."

"Well, that will never do."

"No no, I'm quite all right, I don't actually need that coat anymore. It was something I had twenty years ago, so it's perfectly natural that there's no sign of it anywhere anymore. I just want to know when, where and how on earth I lost possession of that coat. When . . ."

"When did this happen, then?"

"Hmm. I think it was about twenty years ago. Because I'm pretty sure it happened while I was living in Warabi, here at your house, Mrs. Ishida."

"While you were living here!"

"Yeah, that's right. I'm already pretty confident that it happened during those fourteen months."

"Well, what a dreadful business."

"Not really. Actually it's a totally ridiculous business, like some crazy dream, and believe me, I really am embarrassed about it, but still—when was the last time I wore that coat, I wonder? I know it's a silly question, because I can't even remember myself, but I wonder whether you might have some recollection—anything at all, no matter how vague, or small—of when I was wearing that khaki greatcoat, Mrs. Ishida?"

"Well, goodness me, it was twenty years ago, you know . . . for someone like me, that really is a tricky one."

"No, indeed, sorry . . ."

"And, Akaki san, did you report the matter to the police?"

"What?"

"Because you know, he wasn't really a very suitable friend for you, Akaki san."

"No, actually . . ."

"But I suppose it would help if you knew where that Koga san is living."

"Yeah, although it's Kuga, not Koga."

"Yes yes, Kuga, that was the name wasn't it?"

"Well, thank you very much indeed!"

I rose from my chair in the drawing room and bowed before Mrs. Ishida. I had decided that there was probably little point in causing any further unnecessary worry to my old landlady. At the same time, I could hardly keep still anymore in the armchair in the Ishidas' drawing room. Somehow I had to see Kuga. Really, how could I possibly have forgotten about him? I had to see Kuga as soon as I possibly could, and see what I could beat out of that memory of his. I'd have to beat and beat to bring that coat out from the very back of his mind.

On my way out of the drawing room, I remembered to ask to use the toilet. The toilet in the new Ishida residence was entirely Western in style. Behind a half-open plastic curtain, I could make out a cream-colored bathtub. When I pushed the handle after using the toilet, sanitized blue water came pouring into the pure-white, horseshoe-shaped bowl. *Mr. Akaki, that toilet is designed to be used in the squatting position..* That was the voice of old Grandma Ishida, now deceased. Only as I was in the toilet, on the very verge of leaving the Ishidas' house, did I remember the silvery-haired old lady. But I didn't mention that to Mrs. Ishida when I returned to the vestibule. I was in a hurry, so I didn't have the leisure to report to Mrs. Ishida my sudden memory, in the new toilet of the Ishida residence, of the extremely embarrassing scolding I received from Grandma

Ishida one evening twenty years ago. Besides, Takako san had also appeared in the vestibule.

"Sorry about earlier on," she said. "I've remembered your face now, for next time."

"No, no, it was all my fault. Please do excuse me. Please do pass on my very best wishes to Ei'ichi san."

I truly was grateful that she had turned out to be a Takako san. To be perfectly honest, I cannot say I felt entirely comfortable talking with her in front of the entrance. But I had been saved by the misunderstanding caused by the happenstance that she was a Takako san. Thanks to that misunderstanding, I was able to see my old landlady.

I was also grateful for my old landlady's misunderstanding. Her mixing up my coat with some person called Koto or Goto or whatever had been a little bit confusing, but thanks to her misunderstanding I had been reminded of the existence of Kuga, whom I'd forgotten about for some mysterious reason. If it's mysteries you want, the way these misunderstandings and mistakes come together so fortuitously is pretty mysterious in itself. However, in this world of ours, days that are dominated by misunderstandings and mistakes probably do occur from time to time. You can't state for sure that you will never suddenly experience a day that can't be described as anything other than a miracle, however hard you think about it.

After leaving the Ishidas' front gate, I once again dropped in at the rice-cracker shop, and bought the same selection of little rice-cracker nuggets as before. While I was waiting, I put on my coat, which I'd still been carrying in my hand when I came out of the house. Then, emerging from the rice-cracker shop, I set out walking along the old Nakasendo highway in the direction of the Nakamura Pawnshop. Unfortunately it was close to lunchtime, but I might as well go along there anyway, on the off chance. If they were closed for lunch, I could always go and have a bite myself, and return a little later. After that I would go and visit the place where Kuga worked. But I wondered to myself—was the lady who ran the Nakamura Pawnshop still alive?

Chapter 7

IT WAS ABOUT forty minutes after I left the gate of the Ishida residence that I boarded the Keihin-Tohoku line train at Warabi station. The reason for my early departure was that the lady who ran the Nakamura Pawnshop was out. When I slipped through the latticed side door and called out, a woman appeared who looked a little over thirty. Probably she was the wife of the Nakamuras' oldest son. Of course I couldn't get anywhere with the lady who ran the place not there, but for someone like me who's not good at explaining himself, this was at least better than using an intercom. At least there were no misunderstandings. No need for the kind of exchange I had with Takako san.

I started off by announcing that I was someone who had rented a room at the Ishida residence twenty years before, then asked after the lady who ran the shop. It turned out that she'd set out that morning to visit relatives in Ueno.

"Ueno, you say?"

"Yes."

"Whereabouts in Ueno, I wonder?"

"What?"

"Well you see, I'm just thinking of going to Ueno myself. I'd been planning to drop in at your place, then carry on to Ueno, so I was thinking that if Mrs. Nakamura has gone to Ueno, well, as it happens I'll also be heading for Ueno myself."

"Well it's a shame when you've come all this way, but I'm afraid she isn't in . . ."

"No no, it's I who should apologize. I have this friend who works at a bank in Ueno, you see, and I'm going to go see him, but Ueno is such a big place, isn't it. There's no way I'm going to bump into Mrs. Nakamura at Ueno station, just like that. But I fear my question has intruded on your privacy, for which I'm most sorry."

Having said that, I noticed the box of rice crackers still dangling from my hand, and held it out to her. Of course at first, the lady who was probably the wife of the eldest son of the Nakamuras refused the house gift. But then I told her I would explain everything to Mrs. Nakamura later by telephone, so I really wished she would be kind enough to accept the gift. Somehow it would be a little awkward, I added, to carry the parcel with me all the way to the bank where my friend was working. So saying, I handed the gift over to her. At that, her attitude suddenly seemed to change.

For a start, I learned that Mrs. Nakamura would be back from visiting her relatives in Ueno sometime after three o'clock.

"If that time would be convenient for you, I'm sure you could meet her."

"I see. That's a great help. Er, banks stay open until four, don't they?"

"No, three, surely. Though the people who work there have to stay until five."

"Ah, three o'clock, is it? Anyway, I'll just dash down to Ueno as quick as I can, see my friend, then hurry on back here. I'm pretty sure I can get back by four at the latest."

"Er, which bank in Ueno does your friend work at?"

I told her the name of the bank where Kuga worked, then asked her: "Why, do you have an acquaintance in banking?"

"Well, as a matter of fact, my husband works in a bank."

"I see! Is that a fact?"

I realized that her sudden change in attitude had come about when I mentioned the bank, not because of the house gift.

"Well, I'll take my leave. Sorry to have troubled you."

"No, not at all. Excuse *me* for asking all those questions."

"Well then, excuse me for asking, but would your husband possibly be the eldest son of this house, who, if I recall correctly, went to Hokkaido University?"

My guess was right on target. Now her attitude really did change. A cushion was brought out before me. Did I ever sit myself down on a cushion at the Nakamura Pawnshop twenty years ago, I wonder? I remember sitting down on the entrance hall step, just short of the tatami mats, quite a few times. But I don't think a cushion was ever produced. Why did she try to make me sit down on a cushion now? Needless to say, because she wanted to keep me there longer. She probably thought I knew something about her husband from twenty years ago. It made me think of Takako san, from my previous visit. It had been exactly the same in her case.

"Oh yes, Mrs. Nakamura often used to talk about your husband."

Actually the oldest son of the Nakamuras seemed to be his mother's pride and joy. She always referred to his university as Hokkaido *Imperial* University, though the *Imperial* had been dropped since the war ended. Having failed the Early Bird Exam myself, I found that the name made an exceedingly enviable ring in my ear. The fact that he'd passed the exam that very year made it all the more dramatic. However, that was all I knew from twenty years ago about the oldest son of the Nakamuras. I didn't even know what subject he'd studied at Hokkaido *Imperial* University. And of course, I'd never seen his face.

"Tea, perhaps?"

So saying, the wife of the former Hokkaido University student made as if to stand up. I declined the tea. Not because I had virtually nothing to tell her about her husband from twenty years ago. It was because I was in a hurry. Actually, it was something of a surprise to learn that the son and heir of the Nakamuras was working in a bank. Although I had never seen his face, I seem to have somehow imagined a future different from that of a bank clerk for the Hokkaido University student of twenty years ago. Was it because of the school's famous motto, "Boys, be ambitious!" I wonder? Then again, he was just the oldest son of a pawnbroker. As such, becoming a bank clerk wouldn't necessarily contradict those words of the university's co-founder, Professor Clark.

However, it wasn't the striking difference between my unfounded imagining and the reality encountered twenty years later that made me decline the offer of tea. It had nothing to do with the words of William S. Clark, or Hokkaido University, or any kind of bank. I was just in a hurry. I was in such a state that I had even forgotten to light my cigarette. Of course I hadn't sat down on the cushion, either.

Promising to return at four in the afternoon, I left the Nakamura Pawnshop by the side door. I had been there for about ten minutes, I suppose. I had been made to wait at the rice-cracker shop for another ten minutes or so. It took about fifteen or sixteen minutes to walk from the Nakamura Pawnshop to Warabi station. I waited four or five minutes for the Keihin-Tohoku line train. Altogether, that totals around forty minutes.

In Ueno, needless to say, I did not bump into Mrs. Nakamura. It was pure coincidence that the eldest son of the Nakamuras was a bank clerk just like Kuga. It was also pure coincidence that the bank where Kuga worked was in Ueno, and that Mrs. Nakamura from the pawnshop happened to be going to that very place on this particular day. But things didn't reach the point of my actually happening to bump into Mrs. Nakamura in Ueno.

The moment I emerged from Ueno station, I plunged into the public telephone hall right before me. The phone hall was crowded. Maybe because it was the time for office lunch breaks? Several dozen people stood in their various postures, jabbering away about this or that. Using my eyes and ears, I cast around for a phone where the conversation was likely to end pretty soon. Since they'd introduced time limits for calls, after three minutes you had to hang up, put in another coin and redial. This meant the trick of picking long callers from short callers by gender no longer worked. Whether it was a man or a woman on the line, you only had to wait three minutes for the call to end. It followed that one way of spotting a good phone was to check out the hand not grasping the receiver. If it held an open memo pad, it meant the caller was looking up phone numbers jotted down there, and possibly intended to make a whole series of calls.

But before I could even start lining up, I first had to find the telephone number. After all, I had set out today with no intention whatsoever of meeting up with Kuga. I found the number for Kuga's workplace right away in the yellow pages. I jotted it down in my little memo pad, then stood behind a man who was smoking a cigarette held in one hand and waited for him to finish talking on the phone. Or would it be a more effective use of time to go grab some lunch before making the call? My wristwatch said 12:45. In the end, though, I did dial up Kuga's workplace, thinking I might as well give it a quick dial on the off chance. I was sure the New Year greeting card he sent me said he was working in the planning office of the Ueno branch, but you couldn't say for certain he wouldn't have switched jobs in the month or so that had passed since then. Besides, people working at banks might have different lunch break times from other folk.

As it turned out, Kuga *was* still working at the Ueno branch, but he wasn't at his desk, and they couldn't say whether he was at lunch or not. Are bank telephone operators not supposed to give out information like that, I wonder? I left a message saying I would call back around one o'clock, and hung up. Then I joined the crowd of people jostling together as they waited for the lights to change, and crossed the road underneath the elevated tracks in front of the station. Now, what to have for lunch, and where? It was the time of day when you'd naturally feel hungry. I had got up early. I'd had a very hurried breakfast and left the house before nine. And indeed, I was hungry. Pork cutlets? Tempura? Or should I make do with curried rice or noodles? Whichever I went for, I didn't have time to dawdle over lunch. You couldn't rule out the possibility that Kuga might come back to his seat precisely at one and then head off again somewhere else. But the place where I stopped in my tracks was not a noodle shop or restaurant, but in front of a movie theatre. I believe I crossed two sets of lights. If you cross the road under the elevated tracks in front of the station, and then make a sharp right turn across another road, you reach the stone stairway that leads up to Ueno Park. If you go up that stairway and turn right again, you get to the square with the bronze statue of Takamori Saigo. Of course, I didn't go up the stairway. Rather, I think I turned right at the foot of the staircase and passed in front of the shops selling souvenirs to visiting provincials.

There were three cinemas, all in a row. There seemed to be some more of them underground. I went down to the underground level. Of course I wasn't planning to watch a movie. I went down because there seemed to be some kind of cafeteria down there as well. I'm pretty sure there was a counter, and I could see a number of men eating something. It was a kind of underground snack bar. It had no door, and there was no discernible borderline between it and the walkway. Here in the underground, cinema posters and cafeteria posters mingled together on the walls. There were some electronic games, too, where you put ten yen in a slot to have a go. They weren't neatly lined up—they'd been installed here and there, to make use of the very cramped space available.

I stopped in front of one of the posters. A woman was holding up her jaw in stereotypical supplication, her arms outstretched and curved. You could see her armpit hair. The woman seemed to be a high school girl, and beside her sat another woman, who'd already finished taking off her skirt and was now on the point of removing the top half of her schoolgirl's sailor suit by pulling it over her head. A high school girl's armpit hair is attractive. The face of the woman, however, was of an indeterminate age, though she was definitely young. She was probably about the same age as a real high school girl, plus another year or two for the hair to develop. Even so, her face was of indeterminate age. All you could say about it was that it was young. "What do you think of me, mister? Am I young or not?!" It was that kind of face in the poster, in her case not even that beautiful, with maybe the one advantage being her armpit hair. Why do women always shave their armpit hair, I wonder? Doesn't anyone complain about that?

Halfway up the stairs, the same poster was stuck on the wall. Which of the movie theatres was showing this film, anyway? I wondered. The fact was, the posters were so mixed up it was very hard to tell. Even after coming back up to ground level from down below I had the same problem. It was no easy matter to distinguish among the three cinemas lined up at ground level. Each was probably showing three films. Just counting the aboveground movie theatres, that made nine films. And then there were posters advertising the underground films mixed in as well. That was only natural, I supposed, since posters for the aboveground theatres were mixed in among the underground posters too. Well really—which entrance led to which film? Which theatre was showing the high school girl with the armpit hair?

I walked back and forth in front of the three theatres, stopping and starting. Finally I figured out that the high school girl with the armpit hair was at the first of the three. I had a quick look at the screening times for the three films showing there. The schedule was stuck to the window of the ticket booth. Just below it someone had placed an old-fashioned alarm clock. It was five minutes to one. Hastily I left the ticket booth. Because I had only five minutes left to grab some food before phoning Kuga at precisely one o'clock? No—the reason was, when I saw that old-fashioned alarm clock under the film schedule, I had a strong feeling I'd seen it somewhere before.

Where on earth had I seen it? Old-fashioned though it was, it was not so old-fashioned as to have a bell above the dial, like a cap on its head. *Time is money!* It wasn't as old as the picture of an alarm clock I'd drawn underneath that slogan on my poster for "Time Commemoration Day" during my elementary school days. This one had a round dial, with no blue or red coloring, and two legs to stand on—that was about as far as its old-fashionedness went. Of course it didn't have any Disney characters or stuff like that. But where on earth had I seen this alarm clock before? I'd never gone to see a film at the movie theatre with the high school girl with the armpit hair. Of course, the alarm clock was an exceedingly ordinary one. You'd not be particularly surprised to find it placed in the ticket booth of any movie theatre. Just a meaningless little illusion? Could be. What would be the point of wandering around vacantly like this if it didn't provoke some kind of illusion? Quite. Then again, even supposing it wasn't an illusion, and I really had remembered that alarm clock from somewhere, I don't suppose it would have signified much. Quite right, again. However, at that moment the alarm clock suddenly started ringing, and in an instant the sound of it overturned all these speculations.

The alarm clock was still ringing. No—it wasn't the alarm clock ringing at all. It was the theatre's entrance bell. Entrance bell? Yes indeed, the sound of the bell calling customers to get through the doors in time for the next showing. This was the sound I'd heard twenty years ago, right in front of this movie theatre. Could that have been the same occasion on which I caught sight of the old-fashioned alarm clock under the screening times in the ticket booth? Well, is an alarm clock the kind of thing that keeps on running for twenty years? Or not? I didn't know, of course, and at the same time I no longer gave a damn about the alarm clock, whether or not it was the same one as twenty years ago; at least I felt no inclination to try to confirm or disprove the truth of the matter. Either way, the reason I had seen the alarm clock under the screening schedule twenty years ago was not that I was there to buy a ticket.

Of course the film on the posters then was not the one with the high school girl with the armpit hair. It was *A Tale of Privates Second-Class*, a drama starring Junzaburo Ban and Achako Hanabishi, known as Banjun and Achako, as a couple of privates (second-class) in the army. The movie theatre was decked out with more than just posters: larger-than-life cardboard cutouts of the two famous comedians stood on either side of the theatre entrance, and in front of the two cardboard privates second-class stood a dozen men in a row, shorter than the pair of cardboard cutouts, but dressed in exactly the same uniform.

They wore army caps, each with a single yellow star in the middle. The single yellow star on the bright red tag attached to their shirt collars indicated their rank—which was also the symbol of the movie. These "privates second-class" also wore puttees and clunky marching boots, but the hands of each private held not the standard type 38 infantryman's rifle, or even a wooden imitation, but a sort of mop, made of a bamboo pole with bits of rope stuck on the end. The theatre bell was still ringing away. The sound of the movie's theme song came from the theatre's speakers and mingled with the ringing of the bell.

We may never become splendid high-ranking officers
But at least give us our second star
Under the starry skies dressed in just a loincloth
Hold your mops upside down, present arms!

As the song reached this line, the dozen or so privates second-class would all hold their mops in front of them as though presenting arms. The theatre bell kept on ringing. I didn't go into the theatre, however. There wasn't even the slightest question of my going in. Why not? Because I was one of those second-class privates presenting arms with their mops.

I wonder whether my visit to the red light district in Kameido Third Precinct occurred on the evening of that day I presented arms? Sometimes I used to teach English to Little Koga. Maybe that explains why he cut me into that casual employment opportunity he came across at Koryo University. I'd have used the money from that little job to head off over the river. Still and all, it's a funny story, a guy like me who'd failed the Early Bird Exam teaching English. However, Little Koga was grateful.

"*Osu!* Thanks to you, *shenpai*, I got me perfect marks on today's test."

The previous evening, Little Koga had come to my three-mat room holding a collection of short stories by H.E. Bates. "The Ship," "Elephant's Nest in a Rhubarb Tree," "The Dog and Mr. Morency." A passage covering a couple of pages of "The Ship" in Little Koga's textbook was enclosed by pencil marks, indicating it was to be tested. I read the passage and, for a start, I penciled in the pronunciation of the English words in Japanese characters above each line of text. Then, below each line, I wrote in a Japanese translation. Of course my translation may have been littered with errors. But after that, Little Koga showed up frequently at my three-mat room, always clutching his H.E. Bates.

"*Osu! Shenpai,* can you do this bit from here to here? I need it by next Wednesday."

I never refused his requests. On the contrary, I even got him to buy me a copy of the school textbook with the three H.E. Bates stories. I read all three of them, making heavy use of the dictionary. That's how I got to know Bates's name. Of course I was reading him for the first time. Maybe I should have been the one expressing gratitude. You see, though I never read a word of Bates before or after, I still haven't forgotten those three short stories. When I saw the model sailing ship in the new drawing room at the Ishidas' residence, it was almost a conditioned reflex that made me recall "The Ship," maybe just *because* I was back in the Ishida residence. That could be it. Still and all, what a mysterious connection, between H.E. Bates and the Takushoku University karate club!

It could even be that my continued residence in Warabi was related to that mystery. Little Koga sometimes told me about part-time work opportunities: that could have been thanks to Bates. At any rate, it was certainly one of the reasons I continued to stay in Warabi after failing the Early Bird Exam. When did I get the private second-class job, I wonder? *Under the starry skies, dressed in just a loincloth; hold your mops upside down, present arms!* Come to think of it, I imagine it was pretty cold, that day I presented arms with a mop. Was it winter? If it *was* winter, would that mean I'd have been wearing my greatcoat when I set out for this casual job as a private second-class? The gathering place for us privates second-class was at the reception desk of the film production company, in Tsukiji. What time were we all supposed to be there? Whenever it was, it was certainly during the morning rush hour. I got off the train, as instructed, at JNR

Yurakucho station, and walked straight there. But when I looked up at the clock over the Hattori clock shop at the Ginza Fourth-Precinct crossroads, I broke into a run just like a real private second-class.

> *That bugle sounding now means half past eight*
> *Late on parade and they'll chuck you in the brig*
> *Bang, there goes another precious Sunday*
> *Let go, that sword is covered in rust*

The moment I broke into a run, this song came floating back to me. Not through my ears—it started somewhere around my heart, then started to reverberate somewhere in my throat. The accompaniment was a *shamisen*. It was my grandmother hitting the strings with the big wooden pick. Grandmother was in the house where I was born, in northern Korea, sitting in the room with the *ondol* under-floor heating. The ondol room was alive with the partying old ladies of the Sixteenth Night Society. It was a social group for grandmothers, which met on the sixteenth night of every month. Members took turns hosting the party. Apparently men were not allowed. It was a society of about a dozen retired old ladies.

It seems my big brother disliked the shamisen. Or maybe he held it in contempt. "She's tone-deaf anyway," he used to say, "all passion, no talent." My brother never showed his face at meetings of the Sixteenth Night. But I always went, and made sure I got some of the red jelly sweets they'd have on the table. In winter they always brought in some hot dumplings from the local Chinese restaurant. I'd be sure to get some of those on my plate, too.

The old ladies took turns playing the shamisen and singing songs. You might hear the theme song from some festival in Kyushu, then a patriotic war song. I don't suppose any of those old ladies are still alive today. My own grandmother has died. The war was lost, and the house with the ondol room where the old ladies of the Sixteenth

Night used to party was impounded. My grandmother was put in a concentration camp for Japanese nationals, and at that point she started to lose her mind. She ran away from the concentration camp and sneaked back to the impounded house to get something. She was found by some Korean civil guards and was sent back to the camp, clutching a single jar of pickled plums. Then, when we were on our way to Japan to be repatriated, we had to sit out the winter in some unknown hamlet, and that's where she died, and became part of the soil of northern Korea. Now I heard her, twanging away at the shamisen and driving me into a run.

> *Let go, that sword is covered in rust*
> *Tokotottottoto*

The final *tokotottottoto* was supposed to be the sound of a bugle fanfare. I was no high-ranking officer with a ceremonial sword, however, but a mere private second-class. A part-time private second-class who was in danger of being late on parade. Was I wearing that greatcoat? If I had been, it would not have sported a double row of buttons like an officer's greatcoat, since it had been made for a common enlisted man. Suddenly Grandmother's shamisen started playing a different tune. "The Burgeoning Cherry Blossoms," was it? No— those were lines from the song, but the title of it was "A True Foot Soldier." The words I now heard with the tune were totally different:

> *Workers of the world, hearken!*
> *To the thunder of the footfall*
> *Of the May Day demonstrators*
> *Their war-cries proclaiming the future is here*

When was the first time I heard this workers' movement song, set to the tune of "A True Foot Soldier"? The one thing I can say for sure, of course, is that it must have been after we lost the war. Was it after we'd been repatriated to that little officers' town in Chikuzen? If so, it would have been there that I heard it. Maybe it was that obscure artist, the town hall treasurer's oldest son, who sang that song as he came slouching down the street in his wooden sandals and thick glasses with their thick black frames, delivering *Red Flag*, sucking on a popsicle that was virtually down to the stick. Or was it my big brother, going off from the officers' town to work at the American base wearing the uniform of a civilian guard? My brother used to read the *Red Flag*, as delivered by the town hall treasurer's oldest son. Or could it have been that I first heard the workers' movement song that was set to the tune of "A True Foot Soldier" in Yonghung, northern Korea? Yonghung was the town where I was born. I went to Yonghung Public Ordinary Upper Elementary School. *Blooming blooming, cherry blossom blooming. Come come whitey come, come down little dove from the roof of the shrine.* The following year the school was redesignated a National Elementary School. *Ah, guardian dog, oh guardian dog of the shrine.* But the theme song for the piggyback battle during school Sports Day didn't change. It was "A True Foot Soldier."

> *The color of burgeoning cherry blossoms are our collars*
> *Wild ones, perhaps from Mount Yoshino. Let the storms blow*
> *If we are born true sons of Yamato*
> *We will lie scattered on the battlefield like fallen flowers*

There could have been no song more suitable for Sports Day at Yonghung Upper Elementary. Because Sports Day was held every year in April, at the peak of the cherry blossom season. Well come to think of it, possibly in northern Korea the cherry blossom season could have peaked in early May. But either way, the moment we finished the entrance ceremony for the new academic year, we immediately started practicing for Sports Day. I didn't really know why they held Sports Day in the spring. Maybe so that the adult spectators could combine it with some cherry blossom viewing. All the Japanese people in the town came to watch. It was only a little Japanese school—from the first year of elementary to the second year of the high school section, there were about 120 or 130 pupils in the whole school. I believe there were eleven pupils in my grade. Pre-dawn fireworks would be the signal for us to head for the school, carrying straw mats that we'd lay out under the cherry trees planted around the school grounds, to lay claim to the best viewing points. The piggy-back battle was contested by a mixture of fourth, fifth and sixth graders, plus the boys from the high school section. When I was in the sixth grade I got to ride on the shoulders of a high school boy and managed to stay upright and unbeaten right to the end. Then, when I went running back to where my grandmother and grandfather and others were sitting on their straw mat, next to some other relatives, opening up their picnic boxes, all the grown-ups suddenly burst out laughing. My sports shirt had been ripped to shreds, front and back, and it looked like a torn paper door. I reached out my hand for one of the sushi rolls in the picnic box. I'm pretty sure a few cherry blossom petals had drifted into the box.

Yes, "A True Foot Soldier" was indeed a fitting song for Yonghung Elementary School Sports Day. However, one day the words of that song suddenly changed. It happened about four months after I left Yonghung Elementary School to go to Wonsan Middle School.

"The war has definitely not ended. Due to certain circumstances, a temporary truce has been called. You will therefore return to your own homes, with all the alertness, pride and resolve of true Wonsan Middle School students, there to await further communication."

I heard these instructions from the headmaster of Wonsan Middle School on the grounds of Wonsan Izumi-cho National Elementary School. The buildings of the middle school had been commandeered by the army, and apparently various munitions had already been taken in and stored there. We boarders were taking turns, dorm by dorm, to stay up all night and guard the munitions. It was my dorm's turn on the night of August 12. After dinner, we followed the third-grade student who was the dorm prefect, and went into the night watchman's room, which was to the left of the front entrance as you faced the middle school. However, as it turned out, I never did find out exactly what sort of weapons had been carried into the middle school by the army, nor how many. There were four of us on duty that night—the third-grade dorm prefect, one second grader, and one other first-grader besides myself—but just as we were setting out to do our rounds of the munitions cache, there was a sudden roaring sound and the school buildings started shaking violently. At the same time everything went pitch-dark. On the tatami mat just in front of the door to the night watchman's room, I instinctively went down on all fours. I hadn't the slightest idea what was going on. Maybe that's why I forgot to do all the things I'd been taught in the air raid drills I'd been doing since elementary school—adopt a prone position, put your head down, spread out the fingers of both hands to stop up your eyes and ears.

"Hey, where's the flashlight?!" cried out the third grader.

Just then, there was a second mighty roar, and the ceiling started creaking violently.

"Quick, open the window!" cried out the third grader, in the darkness.

But the window wouldn't open. I pulled sideways at the glass window of the night watchman's room with all my might, but the frame wouldn't budge to right or left. I had forgotten that I had locked it myself, on orders from the third grader. Apparently the third grader was planning some prank for when we did the tour of inspection of the munitions. I don't know exactly what he was plotting. I think I vaguely imagined he was planning to help himself to a submachine gun and smuggle it back to the night watchman's room to disassemble it or something. It would be awkward if someone came in right in the middle of that. Interpreting the third grader's order along those lines, I had dutifully locked the window from the inside.

"B-29s!"

So screamed the third grader, as the ceiling rocked wildly to the roar of a third explosion. By the time we finally got the window open and tumbled out of the building, the thunderous roar had faded to silence. The following day we learned that in the attack we had been startled not by B-29s at all, but by the Soviets, who were making their first bombardment since joining the war. The bombing lasted two nights, as I recall. But apparently, not a single Zero went up from the naval air squadron at Yonghung Bay. Why not, I wonder? Of course, I didn't know. There was a rumor that the Soviet bombers had been dropping mines rather than bombs. They'd been trying to drop them in Yonghung Bay, but they missed their mark and fell on the slopes of the surrounding mountains. Another rumor going around had it that some of the local Koreans had dressed up in pure white robes—traditional Korean *ch'ima* skirts and *chogori* coats— and had secretly gathered on the hillside and stood in patterns to form words that would send some kind of signal to the Soviet bombers. We had no idea whether either rumor had any truth to it. Nor did we know what sort of damage the raids had done. On the night of the fourteenth, there was no bombing. Why not, I wonder? Once again, I didn't know. It was the following day that I heard the headmaster's instructions on the grounds of Izumi-cho Elementary School. I understood nothing. I didn't get to hear the Emperor's famous radio broadcast. After we dispersed from the grounds of Izumi-cho elementary school, I made my way back along the hills to the dormitories, and I was still on foot when noon came. I happened to be passing a cluster of four or five houses with concrete walls, so I went up to the entrance of one of them and tilted my ear toward the sound of the radio, but strain as I would, all I could make out was that someone or other was saying something. I suppose that someone was the Emperor. There may have been something wrong with the speaker or the antenna. The voice sounded like that. Anyway, the Emperor had spoken! That, however, was all I knew. I was sleepy. Ever since the surprise of the first air raid, we'd been spending our nights catnapping on the tatami mats in puttees and lace-up boots. By mid-April the snow is gone, and in summer the water boils, it's over a hundred degrees! It was so hot we could barely sleep a wink. On top of which, I had listened to the headmaster's instructions on August 15, under a blazing sun in a cloudless sky. It was an absolutely gorgeous day. Though of course there was no question of heading down to the beach for a swim.

The moment I got back to the dorm, I just crawled under my desk headfirst, not bothering to undress, and fell fast asleep. About how many hours did I sleep? When I awoke, just opening my eyes a crack, I could see the third grader who was dorm prefect sitting on his own desk, naked from the waist up, holding a wooden sword as though he were a samurai about to commit hara-kiri, and crying. However, I did not know why he was crying. The only thing clear to me was that something had come to an end before I even knew it.

From the Wonsan Middle School dormitory I returned home to Yonghung. My big brother, a fourth-former at Wonsan Middle School, also came home, from the fertilizer factory in Hungnam where he'd been put to work. How long after that was it, I wonder, that the words of "A True Foot Soldier" were suddenly transformed into a workers' movement song?

Chapter 8

THE THEATRE BELL was still ringing. It seemed that I was still gazing vacantly at the poster of the high school girl with the armpit hair. But I couldn't seem to bring to mind the Korean-language version of the workers' movement song set to the tune of "A True Foot Soldier." Would I have remembered it twenty years ago, I wonder? Twenty years ago? Yes, back then when I set off at a run towards the film production company in Tsukiji to the accompaniment of my grandmother's plucking the strings of the shamisen. The time I was in danger of being late on parade for my casual job as a private second-class and broke into a run like a real private second-class. Did I remember the song in Korean then, I wonder?

Either way, I couldn't bring it to mind now. The ones I *could* remember clearly were "The Light of the Firefly" and "Painopai." No, actually I'm talking about the Korean lyrics sung to the tunes of those two songs. Of course, it wasn't so simple as translating the Japanese lyrics straight into Korean and singing them just like that. The lyrics were totally different—only the melody remained the same. Both were songs of the Korean people, made newly independent with the defeat of Japan. The one that came to me first was "The Light of the Firefly." I could hear it being sung on the train on my way to Yonghung, after I'd got my luggage together at the Wonsan Middle School dormitory and set out for home. It was already night. And it was an open-top freight train. The stretch from Wonsan to Yonghung usually took around two hours. But this freight train seemed to dawdle more than most. The train was packed with passengers. I was seated in one small corner of an overcrowded car, with a second-form boy from the dormitory who was also heading home, for Hamhung. We were wearing trousers with puttees and the military-style caps that went with the uniform of Wonsan Middle School, and carrying khaki knapsacks on our backs, and we were being stared at. The Korean language came to our ears. Every time the freight train stopped at a station, great shouts went up from the people inside and on the platform.

"*Mansei!*"

"*Mansei!*"

The Koreans all had little flags in their hands and were waving them furiously. They had taken the Japanese Rising Sun flag, divided the red spot in the center into a pair of commas with a curving line, painted half of it black, and painted things like divination symbols in the four corners. That flag has now become the national flag of South Korea, but in those days it was used in northern Korea too. The division of Korea along the 38th parallel had yet to happen, of course. All I understood at the time was that "*mansei!*" was the Korean pronunciation of "*banzai!*" I didn't even know that the flag with the red and black commas was the flag of the Korean people, now independent since the defeat of Japan. I was just very, very uneasy. The way the red sun on the Japanese flag had been painted into red and black commas—was that a way for the Korean people to curse the Rising Sun flag? The divination symbols in the four corners were particularly spooky. It may have been foolish, but I saw in that flag a kind of spell of damnation upon the Rising Sun, and I shrank into the corner of the freight car.

At every single station people were waving the little flags with the red and black commas, and from somewhere amid the mighty cries of "Mansei! Mansei!" came the sound of a Korean song being sung to the melody of "The Light of the Firefly."

A day later I could confirm with my own eyes that something had ended before I even knew it. I finished a breakfast of miso soup and fried eggs, the first I'd had cooked for me by my mother in several weeks. Immediately afterwards, a foolish illusion came to me: namely, that with the passing of August 15, the students of Wonsan Middle School had finally been allowed to have a summer holiday— a holiday that was to have been sacrificed to the cause of annihilating the Americans and the British. Maybe that was why I'd come home from the dormitory. Was it the miso soup and fried eggs that brought on this exceedingly foolish illusion? Maybe. After all, during the last month I'd lived at the dormitory, both breakfast and the midday lunchbox had consisted of nothing but pickled bracken and salted cod roe. My father owned several cod-fishing boats too, and I guess there was more cod to be had in the Sea of Japan than you could possibly plow through—whole rotting mountains of cod. When we sat down at the worksite where we'd been grubbing up pine roots, on the red-soil slopes of a hill covered in pine logs, and opened the lid of our lunchboxes, the red cod roe smeared across the rice looked like some kind of dead body. Or when it was bracken, it smelled foul from being steamed up in the noonday heat.

The first thing I did after finishing off the first breakfast cooked for me by my mother in several weeks was to inspect my school cap. I adjusted the badge. Wonsan Middle School had just about managed to keep up its metal badges until August 15, rather than replacing them with clay ones. But they had already given up using the brass ones that gave out an inner glow if you buffed them hard enough with metal polish. Instead, they were using tinplate badges. Only third form and above got brass badges, or kids with older brothers who'd already graduated. My own badge, of course, was the tinplate variety. The peg at the back that held it in place hadn't yet been bent out of shape though. Even so, just to make absolutely sure that it wouldn't fall off, I had sewn it onto the cap with white cotton thread. We had been ordered to do so. I remember that if you lost your school badge, you had to wear your cap without a badge for the rest of your time at the school, or at least for a year. Now I removed the supporting cotton thread. Then I turned the cap inside-out and temporarily removed the small coin with a hole in the middle that was used to secure the badge from the inside. I slipped the position of the badge downward just a fraction—a quarter of an inch perhaps. Then, taking particular care of the part where it was soldered to the back of the badge, I gently pushed the peg through a newly opened hole, and replaced the coin with the hole in it to secure the badge once more.

Next I took care of my secondhand lace-up boots. I decided against blacking them, contenting myself with a light brushing. But what was it all for? Who on earth was I going to show my badge and boots to? I had no very clear idea myself. I put on my military-style cap with its newly re-set badge, pulled on my lace-up boots, and left the house. I was in my sports shirt and long trousers without puttees. In Wonsan, I couldn't walk around town without puttees. You never knew when and where you might bump into a senior boy. If you met one, you had to give him a clenched-fist salute. At first I found that whenever I clenched my fist, my feet somehow stopped moving. I finally got used to saluting while walking. At the dormitory I was beaten up almost every night after roll call. If just one first-former gave a sloppy salute, all first formers were beaten. Since April, when all the fourth formers had been mobilized to Hungnam, the third formers had taken over the beating.

We'd be made to stand in a line in the dormitory corridor. First we'd be slapped on the right cheek. How many third formers were there, I wonder? About twenty, I suppose. About ten would do the beating. So you'd get ten slaps just on the right cheek. Once they finished with the right cheek, it was the turn of the left cheek. So altogether I'd take about twenty slaps as the third formers went down the line of first formers slapping one cheek, then came back slapping the other. Of course, some of the slaps didn't hurt. Among the ten third formers who did the slapping, about half were actually more fainthearted than the ten who didn't slap at all. But two or three third formers slapped so hard you just couldn't help crying out even if you gritted your back teeth in the prescribed manner. What made them do that? One of them did it with a cigarette in his mouth. "One more year to go," is all I thought to myself, and once more gritted my back teeth. Probably the next year, I thought, I'd be going to the army preparatory school.

If a first former was found walking in town without his puttees, the same thing would happen back at the dormitory. Now, however, I was no longer in Wonsan. This was Yonghung, and I was walking in the direction of Yonghung Elementary School. No need to worry about being accused of showing disrespect. Far from it. If a junior boy happened to pass me in the street and saw me wearing the cap of Wonsan Middle School, it was not inconceivable that *he* might salute *me*. A junior boy? I mean a pupil from Yonghung Elementary. It was unthinkable that anybody else might salute a first-form student from Wonsan Middle School. However, I met nobody. Of course I wasn't saluted. Not that I deliberately walked along the back streets. Why the hell should I! I walked past Yonghung Police Station, past the civil defense headquarters, past the Kanayama Clock Shop, Ichizen Photography Studio, Miyamoto Hat Shop, the Shiramatsu Clinic, the Tanaka Dental Clinic, Utsumi's Seeds and Saplings, the Korean noodle restaurant, the Hattori law office, Yonghung Town Hall. It was the same road to Yonghung Elementary School that I had walked along every day for six years. Even so, I didn't meet a single elementary school pupil. Why was nobody walking around? I stopped in front of the school gate to make a clenched-fist salute towards the *hoan-den*, the little Imperial shrine located on the sports field behind the school. When I'd been in elementary school, I'd always taken off my cap and bowed to the shrine. Entering the school gate, I turned left and walked along the side of the school building until I got to the lecture hall on the far left. I met nobody. I went round the outside of the lecture hall, and came out on the sports field. But there was nobody to be seen there either.

Where had everyone gone? Was it because of the summer holidays that nobody was around? Would I find anybody swimming down at Ryuhung Bay if I went there? I climbed up on the platform in front of the flagpole. There was the statue of Kinjiro Ninomiya, depicted, as always, as a diligent schoolboy reading his book while carrying a load of firewood on his back. There was the sumo ring, surrounded by four stout wooden pillars. The jungle gym. The horizontal bar. The sandpit. The low bar. The swings. The seesaw. These things were all just as they had been before. And they looked like childish things, fitting for an elementary school. The only thing new to me was a row of earthen roofs protruding from the ground underneath the cherry tree. Immediately I knew they were air raid shelters. Dug in haste, perhaps, after the Soviet bombing raids. Actually, there was one more new thing besides the shelters: the area within the running track had been dug up to become a jet-black cornfield. A square area in front of the ceremonial platform was all that was left unplowed: just enough space, I presumed, for the school's 120-odd pupils to stand in rank and file. I could understand that. But what about that other hole at the back? Was it a garbage dump? In winter we always used to dig a big hole on the west side of the sports field to dispose of the ash left over from the coal stoves used to heat the classrooms. But now it was midsummer.

What on earth could that hole be for? As I jumped down from the platform, the intense buzzing of giant cicadas suddenly came to my ears. Sunny skies. Must go to Ryuhung Bay for a swim this afternoon. I took a peek into the hole. Was it maybe two-and-a-half yards in diameter? The hole was freshly dug, but it was about the same size as the ones we used for dumping ash. But what had been dumped here wasn't ash, but a pile of gas masks and steel helmets, the same color as ash. There were six gas masks and six helmets. I clambered down into the hole. And then, instinctively, I froze to the spot. Helmeted skulls! The ash-colored "gas masks" under the ash-colored helmets were actually skulls. The bottom of the hole looked for all the world like a desecrated tomb. Whose tomb could it possibly be? I didn't know. All I knew was that something had come to an end. Before I even knew it, something had most definitely come to an end!

How long after that was it that my big brother and I dug a hole in our own backyard? All I can say for sure is that it was before the two soldiers from the Korean civil guard came to impound our house. One of the civil guardsmen had a Soviet submachine gun on a strap round his neck—we called it a "mandolin." The other had a cavalry rifle on his shoulder—somewhat shorter than the Japanese type 38, probably one of the ones they were using at the Yonghung Police Station. Their uniforms looked somehow like standard-issue civilian clothing. Maybe they had just improvised them. The bottom half included the same kind of lace-up boots that Japanese soldiers used, with puttees wrapped around their legs from the shin down. That was the same as Soviet soldiers. The hats were Soviet-style too. But they had a subtly different feel to them, maybe because of the way they were worn, or because of the shape of the head? Or was it maybe not so much the head as the face and overall physique? Whatever the reason, that kind of peakless army cap doesn't seem to suit Orientals. When the Soviet soldiers used them, they had a

way of wearing them at a rakish angle, but the Korean civil guardsmen just plonked them straight onto their heads. Somehow it made
them look like *inari-zushi*—lumps of boiled rice wrapped in deep-
fried bean curd. I wondered whether Oriental people wouldn't find
the prominent peak of the Japanese-style army cap more suited to
them? The civil guardsmen with the mandolin gun and cavalry rifle
issued orders in exceedingly correct Japanese.

"All the property in this house was stolen from us, the people of
Korea. The same applies to the house itself. This property, the Akaki
general store, is hereby closed by us, the Korean People's Civil Guard,
and henceforth will be administered by us, the Korean People's Civil
Guard. However, we will accord to you items necessary for your living. Take only such things as you can carry in your hands, and leave
this house within thirty minutes."

We put up no resistance of any kind. Japan had been fighting
against America, Britain, China and the Soviets, but it seemed that
we had ended up losing to Korea as well. If the entire family was
taken prisoner, we could hardly complain. Yonghung, where I had
been born, was already a foreign country anyway. And naturally
enough, the Korean people had also become foreigners.

I had realized these things when I dug the hole in the backyard
with my big brother. Here were two warehouses, each with a fat heavy
bolt on its door. One was used to store oil, the other liquor, miso
paste, soy sauce, sugar, etc. The middle part of the yard was enclosed
by a fence. Since Grandfather died, Grandmother had been the only
person with free access to it. Besides flower beds, there was a little
orchard with pear, peach and cherry trees, among other kinds. At
the far back of the enclosure was my grandmother's vegetable plot,
and between the vine trellises and the vegetable plot an air raid shelter had been constructed. This one too may have been put together
hastily after those Soviet air raids. Though as it turned out, it was

used not for protection against Soviet bombers, but for hiding Japanese women from the Soviet soldiers who came looking for them after nightfall. The women who hid there were my mother and Mrs. Tokuyama, wife of the man who lived in the house behind the vegetable plot. Mr. Tokuyama used to help out in our shop, but he had been called up for military service and had not yet returned.

My brother and I dug a hole in front of the air raid shelter. It was right underneath the vine trellises. We each took a shovel and started digging a hole. Each of the two holes was about a yard wide. I was used to digging holes. After all, I'd done nothing but dig for pine roots when I was mobilized as a worker during my first year at Wonsan Middle School. But I didn't know why my brother had suddenly come up with the idea of digging a hole under the vine trellises. Could it be a sort of trap for the Soviet soldiers to fall into? Was that why he wanted it dug in front of the air raid shelter? If a Soviet soldier fell into that hole in the dark, he'd probably at least sprain his ankle. But I didn't bother to ask. And it turned out my theory was off-target. Once we had finished digging the hole, my brother turned to me and said: "Oy, go and get the records from the house."

"The records?"

"You're gonna bury 'em all in that hole you just dug."

"What about the other hole?"

"I'll bring the stuff that goes in that one."

My brother and I spent the whole day in front of those holes, until dusk. My brother brought out a sugar sack with stuff in it, just the size of a bag of cement, and father's ceremonial saber. I brought out all the records from a cupboard in the house, along with the wind-up gramophone.

"I don't think we have to get rid of the gramophone," said my brother.

"OK."

"You gonna listen to it?"

"Can't I?"

"Well, I guess it'll do no harm."

"What are you going to do with the saber?"

"This?"

My big brother removed the scabbard. Then, carefully adopting a pose, he stiffened his right arm, held the saber erect, and moved it right in front of his face.

"Present . . . arms!"

When he was finished, my brother passed the ceremonial saber to me.

"Wanna have a go?"

Then my brother reached into the sugar sack and pulled out Father's army cap. He placed it briefly on his own head. With his round, black-rimmed spectacles, my brother didn't look like Father, even with the army cap on.

"We ended up never having to wear one of these."

My brother passed the cap over to me. It was an infantryman's cap, made of thick, bright red cloth with a gold star on it. It looked almost brand new. The peak was a glossy jet-black, and it reflected the midsummer sunlight. Gleam!

"What's the matter? Not going to try it on?"

Engrossed in looking at Father's cap, I'd apparently forgotten to put it on.

"Uh-huh."

"All *right*, then—no more playing at soldiers!"

My brother pulled some scraps of straw out of an empty box and threw them into the hole. Then he smashed up the box with a claw hammer.

"Shall I bring some more?"

"Yeah."

"Can this be last to go?" So saying, I finally put Father's army cap on my head and stood up. I went and got a couple more wooden boxes from the pile in the corner of the garden. By the time I had carried them back to the hole, the straw kindling was already starting to burn. My brother had just finished bending the ceremonial saber over his raised knee. He chucked the bent saber into the hole, along with broken fragments of the wooden boxes. Then he pulled out the things from the sugar bag: a Wonsan Middle School satchel, a couple of dozen textbooks and exercise books, and surprisingly enough, a Wonsan Middle School cap.

"Why burn them?"

"We don't need them anymore."

"What, even the cap?"

"Well, I guess the cap could come in handy." My brother took the cap in his hand. "But we don't need this."

He pulled the school badge off the cap, held it out between the tips of finger and thumb, and dropped it into the fiery hole. My brother's badge was not made of tinplate: it was a proper brass one. But I just stood there and looked silently into the fiery hole . . . I had already seen the helmeted skulls in the hole in the playing field at Yonghung Elementary.

My brother put the badgeless Wonsan Middle School cap on his head, sat down on a tangerine box in front of the hole, and carried on burning stuff until nightfall. Once he'd finished with the satchel, the textbooks and the exercise books, he started carrying out bundle after bundle of magazines. They were old copies of *Youth Club*. How many years' worth of that did he burn, I wonder? The last bundle he brought out was of back numbers of *Army* magazine. About when was it that they scrapped *Youth Club* and replaced it with two separate magazines titled *Army* and *Navy*? Until I graduated from elementary school, I'd been buying *Army* magazine every month.

"No need for these anymore, either, right?"

"Nah."

I also sat on a tangerine box in front of the hole until nightfall. While my brother kept on burning stuff with the badgeless Wonsan Middle School cap on his head, I sat there still wearing my father's army cap, and listened to records. I guess we had about a hundred of them. Maybe slightly more than that. Half of them were war songs. The rest were children's songs, school chorus songs, popular songs like "The Town on the Border," "Lullaby of Akagi," "The Gondola Song," and so on, *rokyoku* by Torazo Hirosawa, and so forth. I can't remember any Western music except Tamaki Miura belting out "Madame Butterfly" in a high-pitched voice. Who listened to that, I wonder? My mother? But I can't seem to remember seeing my mother listening to records. I do recall hearing her singing in a high-pitched voice a few times, but I don't think she was singing along to records. The *rokyoku*, the musical storytelling, would have been my father's taste, I guess? But I can't remember a thing about that, either. Father used to recite songs from Noh plays. Sometimes my brother and I were set down in front of the alcove where we displayed the family ornaments and made to listen to him. "The Goblin of Mount Kurama;" "Hunting for the Red Leaves of Autumn"—those are the only two Noh plays I can remember having in my hand. Father would sometimes recite Noh songs in the bath or while out on a walk. But I never heard him reciting *rokyoku*. I never saw him listening to Torazo's records, either. And as for Grandmother, she was only interested in the shamisen.

By and large, the grown-ups in our family don't seem to have listened to records much. It felt as if the windup gramophone had already been relegated to the status of a toy for the children. I myself particularly loved it. You see, I didn't read books like my brother. He would read aloud to me—everything from Mimei Ogawa's fairy tales to *The Adventures of Tom Sawyer*. Maybe that's why the name "Injun Joe" remains with me to this day. After that, I looked for stories only from the war songs on our records. Yes indeed, war songs were much more than just songs to me. To me, they were tales to be told, they were drama, they were history. To put it more grandly, they were my lyric and epic poetry.

I had listened to those war songs over and over again on the windup gramophone, and I could recite the lyrics from memory. I loved the ones with a strong narrative thread, like "Lieutenant Colonel Tachibana, War God," "Commander Hirose," "The Meeting at Suishiei," "The Brave Marine," "The Charge of Bredow's Brigade," "Elegy of Poland," "The Song of Iwao Oyama," "The Three Brave Suicide Attackers," and "In Honor of the Defenders of Attu Island." Since they were tales to be told, it would be out of the question *not* to memorize the words. The longer the lyrics went on, the better. They should be as long as possible, and they should be sung from beginning to end. Thus the greatest war song of them all had to be "Lieutenant Colonel Tachibana, War God." From its opening line, "It was the dead of night over Liaoyang Castle," this epic tale from the Russo-Japanese War told of a fight to the death. It had two parts that stretched on for nineteen and thirteen verses respectively.

I also liked extremely sad war songs like "Bandit Patrol" and "Ah, Our Comrades in Battle." And I loved to listen to the female chorus in "Song of the Women's Volunteers" and the solo female vocal on "Flower of the Beloved Country."

Several of my albums were collections of war songs, starting with old favorites like "Miya san, Miya san," "The Naked Blade Brigade," and "The Mongolian Invaders." They covered the Sino-Japanese War, the Russo-Japanese War, and culminated in songs about the current war like "Wheat and Soldiers," "Praying at Sunrise," and "The Blazing Heavens." The most recent ones, starting from "Song of the Great Battle for East Asia," and going through "Hayato Kato's Fighting Unit," "God-warrior of the Sky," "Song of the Young Eagles," and "Sunk at One Blow," were not yet collected in albums. I had bought each of them separately.

I wonder when all the album collections had been bought for me? Placing the windup gramophone on top of the tangerine box, I started playing the records, starting with the albums. The records were slightly smaller than the usual kind, and wouldn't break if you dropped them. What were they made of, I wondered? I quickly discovered they were made of a kind of cardboard-like stuff with other stuff laid over it. I discovered this because as soon as I finished playing each record, I broke it over my knee and threw it into the hole. Until nightfall I sat in front of the hole we had dug under the vine trellises, playing each war-song record, then breaking it, then playing the next one. Well, actually, I not only played them but I also sang them before breaking each record. My brother, who was standing in front of the hole on the opposite side, still burning stuff, sometimes joined in the singing. How many songs did I sing altogether, I wonder? With all long ones and short ones, would it have made a hundred? Actually, it could even have been more.

The children's songs, school chorus songs, popular songs and spoken word records—those I just broke and threw into the hole without playing. I didn't play "Madame Butterfly," either. Still, the whole thing took from just after noon all the way through to dusk. What was the last record, I wonder? Was it perhaps "Lieutenant Colonel Tachibana, War God"? No, it can't have been: that was in one of the albums, and one of the earlier ones at that. I remember that on the last song my brother sang along too. It was "Heartbreak Ballad":

Don't let your daughter marry a pilot
Today's sweet bride is tomorrow's widow
Ah, ah . . . heartbreak

Or maybe I didn't play "Heartbreak Ballad" on that old record player. Maybe I just listened to my brother singing it. That may well be how it was. When he'd finished singing, my brother got up from his tangerine box.

"OK, that's it for the war songs."

Then he pointed at my head and said: "That can go too, OK?"

I still had father's army cap on my head. I took it off and looked at it head-on. Truth to tell, I wanted to at least keep the star. But at that moment, I could not pipe up and tell the truth. My brother took the army cap from me and dropped it into the fiery hole along with the last five or six issues of *Army* magazine. Farewell, army of mine! Farewell, my oh-so-foolish dream!

Yet there was one more blow to come. Not only had something come to an end before I knew it, but this time, I learned, something had also started before I knew it. What on earth could it be?

"Hey—do you know this song?"

So saying, my brother, still on his tangerine box, suddenly burst out singing in Korean: *"Panmanmokk, tonmansannu, iribonmudoraa!"*

Immediately I understood the words. "Guzzling and shitting is all you ever do, Jap bastards!" The tune was exactly the same as "Painopai," one of my favorite war songs. "Fires, fires, getting into fights, fuck off you Jap bastards, rip your stupid carp streamers to shreds. *Mansei, mansei, manseguruse, hebomatsumukuha, koppindonsase, hegukinoppitsurugo, henjinayora!"*

The first time I ever heard "The Red Flag" it too was sung in Korean. I can still remember the Korean lyrics. Of course it's my own, self-learned, sloppy sort of Korean, but I haven't totally forgotten it. I've never checked the accuracy with anybody, but it still remains in my ear, as sound rather than meaning. Somehow, though, try as I might, I couldn't bring to mind the Korean words of the workers' movement song set to exactly the same melody as "A True Foot Soldier." Or maybe I never knew the words in the first place? Could be. Or, like those other songs, could I still remember them twenty years ago but not now? That's possible too. Either way, the problem wasn't the Korean language. The problem was the words themselves. The song was sung to exactly the same melody as "A True Foot Soldier" but had suddenly changed from "The burgeoning cherry blossoms are the color of our collars" to "Hark, workers of the world!" Maybe it hadn't changed, maybe the workers' version had been there all alon —I bet that even on Sports Day at Yonghung Elementary School, while I was engrossed in the piggyback battle, the workers' movement song already existed. To me, however, it was just as if the song had suddenly changed.

Alternatively, you could argue that it did change, but that the change was not sudden but natural, and inevitable. But to me, it was sudden.

"Panmanmokk, tonmansannu, iribonmudoraa!"

These Korean words that burst from my big brother's mouth were a song with exactly the same melody as "Painopai." Could you really say that wasn't sudden? Around the same time, "A True Foot Soldier" had also suddenly turned into a workers' song, no doubt about it. Why was that? Of course, I didn't know. Because I didn't know, it was sudden. After all, before I knew it something had ended, and now, already, before I knew it, something had suddenly started.

"That wasn't sudden at all, that was natural. At the time you were still just a kid in the first year at Wonsan Middle School. It's so natural it's almost too natural that a kid like you should think of something natural as if it were something sudden. But that doesn't mean you can carry on acting like a kid forever. How old are you now, for god's sake? Surely you're at least old enough to start thinking about acting your age. Aren't you a bit too old to be standing there with that surprised look on your face going on about suddenly this, suddenly that? No adult would be fooled by that face, you know."

Whose voice was that? Was it my big brother's? Or was it my mother? Or was it some other person I didn't know? Either way, it's certain that I was just a kid at the time. Yes, big brother of mine, I was just a kid, as you say. But is it any crime of mine that I was a kid in the first year of middle school at the time? That was no crime—more like fate, right? That's just plain common sense. So at least up to that time there was nothing wrong with my seeing things as "sudden."

So the problem is about the time after that. About how things still seem so "sudden" to me, although I'm not a kid anymore. Here I am, far too old to be called a kid anymore, and you say I'm still standing around with that surprised look on my face, saying suddenly this, suddenly that—*that* is my "suddenly" problem. Is it some fault in me? Is it a brain problem? Could be. If I have got to be guilty of some crime, surely it wouldn't be of my fate which made me a first-form middle school boy at the time, but of what happened in my brain after that. The fact is that this "suddenly" got suddenly stuck to my brain one day, and I just couldn't shake it off.

Come to that, has anything happened to me since I was born in 1932 that wasn't sudden? Wasn't something always suddenly starting, suddenly ending, suddenly changing? Maybe those things weren't sudden to my big brother. Or to somebody other than my big brother, too, they might have seemed not sudden, but natural. When I say "somebody," who on earth could I be talking about? Of course, somebody other than me. I know a few somebodies like that. I can put faces and names to some of them. Things that strike my big brother and these somebodies as being so natural they are almost unnatural, are nonetheless "sudden" to me. And no—not only in the past, but in the future too, things will continue like that, to the day I die.

It's already been like that for forty years. It's not at all true that I've been standing there with a surprised look on my face saying "suddenly," "suddenly" all the time. That's one thing I really want to get straight. It's more like the exact opposite. Here's what I mean. In these forty years since I was born, sudden things have already become like natural things. It's actually natural for things to be sudden. So it follows I simply can't be surprised at these natural things. I can't afford to make a big fuss about it every time. Whatever happens, I can't afford to be surprised. The fact is, I don't know what's going to happen. And all things happen suddenly. Just as if it were perfectly natural for them to happen suddenly, things just suddenly happen! I know that the "suddenness" will strike some people as a perfectly natural outcome. To those people, the causes and reasons for things that suddenly happen will be as clear as the palm of their own hand. It's absurd to imagine anything that might fool a grown-up person. But I just want to say this. Probably I'll still be going on about "suddenness" until the day I die. No doubt at the same time other people exist who think that the things that are "sudden" to me are not sudden at all, but so natural that they're almost too natural. Those who read *Red Flag*, and others who learn karate, and yet others who become lawyers—they certainly exist.

Still and all—when on earth did this kind of stuff get stuck to my brain? After all it was a sudden thing, so I don't clearly know, but of course, it didn't happen yesterday or today. Was it perhaps from *that* time? I mean, from the time I was a first-form student at Wonsan Middle School. Uh-oh, it's my big brother, I can hear my big brother's voice. "For god's sake, stop going on about when you were a kid!" But Big Brother, just let me go on a little longer. Please forgive your poor little brother, whose fate it was to be so ignorant at the time.

By the way, Big Brother—sorry to bring it up all of a sudden—but do you know Saul Bellow? He's this Jewish novelist who lives in America and writes in English. Of course it doesn't matter if you haven't heard of him, but here's something he wrote, a passage from a book of his called *Herzog*. Toshiyasu Uno translated it into Japanese.

"To haunt the past like this—to love the dead! Moses warned himself not to yield so greatly to this temptation, this peculiar weakness of his character. He was a depressive. Depressives cannot surrender childhood—not even the pains of childhood. He understood the hygiene of the matter. But somehow his heart had come open at this chapter of his life and he didn't have the strength to shut it. So it was again a winter day in St. Anne, in 1923—Aunt Zipporah's kitchen."

But, Big Brother, I am not Saul Bellow. Obviously enough, I am not even Jewish. And the reason I come out with stories about when I was a kid is not that I am a depressive like Moses, the Jewish character in Bellow's novel. He knew very well that the reason he could not surrender childhood was that condition of his. He was a person who not only knew the cause of his problems, but even how to deal with the condition. In other words, an intellectual. And actually, that Jewish guy was teaching history or anthropology or something at a university. Which means that even in a civilized society like America, he was one of the people with above-average knowledge. And not only did he have that knowledge, but he was a man who had made his living out of imparting the knowledge he'd stored up to American university students—intellectuals of the future.

That's probably why he had to seek the cause of his inability to overcome his childhood memories in terms of his own depressive character. Of course, it's not as if depression was the only possible explanation. He'd got divorced from his wife even though they had two children, and he'd quit his job at the university, and so appeared to be the kind of person who just can't fit in, so to speak. It was because of all that that he came to think of depression. There's sufficient evidence to back up the diagnosis.

He didn't only need to know the cause of his inability to overcome his childhood memories. He also needed to know the content of a speech given at the White House by President Eisenhower. Because after all, he was an intellectual. Since he was an intellectual, it was probably only natural for him to know both those things. He may even have known the reason why all the women suddenly started wearing trousers and walking around in shoes that made them look as if they'd grown taller. Why is it that students suddenly put on helmets and mask their faces with towels? Why are their helmets divided into different colors? Why do hijacks happen? Why can't that guy become prime minister? Why does a war suddenly break out one day? Come to that, why does a war suddenly end one day? Why are porno movies so popular? Why is that guy less attractive to women than this guy? Why do this guy's books sell better than that guy's?

I expect Herzog could have answered all the "whys" I've lined up here. He'd probably have known all their causes and reasons. Even if mixed in among them there happened to be one or two he didn't know, he'd have used some kind of method to find out. Because he was an intellectual, who presumably knew how to find out things. Anyway, his childhood memories weren't things that just suddenly appeared. They were made to appear by a clearly identified cause, and he was an intellectual who knew perfectly well that the cause was his own depressive tendency.

I, however, am not like that guy Saul Bellow wrote about. It's not because I'm not Jewish, and it's not because I'm not a university lecturer. Nor is it because I don't have a tendency to depression. It's because one day, some unidentifiable thing got itself stuck to my brain. It follows that I come up with the stories about when I was a kid in middle school not because I have a tendency to depression—I just suddenly do. I mean, for some reason, I just don't know the cause. Is it, after all, some fault in my brain? Or is it some kind of punishment that's been imposed on my brain? And if it was my fault that I was a totally ignorant kid at the time, I suppose this would be the punishment for that crime. Crime and punishment, that's what it would be. But if it wasn't a crime of mine to be a totally ignorant first former at Wonsan middle school at that time, whose greatest dream was to go to military prep school, then logically my brain couldn't have been punished for that. What name should we put on my brain, which suddenly had some unidentified thing sticking to it that made it keep going on about things just "suddenly" happening? Fate? Yes, perhaps there's no other name for it. Actually, it's not a crime, and it's not a punishment. After all, at the time I was nothing more than a kid, with neither the knowledge to commit a crime nor the capacity to receive punishment. I was like a puppy that just happened to be owned by a captured criminal—a puppy, with no capacity to receive punishment. And Brother, I am ashamed of my own fate, the way it turned out like that. Why? I do not know. Before whom am I ashamed? I do not know that either. It's a very mysterious sense of humiliation. The sense of humiliation at having been no different from a puppy at the time—totally ignorant and without the capacity to receive punishment. What an extremely ridiculous sense of humiliation!

Big Brother, I wonder if it gets through to you how ridiculous I am? From a certain day on, I completely revered military prep school. Then one day, military prep school suddenly disappeared and ceased to exist. Why was that? At the time, I didn't know. Then one day, some time later, it turned out that the military prep school was a mistake in the first place. I was even taught the reason it was a mistake, at one of the new-style senior high schools with its textbook democracy. But when that happened, was I able, I wonder, to hate military prep school?

Things might have been a little different if I'd already entered school. I was absolutely determined to go there the following year. To have entered or not to have entered. The difference is only one small step. And that one step, that one year of my life, was very hard to judge. Because if I *had* gone to military preparatory school, you can't rule out the possibility that I might have become disillusioned. I might have had experiences that taught me the contradiction between dream and reality. You can't even rule out the possibility that I might have developed doubts about the very objectives of the Great Imperial Army of Japan, that I might have come to hate it, to loathe it, to criticize it. As a result, I might have dropped out of the Great Imperial Army of Japan, I might have been punished, or I might have ended up buried in the ground for eternity. But as it turned out, I was never able to put on the military prep school uniform. I only knew the uniform, and the school gate for that matter, from the cover of *Army* magazine and the photogravure features inside it. Then one day, just when I absolutely revered that school, and was thinking "next year for sure!"—the school gate disappeared and ceased to exist, just like that, as if it had been some kind of joke, or lie. And then we were told that it had all been a mistake. They said: you felt a false reverence. And the textbook democracy at the new-style senior high school offered samples of new things that could be revered without being mistakes, namely—but no, I won't bother listing them all for now.

Nobody knows better than you, Big Brother, how unclear and

vague I was about those new things. I came almost to detest the new-style senior high school. Well in that case, you'll probably ask me, why didn't I quit? The reason I didn't quit was that there wasn't anything else I wanted to do badly enough to quit school. I'm not saying our country high school was a low-level one. As a matter of fact I don't even believe that. New-style senior high schools are new-style senior high schools. But if I could just mention one boring little episode, it would be the time the democracy teacher in the social science department ordered me to come to the staff room. He was also the teacher in charge of my class. The reason I was called to the staff room was a crappy little essay I'd handed in to the Japanese-language teacher titled "The White Bird." It was about this bird who fell into some paint one day and came back home white all over, and was put on trial by the black birds. Was the white bird a real bird, or not? The result of the trial was that a majority of those present decided that there was no such thing as a white bird, and so the black birds executed the white bird. Well, it was a very trivial little tale, but the social studies teacher in charge of my class said it contained dangerous ideas because it rejected the concept of majority decision-making that was the foundation of democracy.

The social studies teacher asked me what kind of things I'd been reading. I couldn't come up with the sort of titles that would satisfy him. As you know, Big Brother, I only once showed my face at the study meetings being run by the barrel maker's son back from the kamikaze squadrons, the clam vendor's son back from basic training, the sandal maker's beautiful daughter who played ping-pong, and the tobacconists' daughters who were in love with the Kyushu University student, and after that I never went there again. But the reason I didn't hate that social studies teacher who was in charge of my class wasn't that he didn't punish me for the "dangerous ideas" in that trivial little composition. The reason was that I myself was such a vague sort of thing that it couldn't be helped if I were misunderstood. Of course I wasn't someone who had "subversive thoughts." But in that case what *was* I?

Well that's about it really. I just suddenly started talking without really thinking about it and I've ended up going on for rather a long time. I wonder if I've managed to communicate something to you, big brother? What sort of something? For instance, well . . . well actually, although I've been going on for such a long time, if you ask me to summarize the points that I particularly want to emphasize, well, that does actually appear to be exceedingly difficult. There's a risk I might set out to summarize but end up just repeating what I've already said. Actually there's probably no other way of doing it. After all, the reason I went on for such a long time in the first place was that I couldn't summarize what I wanted to say. I'll give up on the summary. I'll also give up trying to establish what did or didn't get communicated to you, Big Brother.

By the way, Big Brother, sorry to spring this on you suddenly, but do you know that I once thought of becoming a monk, at a temple? And do you know that one time I went out with the third son of the head priest at the local Zen temple in that country town in Chikuzen, across the long bridge on the outskirts of town, to the whorehouse in the village on the other side of the river?

Chapter 9

However, I fear I have very considerably digressed! Where on earth did I wander off the beaten trail? I think it was the point where I mentioned the song "A True Foot Soldier." It was where I broke into a run, to the sound of my grandmother smacking her pick against the strings of the shamisen. The grand digression was all due to "A True Foot Soldier." Because after all, it was "A True Foot Soldier" that my grandmother was picking out on the shamisen but it had turned into a workers' movement song with the same melody.

Despite the grand digression, however, after I broke into a run just like a real private second-class to the accompaniment of the shamisen, I was not late for my casual job as a make-believe private second-class. The film production company in Tsukiji turned out to be in a brand-new building. I believe I got on the elevator with four or five other people. There were already five or six pickup privates waiting in the big room we were taken to. It seemed to be some kind of meeting room. Large tables had been pushed back to the four corners of the room, and as we entered the room behind the person showing us in, two or three people jumped down from the tables they'd been sitting on. Maybe they'd already got into the frame of mind of privates second-class. Were there in all perhaps twelve or thirteen pickup privates? Each of us was issued with the kit of a private second-class—army cap, uniform, puttees, army boots. They were all new. Were they genuine? Surely not! Probably just theatre props. Either way, however, it was the first time in my life that I'd become a private second-class from the top of my head to the tips of my toes.

I suppose I had various thoughts, memories and feelings while I was getting changed. After all, I think it would be fair to describe this as a weird experience. I don't suppose I'll have such an experience a second or third time in my life, unless I become a movie actor or something. It's just that I don't feel like using some expression calculated to produce a particularly weird feeling to describe that weird experience. And it's not that I was suddenly attacked by nausea or felt a powerful need to go to the toilet the moment I started getting changed. The only thing on my mind was the following: please don't let the private second-class uniform issued me be so big that it flops around all over the place! Fortunately enough, the uniform turned out to be a perfect fit for my five-foot-five body. Of course, that was just coincidence. Likewise, the army boots issued me were a perfect fit for my size six-and-a-half feet. No doubt another coincidence. Still . . . what to make of the fact that, coincidentally enough, the private second class uniform issued to me happened to be a perfect fit? Could it be that my body-build was actually cut out for the role of an infantryman in the old Imperial Army?

"You should be happy—didn't ya always wanna be a soldier when you were a kid?"

But it wasn't a private second-class. I yearned to become a private second-class yearning to become a private first-class. I tried to dismiss the words of my big brother. But in the end I really did become a private-second class, and a pretend one at that.

Did ya forget the toy sword ya took that time?

What I truly yearned to become was an officer. And not just a hastily appointed one-year volunteer. I wanted to become a proper officer, something possible only for someone who has been through military preparatory school and then graduated from a military academy. As my brother pointed out, it was the toy sword, not the toy gun, that I took during that infant fortune-telling ceremony. Not that the ceremony matters a damn. Of course I'm not making out there was anything significant about that old folks' bit of fun. It wouldn't even fool a child. Besides, first and foremost, this was only a fake military uniform. It was just a prop to promote a movie. And I was no more than a pickup private second-class, being paid a few hundred yen a day to help promote a movie. Did I get 350 yen a day? Or was it just 240 yen, like those day laborers they call "two-four men" because they get two hundred-yen notes and four ten-yen coins for a day's work?

Still, I wonder if I really wasn't a little bit fixated on my role as private second-class? I wonder if I could really put my hand on my heart and swear it didn't bother me in the slightest? I felt anxious as I put on my puttees. After all, it was the first time since Wonsan Middle School. Had I maybe forgotten how to put them on? As it turned out, I got them on with no trouble at all. More than that, I even did the legs of one of the other guys.

"You're good at that," said the man next to me.

Where was he studying, I wonder? He was a very tall man. Maybe five foot eight or nine? Even so, he wasn't much of a soldier: C-class at best. You could see two whole inches of his wrist, sticking out just like that from the sleeve of his uniform. Also, his trousers were too short—you could see his spindly legs in the gap between the hem and the top of his army boots. He looked just like one of those intellectual-type soldiers who'd responded to the call-up with the greatest reluctance. And incredibly enough, his puttees were flopping around his feet like some child's kimono sash that had come loose! I mean, the puttees were already laced to start with, and he seemed to think you had to untie them completely before retying them round the legs. Were there already Japanese men who didn't know how to lace up a pair of puttees? What year could this man have been born in, for heaven's sake? I took his puttees in both hands from where they were flopping around his feet. Then I started tying them round his spindly legs.

"You're good at that." He said the same thing over again, that intellectual C-class recruit. "I see. So that's it. You just stick your leg into it like a roll of toilet paper."

My hand paused for a moment in the process of lacing up his puttees. He was sitting on the edge of the table with one knee up in the air, so that his leg was right in front of my eye as I laced up his puttees while kneeling on the floor. In this manner I could hear his voice coming at me from right over my head. Well, we'll let that pass. Since I was lacing up the puttees on his legs rather than his arms or neck, you'd have to say the situation was unavoidable. Still, is it really fair that a man who lets his puttees flop around his feet like some child's kimono sash that's come undone, and the man who's putting them back on the first man's legs and relacing them for him, should both be second-class privates? Anyway, I eventually finished lacing the puttees on both his legs.

"You're good at that." Yet a third time, the intellectual C-class recruit said the same thing, while lowering his leg from the table back to the ground. "Your uniform's a perfect fit—you look just like the real thing."

Just like the real thing? Hardly! But where did this "hardly!" come from? Of course I wasn't fixated on being a fake private second-class or anything. I was actually nothing more than a prop for the movies. It was a farce. Fancy dress. A 350-yen-a-day fancy-dress parade. Even so, I felt my anger rising against the intellectual C-class recruit who was three or four inches taller than me. It may be an exceedingly pathetic thing to admit, but I felt just like a real second-class private second-class who'd been unjustly insulted by the intellectual C-class recruit. What a ridiculous illusion! What a ridiculous contradiction! Still, I wonder how I should have dealt with the intellectual C-class recruit on that occasion? Should I have sat him back down on the table, this guy who didn't know how to lace up his own puttees, and silently peeled off the puttees that I'd laced up for him? Left them flopping around his feet like they were before, like some child's kimono sash that had come undone? Given him a karate punch? Right fist, one punch. I'd learned how to do it from watching Little Koga's early-bird karate practice.

Actually, nothing happened. When the man from the film company eventually showed up, and the privates second-class were lined up in front of him, the intellectual C-class recruit's puttees were not flopping around his feet like some child's kimono sash that had come undone. He was standing on the far right as we lined up—all five feet eight or nine inches of him. I was standing third from left. The man from the film company stood in front of the line of privates second-class and gave us our instructions.

"Ahem . . . I am Corporal Takahashi, the leader of this unit. I know I'm the only one here in a business suit, but nonetheless, please think of me as Corporal Takahashi. That will undoubtedly be better for all concerned. Now then—the Takahashi Unit is composed of twelve privates second-class. For convenience we will divide the unit into three squads, each with a squad leader. Because there are twelve of you, each squad will have four men. Each squad will maintain its autonomy and responsibility to ensure that there are no stragglers or laggards, and I want you all to encourage each other and help each other out. If you discover any abnormality in your squad, please report the matter to your squad leader. Squad leaders will promptly pass on the information to me, Corporal Takahashi. I know that makes it sound damned awkward, but your actual duties are very straightforward indeed. For college students like yourselves, I daresay they will appear excessively simple, and not sufficiently challenging. Among all of us present here, I am probably the only one who has experienced life in the real army. I was a corporal in that army too. But of course today I will not be treating you as if you were in the real army. You may set your minds at ease on that point. Very well, let us divide the unit into squads. Counting from the right, the first, fifth and ninth man, please take one step forward. You three will be the squad leaders: please memorize everybody's names and faces, so there'll be no mistake. Speaking from my own experience, it can be very difficult to tell the difference between one soldier and another when the badge on his collar is that of a private second-class. Very well—call out your numbers!

The Takahashi Unit set out first for Asakusa. It then proceeded to Ikebukuro, before finally arriving at Ueno. We went everywhere by streetcar. What were the numbers of the various lines we used, I wonder? Actually, we may have got on the bus at some point. But I don't think we used the train at all. Whenever we moved to a new location, we walked in single file, with the five-foot-eight-or-nine intellectual C-class recruit at the front, since he was the leader of Squad Number One. Our duties were exceedingly straightforward, as Corporal Takahashi had indicated. After all, we privates second-class were being called upon not to perform, but merely to dress up.

At each movie theatre we visited were cutout cardboard figures of Banjun and Achako, all taller than us twelve dressed-up privates second-class. All we had to do was stand in front of them in a straight line, holding our mops. As he'd explained earlier, Corporal Takahashi didn't treat us as if we were in the real army—in fact he didn't even tell us how to carry our mops. He just left it to each private second-class to decide whether to stand at attention with his mop held like a type-38 infantry rifle, or adopt a bayonet stance and treat it like one of those wooden guns used for bayonet practice . . . or whatever. As a result some of the men, including the leader of No. 1 squad, were actually holding the mops upside down and sweeping the floor with the bits of rope stuck on the end, as if they really were mops. Our one and only duty was to present arms at the right moment in the song. *Under the starry skies dressed in just a loincloth, hold your mops upside down, present arms!*

Could the reason there was no trouble between number one squad leader and me have been that we were both privates second-class, both made to wear the identical uniform with a single star? That may have had something to do with it. I'd laced up his puttees, flopping around his feet like a child's kimono sash come loose, and in the end I didn't undo them altogether so that they returned to their original state. I didn't give him a karate punch either. Why not, I wonder? Was it because of that private's uniform, with its single yellow star on a red tab, that had made it so hard for Corporal Takahashi, when he was in the real army, to tell one man from another? That may well have had something to do with it. Mainly, though, it was because of that voice. *You should be happy—didn't ya always wanna be a soldier when you were a kid?*

And that other voice. *"Bakarashika, chi!"*

Still and all, I wonder whether I was wearing that old infantryman's khaki greatcoat the day I set out for that pickup job as a second-class private. The theatre bell was still ringing. And there in front of my eye was the poster of the high school girl with the armpit hair. She was raising her jaw, twisting at the waist, throwing back the upper half of her body, bending her arms. Was this a performance, I wonder? Or just dressing up? Probably you'd call it a pose. I tried imagining a row of twelve people dressed up as high school girls in sailor suits, lined up in front of her poster. Then I peeked at the old-fashioned alarm clock in the ticket booth, and walked away from the theatre entrance. It was precisely one o'clock. I had to hurry up and make that phone call to Kuga. I crossed at the lights and started walking back to the hall with the telephones. A thought occurred to me: Was that tale of Banjun and Achako, privates second class, really a movie from twenty years ago? This sudden doubt quickened my pace. The question was, in the end, closely connected with that greatcoat. And possibly Kuga might remember. So, to start with, I should call him and check out that point.

"Hi! I hear you called me earlier?"

"Uh-huh. Have you finished your lunch?"

"Finished just now. What about you?"

"I haven't, actually. Didn't quite get round to it."

"Oh. I'm sorry. If you'd called me in the morning, we could have had lunch together. Shame about that."

"Well lunch doesn't matter a damn anyway."

"But it's been ages since we had a chance to meet up. How long has it been?"

"Since your wedding, I think."

"Surely not! But then again, maybe you're right."

Kuga's marriage was what you'd call a late marriage. It happened two or three years ago. He was in the same grade as I, so he'd have been thirty-seven or thirty-eight . . . maybe even thirty-nine. There was no particular reason, apparently, why it turned out that way. I didn't specifically ask him about it. After all, it had taken him four years to get into college. He failed the entrance exam for Hitotsu-bashi University three years in a row. On the fourth attempt, he passed. Maybe it was the same story with his marriage. I didn't ask him for full details, but apparently his bride was the niece of the president of a certain well-known private university in western Japan. All things come to he who waits. The proverb fitted Kuga perfectly. Of course it's not that he didn't have tenacity. He wasn't the type to do anything casually. If he'd been that kind of guy, he'd hardly have taken the same university entrance exam four years in a row. But in Kuga's case, he always seemed to stroll along in fair-weather sandals. Actually, those light wooden sandals suited him well.

Ishida Ei'ichi, the Warabi Ishidas' firstborn and a diligent student at Urawa Senior High School, was another one who had looked good in wooden sandals. But it was only your serious, practical wooden sandals that suited him. Student sandals . . . but not the kind with high supports that they used to wear at old-style high schools. Probably they were just regular sandals, but when he put them on, they just seemed like a real student's sandals. Things were a little different in Kuga's case. For a start, the wooden sandals were themselves of high quality, since they'd been donated to the Zen temple as an offering. They were nice and wide, with a certain roundedness to them, and they looked light. What sort of wood were they made of? Anyway, they weren't the sort of sandals that junior high or senior high school students usually wear. The thongs were a rather refined shade of grey. He got them because one of the patrons of the temple was a sandal maker, who during the midsummer and year-end festivities always donated enough sandals to last the priest's family throughout the year.

You see, under the new system the prefectural middle school he'd been attending was redesignated a senior high school and so a lot of the students, imitating the style in the old-system high schools, started to wear sandals with high supports. Not Kuga; he never wore sandals with high supports. He wore the high-class fair-weather sandals donated to the temple, and he always walked slowly, which was very much the appropriate gait for those sandals. They weren't suited for rushing around in a big hurry. I expect all the wooden supports, front and back, left and right, were worn down to exactly the same degree.

Still and all, I wonder why the son from a Zen temple would apply to a secular school like Hitotsubashi? Was it because he was the third son? His two older brothers had both graduated from Buddhist universities. Neither was living in the temple these days, though. Maybe there was a reason, but for my part I couldn't help feeling that it was a terrible waste. Why didn't Kuga try to become a priest, I wonder? If only Uncle Azuma had talked about a Buddhist university when he said he would look after my education—instead of the Law Faculty—I might just have taken him up on it.

Needless to say, it wasn't out of envy for Kuga's donated wooden sandals or because I felt a particularly strong interest in Buddhism. I had no "dangerous ideas," and I hadn't plunged myself into Buddhist ideas either. I hadn't read any of the relevant books. As for the sutras, well—all I knew was the one I'd memorized as a kid—*kimyomuryojunyorai, namufukashigiko, hozobosatsuisonisoji, zaisejizaiobutsusho.* It's probably thanks to my grandmother that I can still recite by heart virtually the whole of that True Pure Land Buddhist sutra. Every morning until I was in sixth grade, I was made to say my prayers with Grandmother in front of the family altar. In a brass bowl held with both hands I'd carry a pyramid-shaped lump of rice to the altar. I could hear my grandmother's voice everywhere—if she wasn't playing her shamisen she'd be intoning her sutras. That is not to say my grandmother was a totally committed Buddhist. Besides the Buddhist altar, we also had a Shinto one, naturally, dedicated to Amaterasu Kodai Jingu, the sun goddess from whom the Emperor was descended, and in Grandma's room was another Shinto altar, from the Konkokyo sect. I'd even been to the Konkokyo Grand Festival with Grandma a couple of times. It was held at the headquarters in Hamhung, three hours away by steam train. The great drums and flutes I saw and heard there reminded me of the grand concerts at the Shurakudai—the magnificent Kyoto mansion of warlord Hideyoshi that I had seen in picture books. In short, I wasn't brought up in a particularly Buddhist environment. Praying to the great Konko and Amaterasu Kodai Jingu at a Buddhist altar was an exceedingly ordinary environment for a Japanese to be brought up in.

It follows that thinking of becoming a Buddhist priest when I was just a high school boy in Chikuzen was a very selfish yearning of mine. Yearning? Yes, a very fanciful yearning. The thing was, I wanted to achieve enlightenment. I didn't yearn to become the head priest of some Buddhist sect. I yearned to see the world with the eyes of a Buddhist saint like Kanjizai Bosatsu. Why, I wonder? I may only have been a high school student in a rural town in Chikuzen, but I had become as weary of the world as the next person. The world-weariness of a pimply schoolboy? That was probably it. Of course, I thought in a general way about the usual things—infinity, immutability. I didn't associate with the worldly folk who thought Buddhism was a system of thought for backward nations. In fact, I didn't give a damn about "thought" in the first place. I had no desire to study it and master it. Not that I had given it up. (All I thought was, that I myself was someone who had been given up on, by all forms of thought.) At any rate I couldn't imagine a system of thought that might do me any good. I don't know why, but there was no other way I could think. Anyway, the thing to do was to ignore worldly people. Not to have anything to do with them. But was such a life of seclusion really possible? I'd need food, clothing and shelter, of course, and sandals, I suppose. Maybe it was the sandals, after all, that made me envious of Kuga, the third son from the Zen temple.

But there was another reason I longed to see the world with the eyes of Kanjizai Bosatsu, and that was the colonel's daughter. I wonder why I just couldn't ignore that woman? Why couldn't I walk past her along the street without flushing bright red? Kanjizai Bosatsu! Kanjizai Bosatsu!! Again and again I reread the paperback book with the 262 characters of the Wisdom Sutra. Still I couldn't over-come my red-face syndrome in front of the colonel's daughter. Was it because I was the son of a first lieutenant? Surely not! If not that, was it because I was an evacuee? Kanjizai Bosatsu! Kanjizai Bosatsu!! What's the big deal about the colonel's daughter!?! She's made of the same soybean curd and potato-gruel as the rest of us, isn't she? She's just a human being who turns into white bones at night like the rest of us, isn't she? Those three women in their beautiful costumes, oh what a mystery: in a flash the beautiful women are naked! And then, oh my, still more of a mystery, in a flash they are turned into white bones! What's this voice I now hear? The voice of a circus huckster, in my ear when I was still just a kid. Painted on the stage curtain in front of his tent were three images of three beautiful women. The far left of the curtain showed them wearing kimonos. The middle of the curtain showed them naked. And if you moved to the far right, they were nothing but white-boned skeletons, like the plastic models in a science classroom. That's what apparently happened if you applied a thing called an X-ray to them. Oh what a mystery! In a flash the col-onel's daughter is naked! And then, oh my, still more a mystery, in a flash she's white bones! In the end though, the eyes of my beloved Kanjizai Bosatsu did not develop X-ray vision.

On the grounds of the Zen temple run by Kuga's family was an enormous camphor tree. There was also a nursery school in one cor-ner. Next to the school was a little house with a zinc roof, where the nursery teacher lived with her family. Her daughter was in class with me and Kuga at high school. The old-style middle school that we'd been attending had been merged with the old-style girls' high school to become a new-style senior high school. The daughter of the fam-ily that lived next to the nursery school in one corner of the temple grounds looked just like her mother. She was petite, fair in complex-ion and above average in looks. Kuga, however, appeared to have no interest in her whatsoever. Why not, I wonder? His serenity was a source of some irritation to me.

Once a month it was Kuga's duty to go around the neighborhood in those wooden sandals of his, collecting money. The land surrounding the temple was temple property, and every month he would go around, collecting rents. Among the temple tenants were the little snack bar, the cosmetics shop, the fishmonger, the barber, the tobacconist and so on, but apparently the nursery teacher dwelling on the temple grounds lived rent-free. She was a war widow, and she taught in the temple nursery school. Those, it seems, were the reasons she was excused from paying rent. Could that have had something to do with Kuga's complete lack of interest in the teacher's daughter, our classmate at school? She was above average in looks, but her face was clearly not the face of a Chikuzen native.

Kuga's face, on the other hand, was clearly local. It belonged to an elite branch of the local bloodstock. He was also three inches taller than I. It even seemed a bit of a shame that he should have to wear the black robes of the priesthood all his life. However, it seems his indifference had nothing to do with contempt for the daughter of an outsider living under that shabby zinc roof in the temple grounds. In his unschoolboy-like high-class wooden sandals he was very good at bowing, as befitted the son of a priest. It was a proper bow that made the other party feel well and truly bowed to—the generous bow of a man glad to lower his head. I expect he bowed the same way to the war widow who lived on the temple grounds. If so, it's possible that as a parent she even harbored a secret hope that something might develop between him and her daughter. If something had developed, it would have been quite a fairy-tale romance. Of course, there's nothing wrong with that kind of romance. But apparently nothing romantic ever did develop on the grounds of the Zen temple. As soon as he graduated from senior high school, Kuga headed straight to Tokyo. Once there, he took up lodging with the firstborn son of the family, who had graduated from a Buddhist university and then for some reason opened a noodle restaurant, and commenced his long and patient life waiting to pass his entrance examination.

Then again, maybe the reason he was indifferent to her wasn't that she was the daughter of a war widow from some distant parts, but because he saw her with the eyes of Kanjizai Bosatsu? Those donated sandals—had he worn them just for show? Surely not! I don't suppose anything like that was going on. Even so, to me this Kuga— who'd set out on a long and patient life waiting to pass his entrance examination while helping out at his big brother's noodle restaurant, minding the store, delivering meals and so on—was an enviable character. What wasteful things he did! Still, whatever I thought about Kuga, it didn't make me feel like going out of my way to get into a Buddhist university. A contradictory tale, I know, but that's the fact of the matter.

"So, how are things with you these days?"

"Oh, well . . . about the same, I suppose."

"But you're pretty busy, aren't you?"

"Well, sort of. In my line there aren't any Sundays or public holidays, you know."

"I'm just getting dumber and dumber by the day. I never read novels at all these days."

He used *jen-jen* for *never,* and I laughed out loud.

"What? What's so funny?"

"You said *jen-jen* for *zen-zen.* You still can't pronounce *never* without that Chikuzen accent."

"Yeah . . . that's the one thing I just can't seem to put right."

"Of course not! That's one thing I could never master either—*jen-jen!*"

"So what's going on today? Something bring you to Ueno?"

"No, nothing in particular. It wasn't that I dropped in on my way somewhere else. I came here specially."

"Specially?"

"Er, yeah. I suddenly remembered that old coat I used to have. I wanted to ask you something about it too."

"Coat?"

"Oh—before we get on to that, do you remember what year that movie came out, the one about the privates second class?"

"Good grief! Did you come all the way here specially to ask about this stuff?"

"I'm, er, talking about the "Tale of Privates Second-Class," with Banjun and Achako. Didn't you see that movie?"

"Now you mention it, I do seem to remember a movie called something like that."

"I was thinking it was probably 1952 or 1953, about a year after we came up to Tokyo. Or could it have been a little after that?"

"If that's what's bothering you, you can easily find out by calling up the production company, can't you?"

"Ah . . . yes, of course. I see, right, right. Well, yes, that probably would take care of it. But that's not all, you see. It's also whether or not I was wearing that soldier's greatcoat around the time that movie was showing. That's really what's bothering me."

"Soldier's greatcoat?"

"Uh-huh. You know, that old-fashioned infantryman's khaki greatcoat I was wearing when I came up to Tokyo. When was the last time, roughly, you saw me wearing that coat, eh?"

"Er, that's a bit of a tricky one, I'm afraid . . ."

"Is it really that hard?"

"Well, you know—when are we talking about, roughly?"

"Let's see—well, I suppose it would be about twenty years ago."

"Good grief!"

"No, really—actually it was a bit of a sudden decision today, but I've already been to Warabi and back, you know."

"Warabi?"

"Uh-huh. The place I had my lodgings years ago. It's totally changed, you know, Warabi. The Ishidas' house has completely changed too, and that three-mat room where you yourself stayed a few times is gone without a trace. I mean, after all—that son of theirs who was in his second year at high school, well, he's got three children now. It's only natural everything's totally changed, but when I asked about that coat, Mrs. Ishida completely misunderstood me you know. I mean, it was an absolutely ridiculous mistake, but she very nearly got it into her head that you might have walked off with it. Although it was thanks to Mrs. Ishida's misunderstanding that I wound up coming to Ueno like this. Er, hello? Hello, hello? Oh I see, just a sec, I'll call you back right away, so just stay there and wait a moment, OK?"

Chapter 10

ALL IN ALL I was in Ueno for about forty minutes. I spent about half that time having curried rice at a noodle restaurant near the station . . . the bright yellow curried rice you get at noodle restaurants. I didn't manage to see Kuga. He said he was too busy with work to pop out and meet me. I made three ten-yen calls from the telephone hall, each cut off after three minutes. The way things turned out, I might have been better off phoning from Warabi rather than coming all the way to Ueno. If I'd called from the Warabi Post Office, I probably could have spoken for as many minutes as I wanted, even for an hour. Then again, maybe not after all, since Kuga seemed to be extremely busy. He spoke fairly normally for the first three minutes, but after I called him the second time, I sensed a certain indefinable restlessness through the receiver. On the third call, he hardly spoke at all. I did nearly all the talking, and he merely responded with the occasional "What?" or "Hmm . . ." Maybe I was keeping him from an urgent appointment. Or maybe he was perusing some urgent documents at the same time he was listening to me on the phone? Both are distinct possibilities.

In the end, I was unable to confirm the question of the privates second-class. Was the movie released twenty years ago, or was it seventeen or eighteen years ago? Anyway, it was sometime around then. And whichever year it was, it was when Kuga was still a perennial examination candidate, or at the very latest around the time he finally passed the exam on the fourth attempt. Even for a guy like him with his wooden sandals, it was hardly a time for watching Banjun and Achako. Still and all, I was a little taken aback by his suggestion that it would be better to inquire with the film company. It was the same way I felt taken aback when Mrs. Ishida mentioned calling the police. Is that the way people think about things when they work in banks? He said he never read novels these days; maybe that's to blame for his banker's way of thinking.

Of course there was no question of Kuga's mixing my coat up with some long-lost friend like Mrs. Ishida—who'd heard of people called Goto but thought Koto was a peculiar name. Instead, he seemed to be constantly worrying about me. Was that also a banker's way of thinking, I wonder? He didn't mix up coat with Koto and Goto, but it struck me that his way of thinking was to worry about me, Akaki, rather than the coat.

"Look, I'm really sorry about today. You see, life here is dominated by appointments and schedules. Next time, I wish you'd give me a call the day before. Because I'll do whatever it takes to make time to see you, just so long as it isn't too sudden." He spoke the last word with a distinct Chikuzen accent.

"No, no, it's all my fault for calling suddenly like this."

"So . . . where are you scheduled to go next?"

"Schedule?"

"Yep. If you're going to be here around eight o'clock this evening, I should be able to get my appointments finished a little earlier than scheduled and meet up with you."

"Eight, you say . . . hmm, it's just after one now. We-l-l . . . I wonder where I should go now."

"At a loose end, huh? But it wouldn't be right to keep you waiting from now all the way to eight o'clock. We'd better leave it till next time. You'll be going home now, I suppose?"

"Home?"

"Well there's no point waiting around without anything scheduled until eight. That'd be a waste of time."

"But I can't go home yet. You see, at four I have to meet the lady from the Nakamura Pawnshop."

"What?"

"Otherwise what would be the point of my early-bird start today? That really would be a waste."

"Early bird?"

"Absolutely. It was on account of that coat that I was up so early this morning."

"Hmm . . ."

"But it's still some time before four. Oh well, I guess I'll have a think about it while I eat a spot of lunch somewhere around here."

It was while I was eating the bright yellow curried rice from the noodle restaurant that I had the idea of going across the river to Kameido Third Precinct. Was it because of that yellow? As I recall, my lost greatcoat was the color of curried rice. The same color as the noodle-restaurant curry I ate a number of times twenty years ago on the other side of the river. I wonder how many times I ate that curried rice on the far side of the river? I wonder how many times I put on my curried rice–colored coat and went to the far side of the river?

At Ueno station, I let one Yamanote line train go by. To go to Akihabara and change there for the Sobu line for Kameido, the Keihin-Tohoku line would be better than the Yamanote line.

Kameido station had changed too. Several buildings had gone up in front of the station, and there were giant billboards on every floor advertising coffee shops, hostess bars, Chinese restaurants, etc. But the change wasn't as radical as at Warabi station. Had the road in front of the station become slightly wider? Or did it just seem that way because of the daylight?

I turned right along the road in front of the station, and started walking in the direction of the road leading to Kameido Tenjin Shrine. This road was another long road. But I don't think I ever got bored walking along this road, since I'd be looking for Yoko san. Of course Yoko san wasn't in Kameido Third Precinct. So what I was really looking for as I walked along was the Yoko san of Kameido Third Precinct. Every time, I'd be wondering whether I'd be blessed with the good fortune to encounter the Yoko san of Kameido Third Precinct that night.

The one and only woman I had ever known before I first visited Kameido Third Precinct was Yoko san. The person who informed me of her existence was Kuga, the third son from the Zen temple. The two things I learned from him were Yoko san and *shogi*. Shogi he taught me when I was in my second year of junior high school. Until then, the only kinds of shogi I knew were Korean-style shogi and that very simple game, *hasami-shogi*. My father was always playing go, and he never bothered with shogi. I was taught Korean-style shogi, with its hexagonal pieces, by Mr. Cho, who worked in our shop. Hasami-shogi I learned from my great-grandfather. Great-grandpa's room was next to the room where Grandma worshipped the great Konko. It was also an ondol room, but an area of about three mats at the back was elevated about twice as high as the usual alcove in a Japanese-style room, and that part alone was laid with tatami mats. Great-grandpa would roll out his futon there, put a flagon of saké next to his pillow, and spend the whole day drifting in and out of sleep. He lived that way for five or six years, until he died at the age of eighty-eight.

"Left, right, gotcha!" That's what Great-grandpa always said if he managed to take one of my pieces when we were playing hasami-shogi. It's a game where you have to try and surround your opponent's pieces in a pincer movement. If you get two of your pieces on either side of your opponent's piece, you can take it.

"Left, right, gotcha!" I learned to say it just like Great-grandpa.

"Got me good!" That's what Great-grandpa said when one of his own pieces was surrounded and taken.

"Left, right, gotcha!"

"Got me good!"

"Went to getcha but you got me!"

Kuga taught me to play real shogi in his study room, which was in a separate building from the Zen temple itself. When I told him I didn't know how to play shogi, he looked as if he couldn't believe it.

"Really?"

"Really."

"You mean you've never played it at all—*jen-jen*?"

"It's the truth, I've never played it at all—*zen-zen*."

"Hoo-ee! Second year in junior high and never once played shogi! Who'd've thought!"

I don't suppose you could say that about anyone else in that little country town in Chikuzen. In summer there'd be a wooden bench in front of every house, and on each bench you'd likely see a couple of men in summer kimonos facing each other with a shogi board sandwiched between them. Even the desk lids in the junior high school had shogi boards on their underside: kids would break the hinges, then carve out shogi board squares with a pocketknife. Even elementary school kids played shogi. I wanted to learn the game: in that little country town in Chikuzen it was understood that there was no such thing as a person who had reached the second year of junior high school without learning how to play shogi.

To me, shogi was a symbol of the local culture. Until I mastered it, I couldn't hope to assimilate with the locals. Kuga taught me. I managed to learn the rules of the game and a few of the strategies for winning. Still, it's not something I'm proud of, since to this day I have never won a game of shogi, never yet come across a player worse than me. What on earth does that signify? Of course it's presumably a matter of talent. And I expect effort, study and the will to win have something to do with it too. I've certainly been lacking in all those departments. My shogi playing was defective in much the same way as my Chikuzen dialect was marred by my weakness in the all-important Chikuzen accent. I mastered the special vocabulary, ending sentences the Chikuzen way, with *batten*, *tai* or *gena*. But I just could not get used to saying *shenpai* instead of *senpai*, or *jen-jen* instead of *zen-zen*. Chikuzen people always pronounced "s" as "sh" and "z" as "j." I had mastered Chikuzen dialect, but not the genuine "Chikujen" tongue.

It's only natural, really. Because if there's one thing you can't learn or master, it's being a native. Of course shogi's a different matter. I wouldn't attempt to claim I've never won at shogi because of problems with not being a native—that would be too much of a stretch. Basically I just had no talent for it. But besides talent, the reason I gave up on the shogi was probably to do with despair at ever becoming a native. Despair? Yes indeed, a very ridiculous despair. But even looking to the future, I don't suppose I'll ever be lucky enough to meet a player who's worse than I at shogi. *Left, right, gotcha! Got me good! Went to getcha but you got me!*

It was just before the summer holidays of my third year in senior high school when I set out to visit Yoko san's place with Kuga. It was a rainy day. Carrying a coarse oil-paper umbrella, I set off for the six-o'clock rendezvous with Kuga on the long bridge on the outskirts of town. The light was already fading. But we couldn't be too careful. There was a village on the far side of the bridge, and another village beyond it. This long bridge on the outskirts of town was the only route for people from those two villages when they went in and out of town by bicycle or bus on their way to and from school. There was no knowing when you might bump into somebody on the way. Of course we had prepared various excuses, but if it were discovered that we'd gone to a whorehouse we'd be suspended from school for a week. On top of that, we'd be kept after school to clean the grounds for a fortnight: "Since you've got so much energy to spare!" Apparently that's what they would say. After the school trip at the beginning of May, three of my classmates had each got a fortnight's detention.

Kuga was standing around in the middle of the long bridge, under a black umbrella, looking down over the side. We started to walk along, side by side. There was a single 500-yen note in my trousers pocket. When I'd asked Kuga how much money I'd need, he'd said 300 yen, but added that it would be better to take 500 yen if possible. I scraped together the 500 yen by taking it out of the money I'd been paying into the school trip fund. Those of us who didn't go on the trip got our money back before the summer holidays. I believe 500 yen was exactly the same amount as a month's worth of fees at the senior high school.

"It's prob'ly safer to walk than take the bus," said Kuga. "Any road, don't drink no sake, OK? Even if someone finds us, there's no evidence so long as we ain't bin drinkin'." Then Kuga asked if I'd read a novel called "Confessions of a Mask." I hadn't read it.

"It's a damn masterpiece."

As I recall, Kuga was very keen on novels in those days. Maybe from the very beginning he was planning to take his time getting into the university. Come to think of it, he was born the same year as I— 1932. We were both a year older than our classmates. The year delay in my case was from having been evacuated from northern Korea.

In Kuga's case, it had to do with illness. At some point in elementary school he'd already had to repeat a year. Still and all, where on earth did he get to know about Yoko san? That I didn't know. I heard about her from Kuga, during that holiday when the other students were away on the school trip. Neither Kuga nor I went. We were extremely cocky kids. Why should we go along on a childish group outing like that! Once Kuga and I had seen all there was to see at the two movie houses in town, we just killed time hanging around doing nothing much. We did some secret drinking in the shady back street bars, but that was as much as we dared do in our own town. If we'd ventured upstairs to try out the other services offered there, we'd certainly have been busted right away.

But that wasn't the only reason why I didn't venture upstairs there. It wasn't just fear of discovery that made me cross the long bridge to the village on the other side. What made up my mind was something Kuga said.

"She's a very literary whore."

Another thing Kuga said: "I wouldn't want to introduce a woman like her to someone who'd never read any literature."

After Kuga and I finished crossing the long bridge, we steered clear of the bus route by turning left and walking along the river embankment. Apparently this embankment was famous for its sumac trees. Several households in town made a living from collecting and selling the wax from those trees.

"Akaki, have you ever had poison sumac?"

"Nope."

"When I was in elementary school, everyone got it from these sumac trees."

"A bit like shogi, huh?"

"God it was itchy. So itchy! You'd break out in bright red spots all over your face and body."

"Maybe I'll try it out."

"Nah, too late. It seems grown-ups don't get it."

"Why not?"

"I've often wondered the same thing, buddy."

The leaves of the sumac trees on the river embankment turned bright red after midsummer. It certainly made a striking view. But why didn't adults get the rash, I wondered? As I walked along, I pulled a leaf off one of the trees. Was it true I wouldn't flush bright red the way I did whenever I passed the colonel's daughter on the street—even if I squeezed out the sap and wiped it over my face?

"Oy, oy, stop it, stop it!" said Kuga.

Of course I didn't really want to give it a try. For after all, it was partly because of the colonel's daughter that I'd set out to visit Yoko san. Kanjizai Bosatsu! Kanjizai Bosatsu!! What's the deal with the colonel's daughter!?! But my red-face syndrome in front of the colonel's daughter could not be cured by the 262 characters of the Wisdom Sutra. Would a literary whore cure it for me?

Was it four or five hundred yards we walked along the river embankment? Eventually we turned right down the side of the embankment and there was a small settlement. The houses of the settlement were surrounded by a bamboo grove. They all looked absolutely identical. Beyond the settlement lay rice paddies. But as muddy trails go, the road through the settlement was relatively wide, and you could probably just about drive a small truck down it. The rain kept falling, though it was just a drizzle. In their wooden sandals, my feet got wet from the touch of the damp grass. Kuga wasn't wearing his usual fair-weather sandals; he had his rubber boots on instead. How far did we walk along that farm road, I wonder? A thousand yards? Probably about that. Eventually a large camphor tree came into view. Underneath was a single cottage with a thatched roof.

As we approached, I realized that the cottage was surprisingly large, with an upstairs. Passing through the latticed door into the interior, however, we found the broad, dirt-floored room you'd expect in a farmhouse. Kuga made me wait there, while he approached the doorway to the living area of the cottage and called out to someone inside. A woman emerged. Could this be Yoko san? It seemed not. More like the lady of the house. When he'd finished exchanging words with this woman, he came back to where I was standing. He addressed me with a serious face: "Yer in luck."

"Why?"

"Yer gonna be Yoko san's doorman today."

"Doorman?"

"Means her first customer of the day!"

"And what about the money?"

"Hmm, let me see. Should I give it to the old lady? Yeah, maybe that's better."

"Is 500 yen all right?"

"Fine, fine. I'll have a chat with the old lady and sort it all out, no worries."

"And what about you?"

"Me? I'm just here to introduce you. No worries, *chi*!"

I produced the five-hundred-yen note from my trousers pocket, smoothed out the creases in it, and handed it over to Kuga. Then I wiped my feet with a floor cloth and went up the stairs. I was given the floor cloth not by the landlady, or Yoko san, but by some girl who seemed to be a kind of maidservant. She was also the one who showed me to the upstairs room, and brought me a cup of tea.

I wonder how long Yoko san and I were alone together in that upstairs room? Probably twenty or thirty minutes, I guess. As to what happened during those minutes, well—on the one hand, I could go on about it all day long, but on the other, I could treat it as an entirely private matter all my own, with no need to breathe a word to anyone else. Meaning I have the right to maintain absolute silence about the events that transpired during this period. At the same time, I also sense behind that silence an inexplicable urge moving me to confess. It's difficult to say immediately which is the stronger of those two forces. Silence isn't necessarily golden; speech isn't necessarily silver. Or if I may put it more boldly: confession is like a sword, and silence is like a shield. Silence opposes speech, it is contrary to diction. Between them, silence and speech is a contradiction. However, that doesn't mean it's a totally hopeless case. Here's how Ogai Mori puts it in *Vita Sexualis*:

"The madame arose. I followed her out to the corridor. There was a maidservant waiting there, and she took me to another room. There was a geisha there whom I'd never seen before. She seemed a different type from the ones who get called to dinner parties. Slightly hard to describe. This was when I learned that 'doing it without disrobing' is not only something that happens when a virtuous woman is tending to the ills of an invalid."

"This time I can write the truth with no deviation. After that I had other encounters in teahouses, but this was the first and last time that I really had a true teahouse experience."

"For a few days afterwards, I had that uneasy feeling at the back of my mind. Fortunately, however, I turned out to have nothing the matter with me."

The *I* here couldn't possibly be the real Ogai Mori. Even if it was *partly* him, it couldn't be *all* him. Either way, the *I* in the novel was a young man who had graduated from the university, passed an exam qualifying him for overseas study in Germany, and was making a living translating legal books while waiting for the official letter of appointment to come through. The scene describes the first sexual experience in the young man's life.

Still and all—"Slightly hard to describe." Great writing! Vintage

Ogai Mori. The next three lines, from "This was when I learned . . ." are also brilliant. But in my case things were slightly different. Only natural, you may say, and rightly so. Of course I hadn't taken on Yoko san at arm wrestling, as the *I* in *Vita Sexualis* had done with a geisha at a house in the Yoshiwara, shortly before having his "virtuous woman" tend to his ills "without disrobing." Nor did I sit by the brazier chatting in a desultory fashion about this and that, or stand next to the window cooling off with a paper fan, the way the *I* in Kafu Nagai's *Strange Tale from East of the River* did with "Oyuki san." Nor did I ask Yoko san what circumstances had brought her to her profession; and neither did I eat iced dumplings with her.

As Kuga said, Yoko san was a "literary whore." The names of Poe, Rilke, and Rimbaud came from her mouth. Well, strictly speaking they didn't exactly come from her mouth—more like I dragged them from her mouth. Kuga's words had got so firmly stuck in my mind that I must have seemed like a complete literary freak who was taking part in some literature seminar or poetry contest with a rival school. I'm sure that's why I delayed matters until I was surprised to learn that I was running out of time.

"Please don't get too tense."

Yoko san did not go so far as to "not disrobe." But in the end I think maybe you could say that I "had my ills tended to by a virtuous woman." Because in the end, like a patient who mustn't get too tense, I adopted a position lying on my back and looking up. When I went back downstairs, Kuga was sitting on the bottom step, leaning on his black umbrella as if it were a walking stick.

We walked back the same way we came, emerging onto the river embankment. The rain had lifted.

"I never thought you'd be waiting downstairs."

"Well, I was in charge of the introductions today. So, how was it?"

"Uh-huh. Just like you said it would be."

I kept to myself the fact that I'd "had my ills tended to by a virtuous woman." On our way home, Kuga told me about Yoko san's circumstances. She'd been evacuated from Manchuria, and she was now twenty-seven or twenty-eight. That meant she would have been about twenty when the war ended. I wonder if she had also been assaulted by Soviet soldiers? You couldn't rule out the possibility.

"Yaponski madam, davui!"

"Chassui, davui!"

Yaponski madam meant *Japanese woman. Chassui* meant *wristwatch.* And *davui!* was a verb in the imperative form, meaning *give*! Those were the first Russian words I ever heard in my life. I had yet to hear the "P" in Pushkin, the "G" in Gogol, or the "D" in Dostoevsky— instead these were the first Russian words I ever heard. An arch was set up on a street corner, like an enlarged version of the one through which contestants entered on school Sports Day. On the arch were displayed portraits of Lenin, Stalin and Kim Il Sung surrounded by little red flags. Underneath the arch, military trucks packed with Soviet soldiers carrying mandolin guns zoomed back and forth. The smell of the gasoline from those trucks! Down at Ryuhung Bay, the Soviet soldiers in crew cuts were enjoying themselves swimming, their yellow hair glistening and their cocks dangling in full view. At the time the only two Russian names I knew were Peter and Nikolai. Of course when I say "Peter" I don't mean Peter the Great. And when I say "Nikolai" I don't mean Nikolai Gogol. This Peter and Nikolai were a couple of White Russians who used to come to our shop to buy wheat flour and sugar. They did their shopping in broken Japanese rather than Russian.

I wonder whether in those days Yoko san already knew Pushkin, Gogol and Dostoevsky? It occurred to me that I'd quite like to ask her about that. And I imagined for myself what her answer might be: "I did know them. But I don't suppose those men with the crew cuts did."

Yoko san's face was clearly not local. Nothing about it was much like the face of the woman who lived in the little zinc-roofed house on the grounds of the Zen temple where Kuga lived, but still if you were to classify her face you'd say that it didn't belong to the neighborhood. The old lady and the maidservant of the thatched cottage also had different faces. And it wasn't just Yoko san's face: her whole body was pale and thin. And, just as Kuga had said, she was a "literary whore."

But it wasn't literature I did with Yoko san upstairs in the thatched cottage. As proof of that, I got on a train with Kuga to go to a clinic. Was it about a week after our visit to the thatched cottage? I had the same "uneasy feeling" as the first-person narrator of *Vita Sexualis*. And as it happened I, like him, "fortunately . . . turned out to have nothing the matter with me." But in one respect I differed from him. Ogai Mori's *I* only had "that uneasy feeling" at the back of his mind. In my case, there was a certain pain as well as the uneasiness.

"Shall we head out to a clinic?"

"But it's nothin' to do with you?"

"Is too." Kuga laughed. It turned out he'd been to visit Yoko san the very next day. The two of us got on a train bound for Kurume. We'd risk being discovered if we went to a clinic in our own town. We got off the train at the next station. We'd been planning to go a little further than that, but changed plans because Kuga saw a sign through the train window. It was attached to a telegraph pole near the first station, and on it were the characters for "flower willow malady," indicating a VD clinic.

Finding the clinic, however, was no easy matter. We walked around the village, checking the telegraph poles and furiously wiping the sweat off our faces. It was blazing hot. I think school had already finished for the summer holidays. Could it be that the sign Kuga had seen was advertising a clinic that wasn't in this village? We couldn't very well inquire at some farmhouse, and for better or worse we met nobody as we walked along. Maybe we'd arrived just when farmhouses in midsummer took their siesta. I was the one who found the "flower willow malady" sign. It had fallen down in front of the clinic with its face to the ground. When I picked it up and peeked at it, I found the painted characters were already starting to peel off. The house with the gate in front of it did indeed prove to be a clinic, however. We made our way past the shrubbery in the front yard and called from outside the lobby. The doctor in charge of the clinic emerged, a little man with silver-wire spectacles. Then the two of us lined up in the consulting room and confessed to our experiences upstairs at the thatched cottage. Confessed and repented, I should perhaps say. At least that's how I felt. I became acutely aware of myself as totally powerless in front of somebody or something. I also felt a certain satisfaction in having been able to do something so laudable as this confession. I wonder how it felt for Kuga, the third son of a Zen priest?

"Nothing to worry about for either of you," said the old doctor, drying his hands with a towel after he'd washed them, "*jen-jen*." "Still, it's a funny old business, two lads going with the same lass. So, which of you went first?"

"Err . . ."

"Well either way, you're brothers, I can see that."

"Err . . ."

"Anyway, never go unprotected, boys. Never go unprotected."

Kuga and I managed to graduate safely, without being suspended for a week or getting two weeks' detention. But the question of whether Yoko san had any effect on my blushing syndrome went unanswered. The Wisdom Sutras, or the literary whore? In the end I never found out whether either worked, since after my visit to the thatched cottage I never once passed the colonel's daughter in the street again. In school or town, I always avoided seeing her face. If she came walking along the street towards me, I'd duck down a side road. If there were no side road, I'd swallow my shame and turn back the way I'd come.

The summer of the following year, I went off to Yoko san's place on my own. I had come back from Warabi to Chikuzen, and planned to stay a couple of weeks. You couldn't exactly call it a summer holiday since I was neither at college nor employed at the time, but in the end I cut it short and went back to Warabi after less than ten days, probably because I didn't manage to see Yoko san. I learned that she had gone to Kurume. Kuga seems not to have come back to Chikuzen on that occasion, but when I went back to the thatched cottage, it was almost the exact same time of day as the first time. Of course I planned it that way. The woman who appeared at the inner door was neither the old lady nor the maidservant who'd brought me the floor cloth. Probably she was one of Yoko san's coworkers.

"Kurume?"

"Yes. She went to a timber merchant's place in Kurume."

"A timber merchant . . ."

"Yeah, it'd be three months ago, almost to this very day."

That was the second and last time I crossed the long bridge on the outskirts of town for an outing to the thatched cottage. Of course I merely inquired after Yoko san, then left the place. It felt not at all mysterious that the woman didn't try to keep me from leaving. About how long after that was it, I wonder, that I first set out for Kameido Third Precinct? What I do know is that I got on a tricycle-taxi in front of Kameido station and headed off to Kameido Third

Precinct just as if I were heading off in search of a "timber merchant's place in Kurume."

The tricycle-taxi cost one hundred yen. That was the first and last time that I ever used a tricycle-taxi. After that I always walked from Kameido station on my own. About when was it they got rid of the tricycle-taxis? Maybe around the same time the red-light district in Kameido Third Precinct disappeared. I never walked that long road from Kameido station with Little Koga. Not with Kuga either. Kuga came to see me in Warabi on a number of occasions, and sometimes he would sleep in my mosquito net for want of a futon. I sometimes went and stayed at his place, too. The noodle restaurant run by Kuga's brother was near Togoshi Ginza station on the Ikegami line. It was in the shopping street in front of the station, just where it branched off toward the No. 2 Keihin national highway. Kuga's big brother and his wife lived in a house just behind the restaurant, while Kuga himself and a married couple who worked at the restaurant lived in rooms over the shop. Kuga had a four-and-a-half mat room—definitely a cut above my own three-mat room. Moreover, he had on top of his desk a radio with a magic eye that glowed green when the signal was stronger. They were the latest thing in those days. Having your very own radio at home was a sure sign of privilege. The only drawback, it seemed, was the noise from the long-distance trucks hurtling along the No. 2 Keihin highway. But Kuga, being Kuga, had a different problem on his mind.

"It's not the trucks so much as them next door."

To him, the radio was not a luxury at all: it was essential to drown out the sounds made by the shop-hand couple living in the next room.

"Your room's tons better," he said.

"Every night, is it?"

"Pretty much, yeah."

I was treated to a bowl of rice with tempura at Kuga's brother's restaurant, and spent the night in Kuga's room. Truth to tell, I wanted to try switching the radio off just for a bit. But somehow I couldn't blurt it out. And mysteriously enough, the topic of Yoko san never came up in our conversation. And I'm not talking just about that night. The topic never came up at my three-mat room in Warabi either. I never told Kuga about the "timber merchant's place in Kurume." Did he not know about it? Surely he must have. Then again, maybe he also had somewhere he went looking for Yoko san. I never told him about Kameido Third Precinct. Why not, I wonder? I didn't really know myself. When Kuga went out looking for Yoko san, I wonder where he went? Or was it that he no longer needed a literary whore, since now he was taking the entrance exam for Hitotsubashi University?

I stood at a crossroads. If you turned left after the traffic lights you'd get to the great red gate of Kameido Tenjin Shrine. If you turned right after that you'd get to the Third Precinct. I waited for the lights to change. Just then, the aroma of roasted beans wafted past my nose. The same aroma as twenty years ago. I looked around and sure enough, there was the very same bean store I remembered from twenty years ago. I took five or six steps back and stood in front of the bean store on the street corner. Was it about three mats wide, that storefront? Various kinds of roasted beans were displayed in wooden cabinets with glass lids. Beans were sold by the cup. In the days when I used to go to Kameido Third Precinct, I stopped at this store several times and bought a cupful of unshelled peanuts. They say every fool knows one thing, and I had got it into my head that peanuts were the cheapest nutritional supplement you could get. They were also more filling than raw eggs. However, I was not sufficiently at home in Kameido Third Precinct to just stroll around the place, munching on peanuts while checking out the neighborhood. I would only munch on my peanuts as far as the red gate of the Tenjin Shrine. Then I would stuff the remaining ones into my pocket.

One night, I ate peanuts together with a woman. I must have had enough cash on me to afford more time than usual. The woman's room was completely different from Yoko san's place upstairs at the thatched cottage. It wasn't a six-mat room, just four-and-a-half. It didn't have a proper table—just a little lacquered side table with collapsible legs. It was too small to eat off. Of course it wasn't there for meals; there were just a couple of cups of coarse tea on top of it. Next to it was a little red dresser, and on the wall was a letter rack made of white birch. There were no letters in it, though. Two or three magazines were lying around on the tatami, magazines like *Heibon* and *Myojo*. Any woman's room in Kameido Third Precinct would look pretty similar to this. For some reason the magazines were always a month or so out of date—another aspect the women's rooms had in common.

The woman took some photographs out of the dresser drawer and showed them to me. It was the first time in my life that I'd seen such photographs. Were there about a dozen of them? I stood up, went to where my coat was hanging by the window, took the paper bag of peanuts out of a pocket and put it next to the pillow. Then I snuggled back under the futon, stuck my head out like a tortoise peeking out from its shell, and examined the photographs one by one. The woman sat down by the pillow with her legs to one side and helped herself to peanuts, giggling quietly. The photographs were all playing-card size. Did this woman show the same photographs to all her customers? And did she do with them the kinds of things the people in the photographs were doing? Not necessarily, it appeared.

"Want them?" asked the woman, picking off the shell of a peanut with the same finger and thumb she had used to pick it up. "If you want them, I might give you just one."

"But they're not photos of you."

"Ooh, you're good at flattery for a young'un."

"It's not flattery. This is the first time I've done something like this."

"Well, do come again then."

"Uh-huh."

"When I get some new photos in, I'll show them to you."

"I don't come here particularly to look at photos."

"Silly boy. Of course you don't."

However, I didn't go to her place again. The following day, I felt a sudden unbearable itchiness. Even if I went to the toilet I couldn't figure out the problem. I went to the public bath and rubbed myself down with soap, but still the itching did not let up. I had been strictly observing the warning from the old doctor. Never go unprotected, boys. Never go unprotected. But since the cause had to be something other than that, I couldn't for the life of me think what it might be. On the third day I couldn't bear it any longer and went to a clinic. I took a train to Akabane and looked in the yellow pages for a VD clinic. There were plenty of them in Akabane. Afterwards, in my three-mat room, I borrowed the big *Kojirin* dictionary from the Ishidas' son and looked up a certain item. The entry read as follows: "[Fauna] A type of louse, yellowish-gray or grayish-white in color, minute and cubic, dwelling parasitically in the genital region, sometimes spreading to the armpit, beard and eyebrow regions." I spread the jet-black cream I had received over the affected area for three days, as instructed. During that period, for some reason, I never once thought of the photographs I'd been shown by the woman, or even of the woman herself. I didn't think of the woman who'd shared my peanuts until the fourth day, when the moment I'd been so anxiously waiting for finally came—no sooner had the public bath opened for business than I dashed in, hurried over to the tiled washing area before anyone else could get there, stood in front of the faucet and washed off the jet-black stuff I'd had smeared on myself for three straight days. It was just after that, when I thought of the woman with the photographs and my peanuts.

"Er, the old Kameido Third Precinct would be that way, wouldn't it?"

I asked the question while taking possession of a paper bag full of roasted broad beans. They were the kind that had just been roasted, not the ones deep-fried in oil and then sprinkled with salt. My decision not to order peanuts was not connected particularly with my experience that time. Recently I hardly ever eat peanuts. Just occasionally as a snack with beer or something. I never did have a strong attachment to them. It was an exceedingly calculating thing—I simply considered peanuts the least expensive form of vitamin supplement, and now I no longer needed to concern myself with such calculations. Besides, these days I find peanuts a shade too heavy on the stomach.

"The old Third Precinct is still the Third Precinct," replied the man, who was apparently the owner of the bean store. Had he been selling roasted beans at this store twenty years ago, I wondered? He looked about fifty. But of course I didn't recognize him.

"Ah, I see."

"You'd be talking about the old pleasure quarters, perhaps?"

"Yes, actually."

"In that case, you want to cross over there—"

"Past the Tenjin Shrine gate—"

"Yeah, yeah, then turn right and the Third Precinct is about there."

I wonder how long I spent strolling around Kameido Third Precinct? In terms of time, I guess it was about thirty minutes. On my way back, I stopped at the same place again and called out to the bean merchant.

"Hi, it's me—the guy who asked directions to the Third Precinct."

"Oh yeah. Nothing to see there now, eh?"

"No, the place has gone to the dogs. What went wrong?"

"Well, the massage parlors went to Kinshicho and Koiwa. And Third Precinct, like Yoshiwara, has been sinking, and it's no good anymore."

"I see. Sinking, eh?"

"Yep, sinking."

During the thirty minutes or so I walked around the place, I spotted only four or five houses that I remembered from the old days. Even those four or five places showed only a few lingering signs of their old glories—a few pale pink tiles barely clinging to a wall, a pillar or two to the side of a front entrance. Nor was there any sign of the old establishments having switched to related lines of business like love hotels or seedy bars. I took a peek inside one of the houses. I chose it because I recognized part of the old tiled design still there at the top of the wall, but in the gloomy interior some kind of machine had been installed, and a middle-aged man and woman, probably a married couple, dressed in overalls, were operating it by slowly moving their hands and feet.

The houses where the women used to be were identifiable mostly by their entrances. Of course the ones I knew were nothing like the peeping-window type described in *A Strange Tale from East of the River*, where Oyuki san could sit with just her face visible from the outside. The walls of the places I knew were decorated with tiles, or at least with a fake tile pattern, and tall narrow windows. The number of windows indicated the scale of the establishment. At the entrance would be round or square tiled pillars which the women would lean against as they called out to passing men to ask for a light. At least that was the conventional form, and often one did really observe it.

Indeed, some of the houses may have been big and some may have been small, but they all adhered to conventional form.

Conventional form could no longer be seen anywhere in Kameido Third Precinct. Of course I didn't find the house with the woman who giggled softly by my pillow while I nibbled peanuts and looked at photographs. Some of the houses, like the one I peeked into, had turned into gloomy little workshops, others were now little apartment buildings with concrete block walls that looked as if they'd been designed to conceal something that had already gone away. Walking wherever my feet led me, I came out onto the riverbank. I didn't know the name of the river. Walking alongside, I came to the foot of Kurihara Bridge. I hadn't known the name of this bridge either—I found it out from a sign it was written on. There were a couple of temples by the side of the river—Ryuganji and Chojuji. I didn't know them either, though I had a feeling I might have seen or heard their names somewhere. It had never occurred to me to walk along this riverbank. After all, this was the only time I had ever come here by daylight. Twenty years ago I would appear in Kameido Third Precinct after dark, drunk on several glasses of cheap saké, and make my exit in a frantic rush to catch the last train home on the Keihin Tohoku line.

Walking along with an eye on the logs floating on the surface of the river, I came to the foot of Tenjin Bridge. Looking up, I saw before me a high-rise apartment building with a dozen floors or more. It was probably the Kameido Second Precinct public housing project. Who was that acquaintance of mine who lived on the ninth floor of that high-rise housing unit? Tomioka? Tsujii? Or was it Kuga? Come to think of it, maybe it was Tomioka on the seventh floor and Kuga on the ninth. But I didn't just stand there at the bottom of the bridge, thinking I had to confirm at all costs the identity of my acquaintances who lived in that high-rise apartment building. My pilgrimage was not going to come to an end at the foot of Tenjin Bridge. By four o'clock I had to be back at the Nakamura Pawnshop in Warabi. *He's not the man he used to be* . . . Muttering to myself, I turned left in front of the high-rise and started walking towards the crossroads with the bean store. The cupful of roasted broad beans remained in my pocket, untouched.

Chapter 11

MY FIRST ENCOUNTER in twenty years with the mistress of the Nakamura Pawnshop went largely as I had imagined. Her face and general physical appearance were much as I'd pictured: round face, slightly chubby. Unlike Mrs. Ishida, she had a face that did not easily wrinkle. But most of all it was her voice that was exactly as I'd imagined it.

"Well hello, sonny!"

With those few short words, she made me forget a gap of twenty years. "I understand you've been to Ueno today."

"Yes indeed, sonny. My youngest daughter had a baby about a week ago. So I thought I'd pop over there."

"Actually I've just been to Ueno and back myself."

"Yes, so I hear. My daughter-in-law told me that you'd gone to a bank in Ueno or something?"

"Well, I have an old friend there, you see."

"Sonny, that friend you went to see, was it that old—you know—what's his name?"

"Kuga, perhaps?"

"Well now, I wonder. That fellow who was always bowing his head and saying *osu!*"

"Ah, you mean Koga san!"

"Koga san, was that his name. Anyway, he's really made something of himself, hasn't he? Though he often used to come here with you in the old days."

"Oh. Err . . ."

"Oh I remember him well, even now. After all, you and he were about the only people who ever came here carrying a mosquito net."

"Please excuse me for my rudeness earlier on." This last was spoken by the bride of the Nakamuras' son and heir, as she came into the room with some tea for us.

"Mother, you shouldn't be talking here—why not come on inside?"

"No, no, I'm absolutely fine here, really." While answering, I remained sitting on the step that led up from the entrance hall to the interior of the house.

"Oh and sonny—thank you so much for that present you brought us before when you stopped by. You shouldn't have, really."

"My husband should be back after five, so please don't rush off straight away."

"Oh. Err . . ."

"I'm sure you've got lots to talk about, about the old days. I'd like to hear some of the stories too."

"Ooh sonny—did you know our boy?"

"I heard quite a bit about his life in Hokkaido from you."

"Is that so. Well goodness me, it must be all of twenty years, if we're talking about when our boy was at Hokkaido Imperial. Well I never! I've got five grandchildren now, you know sonny."

"I dropped in on the Ishidas earlier, and Mrs. Ishida was saying that she's got, let me see, seven grandchildren, I think she said."

"Really. Their eldest, he's got three children, I believe."

"By the way, Mrs. Nakamura. Just to get back to the mosquito net for a moment, can you remember anything about it?"

"Let me see now. The color was dark green, wasn't it?"

"Yes! That's right, that's right!"

"I also recall it was an extremely *heavy* mosquito net."

Indeed, it had been a heavy mosquito net. I was impressed. Maybe it had something to do with her profession, but Mrs. Nakamura seemed to have truly amazing powers of memory. Or did it have something to do with the territory? Warabi was a town with an awful lot of mosquitoes. According to Little Koga's theory, it was on account of the drainage canals and low-lying terrain. *"Cause this place is only six feet above sea level, ya know."*

Maybe Little Koga had been right. There certainly was a drainage canal nearby. It'd be more accurate to describe it as a stagnant pool, really, the color of liquefied soap. In what month had I asked for the mosquito net to be sent from home? Anyway, it was definitely before I went back to Kyushu for that visit that was supposed to last two weeks. The mosquito net my mother sent me wasn't new. The heaviness was because of the materials, I guess: it was rough to the touch, and if it touched your face a pungent botanical odor would rush up your nose. It was designed for a four-and-a-half-mat room, so in my three-mat room quite a bit of spare material ended up on the floor. When I hung it up, the whole room felt like the inside of a tent. Everything in the room fit right inside, even my little desk and its old-fashioned desk lamp, little more than an aluminum bowl over a lightbulb.

Roughly when was it, I wonder, that I hocked the mosquito net at the Nakamura Pawnshop? According to Mrs. Nakamura, I was with Little Koga at the time; I guess it was probably August or September. I say that because I can still remember trying to smoke out the mosquitoes. That's to say, I took the mosquito net to the Nakamuras at a time of year when I still needed it. In Warabi, you hung your mosquito net up before the rainy season began in May, and you still had it up after the school summer holidays had ended. Except in my case, that is.

It was Little Koga who suggested smoking out the mosquitoes. He fetched the little earthenware charcoal stove from Big Koga's kitchen and placed it at the entrance to my room. The stove was already stuffed with old newspapers crumpled into balls. On top were some very green pine needles, still on the branch, that he'd collected somewhere. We also had some old torn paper fans ready and waiting.

"*Osu*! This'll be a cinch, *shenpai*. Thirty minutes will do it."

But the mosquito fumigation project ended in failure. We placed the stove on the dirt-floor area in front of the entrance to the room, closed up the latticed window on the north side, and flapped the old paper fans around for—what—twelve or thirteen minutes? First Little Koga, who'd proposed the strategy, did some fan-flapping, then I took a turn myself, but neither of us could bear it for more than three minutes. We could hold our breath for one minute at a time, and we could do that three times before we needed a break. Little Koga would come stumbling out of the room, coughing and spluttering. I'd go in. Then I'd come stumbling out of the room, coughing and spluttering. The two of us each did that twice. Then we left the stove where it was in front of the open door to the inner room, closed up the room from the outside with the door that worked like a storm shutter, and went to the well to wash our faces. After that would it have been about thirty minutes that we waited outside? Little Koga did his karate practice. While I stood watching him in my wooden sandals in the already darkening garden, just in front of the house, mosquitoes bit the tops of my bare feet again and again. That part of it couldn't be helped. The problem was what happened afterwards: I just couldn't bear to be in the fumigated three-mat room. Driven out by the pine needle treatment, I spent most of the night in the Ishidas' garden, chasing mosquitoes with a broken fan.

"For some strange reason, I remember that day very well."

"Do you now?"

"Was it right after dinner that you arrived with that fellow who always said '*osu*,' carrying that mosquito net on your shoulders?"

"I wonder."

"And then, two or three hours later, I heard the two of you coming back home, in a very good mood. I remember the sound of your wooden sandals ringing out clearly."

"Mine and Koga san's?"

"Oh yes. One of you was singing some kind of song. Was it the other fellow? Oh my, we laughed and laughed. We told each other you'd probably made a beeline for the bars around the station the moment you left our place."

"I see. Well, something like that could have happened, I guess."

Probably we had done just what Mrs. Nakamura had guessed—headed straight from the Nakamura Pawnshop to the drinking alley in front of Warabi station to shake off the summer heat with a few glasses of shochu. I wonder what sort of price we got for that heavy mosquito net? Would it have been worth more than the old khaki infantryman's greatcoat? No, I doubt that very much.

"So, how was it, I wonder, Mrs. Nakamura?"

"What?"

"Which brought the better price—that coat, or the mosquito net?"

"Coat, you say?"

"My overcoat, Mrs. Nakamura. The one you were kind enough to value at eight hundred yen."

"An eight-hundred-yen overcoat, sonny, that belonged to you?"

As she spoke, the mistress of the Nakamura Pawnshop cast her eyes upon the overcoat I had taken off and laid on the doorstep beside me. "An eight-hundred-yen overcoat, eh?"

"No no—when I talk about my overcoat, I don't mean this one here."

"It's a very nice overcoat, isn't it, sonny."

"You think so? Well, thank you."

"English wool, isn't it?" she said, running a finger along the coat as she spoke.

"Yes, err . . ."

"It's really a very nice piece of cloth you've got there, sonny."

This time she reached out for the overcoat and laid it over her knee.

"Really? It's good of you to say so, Mrs. Nakamura."

"The pattern's rather elegant too, and just right for a man of your years, sonny."

"You really think so? Well then, Mrs. Nakamura, just for fun, how much do you think you'd be able to lend me now, if I pledged this coat?"

"Now, you say?"

"Only asking for fun, you understand."

"I see . . . now, you say . . ."

She spread out the sleeves of the overcoat, across her knees. Then delicately she spread out the hem of the coat on the tatami mat. The moment she did that, my overcoat suddenly took on the look of a real pawnshop pledge.

"Well, sonny, it really is a nice piece of cloth, and the pattern's not bad. But I have to say the cut is . . . well, how can I put it? A bit old-fashioned."

"Oh . . ."

"It's this collar. This style of collar—it's not really what people look for these days."

She ran her finger along the lapels to illustrate.

"I see, uh . . . the collar style."

"Anyway sonny, how much do you want for it?"

"Well, let's see . . . just for the sake of argument, let's see now, maybe I'd settle for five thousand yen."

"*Five thousand yen!?*"

"Well, just for the sake of argument, you know."

"I don't mean to be rude, sonny, but I really think five thousand yen's going a bit too far."

"I wonder."

"But sonny, take a look at this."

So saying, the mistress of the Nakamura Pawnshop seized the back of the collar with both hands and turned it smartly inside out. A few faint black grease stains showed on the inside of the collar. My grease.

"And this elbow's also quite badly worn."

"Hmm . . ."

"And what about this spot, near the seat?"

She flipped over the coat as if she were turning over a dried mackerel and showed me the back. "The wool's already been worn quite thin here. Though it's the kind of thing you tend not to notice when you're wearing it all the time."

"But you know, Mrs. Nakamura, twenty years have passed since then!"

"Twenty years?"

"No, of course I don't mean I've been wearing this overcoat for twenty years. I'm not talking about *this* overcoat, which is only . . . well let me see now, I bought it sometime after my younger daughter was born, and she's five now, I think, seeing as she's in her last year at nursery school. So I can't have been wearing this overcoat for more than four years or so, Mrs. Nakamura."

"Four years is a good lifetime for an overcoat, sonny."

"Well, yes, I suppose so . . ."

"This is made in England, right? That's why you've got four years' wear out of it. But oh dear, sonny, just take a look at this."

And so the mistress of Nakamura's went on, sounding just like Petrovich. Petrovich? Indeed, I'm talking about the drunken, one-eyed tailor with the pockmarked face, the one Akaky Akakievich took his worn-out old overcoat to, in hopes of getting it repaired.

As he made his way up the stairs to Petrovich's (these stairs, to describe them accurately, were running with water and slops, and were saturated with that strong smell of spirit which makes the eyes smart and is a perpetual feature of all backstairs in Petersburg), Akaky Akakievich was already beginning to wonder how much Petrovich would charge and making up his mind not to pay more than two rubles . . .

Akaky Akakievich was really just clutching at straws. However, Petrovich brusquely turned down his request. Here's how it happened:

"What on earth's that?" Petrovich said, inspecting with his solitary eye every part of Akaky's uniform, beginning with the collar and sleeves, then the back, tails and buttonholes. All of this was very familiar territory, as it was his own work, but every tailor usually carries out this sort of inspection when he has a customer.

"I've er . . . come . . . Petrovich, that overcoat you know, the cloth . . . you see, it's quite strong in other places, only a little dusty. This makes it look old, but in fact it's quite new. Just a bit . . . you know . . . on the back and a little worn on one shoulder, and a bit . . . you know, on the other, that's all. Only a small job . . ."

Petrovich took the "dressing-gown," laid it out on the table, took a long look at it, shook his head, reached out to the windowsill for his round snuffbox bearing the portrait of some general—exactly which one is hard to say, as someone had poked his finger through the place where his face should have been and it was pasted over with a square piece of paper.

Petrovich took a pinch of snuff, held the coat up to the light, gave it another thorough scrutiny and shook his head again. Then he placed it with the lining upwards, shook his head once more, removed the snuffbox lid with the pasted-over general, filled his nose with snuff, replaced the lid, put the box away somewhere and finally said: "No, I can't mend that. It's in a terrible state!"

With these words Akaky Akakievich's heart sank.

"And why not, Petrovich?" he asked in the imploring voice of a child. "It's only a bit worn on the shoulders. Really, you could easily patch it up."

"I've got plenty of patches, plenty," said Petrovich. "But I can't sew them all up together. The coat's absolutely rotten. It'll fall to pieces if you so much as touch it with a needle."

"Well, if it falls to pieces you can patch it up again."

"But it's too far gone. There's nothing for the patches to hold on to. You can hardly call it cloth at all. One gust of wind and the whole lot will blow away."

"But patch it up just a little. It can't, hm, be, well . . ."

"I'm afraid it can't be done, sir," replied Petrovich firmly. "It's too far gone. You'd be better off if you cut it up for the winter and made some good leggings with it, because socks aren't any good in the really cold weather. The Germans invented leggings as they thought they could make money out of them." (Petrovich liked to have a dig at the Germans.) "As for the coat, you'll have to have a new one, sir."

The word "new" made Akaky's eyes cloud over and everything in the room began to swim around. All he could see clearly was the pasted-over face of the general on Petrovich's snuffbox.

Of course, the mistress of the Nakamura Pawnshop was not

Petrovich. Far from being pockmarked, her face was round, glossy and almost without wrinkles. Far from being one-eyed, she had a pair of clear and round, if not exactly large, eyes. Why, then, did she suddenly look like Petrovich? Could it have been the way she handled my overcoat? The truth is, her handling was consummate perfection. And those eyes of hers would not overlook the tiniest tear in the stitching of a seam.

"Oh dear, sonny, just take a look at this," she said, pushing the forefinger of her right hand through the top buttonhole on my overcoat.

"This button, and the one just below it. These are the two buttons most often done and undone on an overcoat. When you put on your scarf, or take it off. And sometimes people reach into an inside pocket with their coat still on, to take out their wallet or something. You too, sonny."

"I see . . ."

"So the stitching around these two buttons is frayed to pieces, as you can see. And it's not just the buttonholes. They've been roughly treated, you see, so the area around the buttonholes is a mess as well."

"I see, I see. Every single little thing you say is absolutely correct, Mrs. Nakamura. I must admit I'd never noticed the little things you point out. But you know . . . eight hundred yen twenty years ago is equivalent to at least eight *thousand* yen today, no? Not that I'm the kind of person who knows anything about that kind of thing, but as a matter of plain common sense, surely the ratio would be something like that, wouldn't it, Mrs. Nakamura?"

"You're saying that eight hundred yen twenty years ago would be eight thousand now?"

"Yes—although it's only a rough comparison, of course."

"It'd be a lot more than that, sonny."

"What?"

"But it all depends on what sort of item you're talking about. It's a different story for overcoats."

"But overcoats were the very example I was talking about. Specifically, my own overcoat."

"Well anyway, the thing is that nobody wears coats like this anymore. And I'm not just talking about being out of fashion, you know. Young folk go everywhere by car these days, and the buildings are all heated as well. And then I'm pretty sure the winters have been getting warmer the last few years. I've lived a long life, you know, and I really do think that. But why is that, eh, sonny?"

"But Mrs. Nakamura, you're still young!"

"Twenty years may sound like a long time, but when you come to think of it, it seems to have slipped by just like that."

"But Mrs. Nakamura, you seem to have forgotten about the overcoat I had twenty years ago."

"*Your* overcoat, sonny?"

"That's right. Although at the time it was a good enough overcoat for you to value it at eight hundred yen."

"Eight hundred yen, you say, twenty years ago?"

"That's right. It was eight hundred yen, no mistake about it. It was exactly the same as the rent I was paying for my room at the Ishidas, so I couldn't possibly be mistaken."

"Well, sonny, if we were looking after it as collateral for eight hundred yen, it must have been a very fine overcoat indeed."

"No, it wasn't that special."

"You don't say so . . ." With these words the mistress of the Nakamura Pawnshop started to fold up my overcoat, which lay open on her knee. Her manner somehow suggested a world-weary pawnbroker at the end of a lengthy negotiation with a customer that has failed to produce a compromise on the value of an item. The customer had been hoping to hock it for five thousand yen. The mistress had demurred. The ensuing battle of words had continued for some thirty minutes and ended without agreement. The mistress started to fold away the overcoat on her knee. "Last chance to change your mind, sonny. Why not take what's on offer? Go round to the other places if you like, but I doubt you'll get more than four thousand for it. How about it, sonny? Are you going to carry it round two or three more shops? Or shall we look after it for you here? Can't help thinking you'll be wasting your time wandering around the pawnshops out there, on a cold day like this . . ."

But at that very moment something unexpected occurred. Just as the mistress of the Nakamura Pawnshop was lifting up the hem of my overcoat to fold it on top of her knee, two or three roasted broad beans tumbled out of a pocket in the overcoat and skittered across the tatami mats.

"Oh!" Mrs. Nakamura exclaimed in surprise, and picked up one of the beans. There was something more significant to this, however, than the mere fact of two or three roasted broad beans suddenly tumbling onto the floor.

"Sonny, I remember now!"

"What?"

"You know—eight hundred yen! The eight-hundred-yen overcoat."

"Eight hundred yen, you say?"

"That's right!"

"But Mrs. Nakamura, you can't possibly mean this overcoat's only worth eight hundred yen, the same as the one twenty years ago? Besides, that one was only an infantryman's greatcoat, Mrs. Nakamura."

"Yes, yes! It was a khaki coat, wasn't it, sonny? The kind soldiers used to wear long ago."

"Yes, that's right, that's right."

"Well, it really is most peculiar. You know, sonny, it's all thanks to these beans. They popped out and skittered across the floor, right? And then, sonny, well it's really most peculiar, but that old soldier's coat you had twenty years ago, well—one time a monkey nut fell out of the pocket of *that* coat. I just suddenly remembered that."

"A monkey nut?"

"Yes, you know—a peanut."

"With or without the shell?"

"Hmm, now you're asking . . . yes, yes, that's it—an unshelled peanut. There were bits of broken shells in the bottom of the pocket, I recall."

However, that was as far as Mrs. Nakamura's memory would take us. I asked what date it was twenty years ago when the unshelled peanut popped out of the pocket of the khaki greatcoat, but she didn't know. The one thing I did know was where the nut came from. Needless to say, the unshelled peanut that popped out of the pocket of the khaki greatcoat twenty years ago, like the roasted broad bean that popped from my English-made overcoat twenty years later, had been bought at the bean store next to the traffic lights. But had the peanut been left over from *that* night, or another? I didn't know. Nor whether that was the last time Mrs. Nakamura handled my coat.

I was looking at the big padlock on the door of the Nakamura storehouse. Seen from outside, the storehouse looked like a separate building from the pawnshop with its latticed doors. But in fact, it was possible to access the storehouse from inside the pawnshop. I tried to imagine the gloomy interior, behind the thick metal doors with the big padlock hanging from them. How many times was my khaki greatcoat carried into that storehouse, I wonder? And when was the last time? Whenever it was, there seemed no possibility my khaki greatcoat might still be in there. At any rate, it wasn't registered in the Nakamura account books. In fact, according to Mrs. Nakamura, the account book for twenty years ago no longer existed. In other words, the old khaki infantryman's greatcoat I was wearing when I came up to Tokyo from that little country town in Chikuzen to take the Early Bird Exam no longer existed—not in the Nakamura Pawnshop storehouse, nor in any written record. All that was left were a few fragments of peanut shell lingering faintly at the bottom of Mrs. Nakamura's memory well.

I don't suppose my overcoat can possibly have been anything more or less than that. That much was clear enough from her response to my final question.

"All right then, Mrs. Nakamura, there's just one last thing I'd like to ask you."

Mrs. Nakamura had picked up the two or three broad beans that had fallen onto the tatami, and was rolling them around on the palm of her hand.

"I know it was twenty years ago, but do you recall ever hearing talk of that greatcoat of mine being stolen by somebody? At one of the bars next to the station or somewhere?"

"That soldier's greatcoat of yours, sonny?"

"That's right. For instance, might I myself have said something like that to you, Mrs. Nakamura?"

"But sonny, if you'd said it yourself, you'd surely remember it yourself."

"Well, you're right, of course, but the fact is there are things I've forgotten myself that you still remember. Like those peanut shells in the bottom of the pocket! There's a case in point for you."

"But sonny, now you're asking too much."

"Too much? Well, maybe I *am* asking too much. It was twenty years ago, after all. But . . . the peanut shells, you know? If you could manage one more flash of memory like that . . ."

"But sonny, never mind memory and all that. The thing is, who on earth would *want* to steal that soldier's coat of yours?" And with that, the mistress of the Nakamura Pawnshop burst out laughing. I could see that she was missing four front teeth, two each top and bottom.

Two or three minutes later I emerged from the interior of the Nakamura Pawnshop through the latticed door. After I said my farewells and closed the door, I took the paper bag of roasted broad beans out of my coat pocket and quietly left them on the inside door-step as a little souvenir.

Chapter 12

THERE WAS NO particular significance to my decision to make Ochanomizu Bridge the site for meeting Yamakawa. One time, Yamakawa and I missed each other at Ochanomizu. I guess it was about a month ago. Due to an exceedingly foolish illusion on my part, I went to the wrong café in Ochanomizu. I arrived at JNR Ochanomizu station about an hour earlier than our appointment. Was it six o'clock we'd agreed on? If so, then I'd arrived in Ochanomizu at about five and walked past the café where I was supposed to meet Yamakawa about an hour before the time we'd agreed.

I didn't pass in front of that café just by chance. I didn't exactly go out of my way to pass it either, but the thing is I'd never been to the Tiger Café before. So I walked in roughly what I took to be the direction of the café according to what Yamakawa had told me on the phone, and a sign saying *Tiger Café* came into view around the place where I would have expected to find it. It was a vertical sign, mottled black and yellow, with "Tiger" written on it in big, simple characters, running from top to bottom. I thought: I see, that makes sense. Apparently Yamakawa uses this café for business meetings, and even if you were meeting someone for the first time there'd probably be no problem. You had to be careful, because there were an awful lot of cafés on this street, but you could hardly fail to find a signboard like this one. The Tiger Café has the further advantage that for some mysterious reason it doesn't get crowded.

Each and every café around Ochanomizu tends to be packed with students—even I knew that from things I'd seen and heard. They really are crowded. And it's only natural that they should be crowded. Why is it, then, that the Tiger Café alone always has plenty of room? Yamakawa says he doesn't know the reason himself. Of course I didn't know either, but that didn't much matter. Actually, it wouldn't have mattered that much even if it had been crowded. Yamakawa and I weren't meeting up for some important discussion. Of course, we weren't just going to sit around sipping coffee or tea and chatting idly about this and that. Nor were we just going to kill time the way university students do. In short, nothing required me to sit in a café for a long time face-to-face with Yamakawa.

I walked past the sign of the Tiger Café. Then, jostling with college students all the way, I walked along the street with all the cafés, towards the main exit of Ochanomizu station. This was because I had left the station by the rear exit, close to Nikolai Cathedral. Having walked round to the main exit, I now started walking in the direction of the bridge. Not that I had any particular plan in mind about how to kill the hour or so before the appointment. I wandered idly across the bridge. Then I waited at the traffic lights in a big mass of people and went over the crossroads. Most of the people who crossed with me went rushing down the stairs into the Ochanomizu subway station. Maybe I'd pop over to Yushima Tenjin Shrine? The thought occurred to me after I'd negotiated the crossroads, turned right and walked a little way, just as I started to go up the stairs on my left that led up to another bridge. An hour would be plenty of time to stroll over there and back.

I had been to Yushima Tenjin just once before. Had it been about a year before? You could say it had been a matter of chance that time as well. An acquaintance of mine had been running a small publishing house near there for well over a decade, producing books for elementary and junior high school pupils, and I'd been thinking of going to see him for some time without ever getting round to it. But then one day I got on the newly opened subway line from Kita-Senju, and the third or fourth station turned out to be Yushima Tenjin. On the spur of the moment I got off the train, met this old acquaintance of mine for the first time in well over a decade, and the two of us went out to the famous shrine and had a look at the memorial stone tablet erected to honor the pre-war novelist Kyoka Izumi. Then again, maybe I wasn't heading out from Kita-Senju but on my way back home *towards* Kita-Senju. Either way, I didn't set out for Yushima Tenjin that day—I just happened to be passing by. I haven't seen that acquaintance again since then, either. Nor was the relationship between him and me anything particularly worth discussing here.

So it wasn't on account of my acquaintance that it occurred to me to go to Yushima Tenjin. Nor did I feel a pressing urge to see Kyoka's memorial again. Right in front of the Kyoka Izumi Memorial they'd just put up one of those new-style high-rise condominiums, and it was shining like silver. Did it have a dozen or more floors? Actually it could have had more than twenty. The silver condominium looked taller than the literary memorial on the hill at Yushima Tenjin. Was that an outrage? Of course, Yushima is not only the Yushima of Yushima Tenjin, not only the Yushima of Kyoka Izumi—it is also the Yushima of shiny silver new-style high-rise condominiums, the Yushima of the newly opened subway line. And what I'm saying is in no way limited to Kyoka's memorial and Yushima.

The reason I thought of going to Yushima Tenjin was that I reckoned the journey there and back would be just long enough to kill the hour I had in hand until I was due to meet up with Yamakawa. That's not to say, however, that I had no desire whatever to have a look at the grounds of Yushima Tenjin and the literary memorial there. I even thought that once there I might buy a fortune-telling slip. I like to visit literary memorials, and I'm not a person who is averse to seeing scenic spots and historic sites in general. If I go to Nikko, I want to see Toshogu Shrine. If I go to Toshogu Shrine, I want to see Higurashimon Gate, and I want to see Jingoro Hidari's carving of a sleeping cat. As a matter of fact, I've stood on tiptoe, buffeted by crowds of tourists and at risk of being pushed down the stone steps at any moment, just to get a look at those buildings and sculptures so familiar to me from picture postcards. I've been to the famous Kegon waterfall, though I came home having only *heard* it. Unfortunately it was a very foggy day and the waterfall could not be seen. *"But the Kegon waterfall is in that direction."* That was how the guide from the bus tour company explained it, sounding almost as if it were half her fault that we couldn't see the waterfall. Of course she only spoke that way for form's sake . . . and it can't possibly have been the first day ever that it was too cloudy to see the waterfall. The guide was just dutifully explaining the situation to us, the way she'd been taught to. Half the responsibility for the waterfall not being visible lies with the foggy weather, but the other half lies with me . . . I'm sure the girls are taught to convey that sense of responsibility to the customers. At least it got through to me, and it probably got through to the other tourists as well. It's all right darling, it's not your fault we can't see the waterfall. It's quite amusing, really, to listen to the sound of the waterfall and imagine it somewhere behind the dense fog; at least I'm pretty sure the people who followed the bus guide away from the waterfall-viewing point were so persuaded in their hearts.

When I went up to Komoro, I wanted to go to Kaikoen Park, famous as the site of the ruins of Komoro Castle. I also wanted to take a peek at the Toson Shimazaki Museum, and to see the archery ground mentioned in *Chikuma River Sketches*. Of course I also observed the Chikuma River from the observation deck. The river had been dammed up by Chubu Electric Power, and the characters advertising Yushien Garden on the sandbar in the middle of the river were dwarfed by the four characters of the electricity company's name. I guess it was the same kind of relationship as the one between Kyoka Izumi Memorial and the shiny silver high-rise in Yushima.

I am a person who is profoundly ignorant of the history of every country, east or west. Though it's not something I'm proud to admit, Japan is no exception. I'm also very poorly read when it comes to historical novels. I'm almost totally ignorant of anything that has to do with fortifications, needless to say, and the same goes for swords and armor. I don't know what the Komoro clan used to get up to in the Edo era, and I don't have any idea what Toshogu Shrine in Nikko was built for. Why is it, then, that despite my ignorance I just cannot deliberately ignore places like that? Does it have something to do with adhering to convention? Or is it because I'm a country boy? That's probably got something to do with it too. But whatever the reason, you can bet that I'm the sort of person who in Moscow would head straight for the cemetery behind Novodevichy Convent where you find Gogol's grave. I'm also the sort of person who in Leningrad would want to go sightseeing on Nevsky Prospect, and cross the Neva River, inseparably bound up with Nevsky Prospect in my mind. I'd also want to stand on Isaakievsky Bridge where, in Gogol's "The Nose," Yakovlevich the barber stood as he wrapped the nose of Collegiate Assessor Kovalyov in a bit of old cloth and desperately tried to get rid of it by chucking it into the Neva. Speaking of bridges, the rumors about the ghost of Akaky Akakievich haunting the streets of Saint Petersburg and ripping the coats off people's backs first started in the vicinity of Kalinkin Bridge. And the place where Akaky's ghost made its final appearance, before disappearing for good into the night, was Obukhov Bridge.

Of course, some people just aren't interested in places like that. You couldn't even call it a mystery if some people were not just uninterested, but positively contemptuous of places like that. Whether it's Leningrad, Moscow, Nikko or Komoro, people have a right not to go sightseeing in places they don't want to see. They're free to think that it's quite enough to see those famous places on picture postcards. Maybe that's precisely why picture postcards are mass-produced in such numbers: for people who think that way. And if the number of people who thought that way increased till it was the same as the number of picture postcards, then scenic spots or historic sites might not get quite so crowded. In practice, however, things are going in the exact opposite direction, and I hear that both Nikko and Komoro are attracting more and more sightseers. I daresay it's the same story in Moscow and Leningrad. It would appear, then, that people who show no interest in scenic spots and historic sites are in the minority.

Truth to tell, I have something close to a sneaking admiration for this minority. Admiration? No, maybe it would be better to say I'm interested in them. Interested in people who're able to gaze with contempt on people who're interested in places they aren't interested in. Let me put it another way. It's the kind of interest contained in the following question: Is it really possible to believe that you alone are not being gazed upon with contempt? If so maybe I *should* admire that happy minority. However, I doubt the existence of this admirable minority. Why? Because if I'm capable of looking on someone else with contempt, surely I cannot state with absolute confidence that someone else isn't also gazing at *me* with contempt. And because the reverse is also true.

However, in this case, maybe other people don't matter at all. What I mean is: Why is it that a person who not only has very little knowledge about scenic spots and historic sites, but does not even make the effort to acquire such knowledge, nonetheless finds it impossible to ignore those places? Of course I'm not talking about the great majority of people who flock to scenic spots and historic sites, but about myself. Why is this so? It's probably because of a self-contradiction. Because when I was halfway up the stone steps leading to Higurashimon Gate at Toshogu Shrine in Nikko, being pushed backwards by the posteriors of the package tourists following their purple flags, starting to fear that the whole crowd might collapse like dominoes, I cannot deny that I viewed each and every one of those tourists with their cameras hanging from their shoulders with contempt. When I was standing precariously on tiptoe, bent backwards like an archer's bow or a sumo wrestler who's been shoved back to the very edge of the ring, I gazed with contempt upon the backs of the tourists who were forcing me into such a posture. What a ridiculous sort of contempt!

Another time, when I was waiting in line for my turn to use the telescope at the observation deck at Kaikoen Park in Komoro, I gazed with contempt upon a mother who made her own child cut into the line and put a ten-yen coin in the slot. In the end, however, I too put a ten-yen coin in the slot and peeked through the telescope across the Chikuma River to Mount Asama, looking just like it did on the picture postcards. What a ridiculous, self-contradiction-riddled contempt!

Probably the only reason I went along sightseeing with these contemptible masses of people at these so-called scenic spots and historic sites was this extremely ridiculous self-contradiction. Probably the reason I felt a faint sense of admiration for people who could consciously ignore such places was that I could not detect in their attitude my own kind of extremely ridiculous self-contradiction. I felt something akin to admiration for a life free of contradictions. But of course I can never be one of them. And every time I go off to a scenic spot or historic site I'm painfully reminded of that fact. You might even say that the reason I can't seem to ignore scenic spots and historic sites is that they're such good places for painfully reminding me of my own self-contradictions.

Incidentally, isn't it a bit of an exaggeration to call the monument to Kyoka Izumi that stands on the grounds of Yushima Tenjin Shrine a historic site? That's probably so, it's far too exaggerated. But whether it's an exaggeration or not, it's a fact that I started walking in that direction, and it is also a fact that I was thinking I might buy a fortune-telling slip at the shrine. As proof of that, I believe I even started humming a song about a couple of characters in one of Kyoka's novels as I walked along: *If you go through Yushima you bring to mind / the love of Chikara and Otsuta*. In the end, however, I returned to Ochanomizu without going to Yushima Tenjin that day. I'd been planning to go round the back of Tokyo Medical and Dental University, then up the hill towards Yushima Tenjin, but somehow I strayed off into the hotel district. Motels with automatically opening and closing doors. Spaceship-style rotating double beds. Etcetera, etcetera. Wandering around amid all the signs, aimlessly of course, I found that the appointed time for meeting Yamakawa was almost upon me.

However, I was not only unable to get to Yushima Tenjin, I failed even to meet Yamakawa. Returning to the main exit of JNR Ochanomizu station, I turned left. Then I walked down the same street of cafés as before, looking for the sign of the Tiger. I didn't need to search again for the vertical, yellow-black mottled sign, for it was right in front of my eyes. I went in. I could not see Yamakawa. The clock showed five or six minutes before the appointed time of six o'clock. The café was not exactly empty of customers. However, I managed to secure a small table for two by a window some distance from the entrance. I ordered a tomato juice and waited for Yamakawa. I liked my spot. From the window I could look down at the platform of JNR Ochanomizu station. Seated here, I felt certain I wouldn't get cross if I were made to wait a little.

I finished the tomato juice, thought for a bit, then ordered a whisky and water. Truth to tell, it was a spot that made you feel like having a proper drink. Looking down at the platform of JNR Ochanomizu station, I had a couple of whiskies with water. I started to get a little bit cross as I was ordering the third. Of course the reason was that Yamakawa still hadn't shown up. I polished off the third whisky and water, then got up from my seat. The clock showed just after seven. I walked out of the door and looked above me and to my left, to check the sign for the Tiger Café. The Tiger Café, however, was directly underneath the sign, which meant I had just emerged from one door further up the street. In a sudden hurry, I opened the door of the real Tiger Café. There was no sign of Yamakawa. I inquired with one of the waitresses.

"Excuse me—was there a customer in here who was on his own and seemed to be waiting for somebody?"

"Dunno."

"It would have been a man. About the same height as me."

"About what time would it have been?"

"I think he'd have been here, on his own, from about six."

"I wonder if it could have been the fellow who was sitting at that table over there . . ."

"That one next to the window?"

"Yes, that one."

"I would guess that the ashtray had a mountain of cigarette butts in it?"

"Yes, it did. I guess it could have been the customer who was sitting there."

"Wait—he might have ordered whisky and water."

"Err . . . boss, can you come here a moment?"

"Welcome!"

"No no, I'm not here for a drink."

"Oh, sorry. Looking for that customer who just went out?"

"What?"

"He seems to be looking for that customer who was drinking whisky and water over there by the window."

"That's correct. What time did he leave?"

"If it's that fellow you're talking about, well, I think he only left just this minute. Almost the same time you came in."

The reason I had agreed to meet Yamakawa on Ochanomizu Bridge this time was that kind of thing had happened in the past. My illusion was all the fault of the sign for the Tiger Café. That sign was just too prominent. When I arrived an hour before the appointed time, I emerged from the Nikolai Cathedral exit and then, walking round to the main exit, as instructed by Yamakawa over the telephone, I immediately spotted the sign. I didn't just spot it—the unusual vertical signboard, mottled black and yellow, seemed to adhere to the back of my eyeball with a mysterious intensity. When I returned from my stroll around Yushima, I was coming from the opposite direction—from the main exit this time, heading towards the Nikolai Cathedral exit. Then, looking up at the tiger-striped sign that seemed to have adhered to the back of my eyeball, I opened the door of the shop right before it. An exceedingly ordinary illusion. And that's the reason I'm waiting for Yamakawa on Ochanomizu Bridge—nothing more, nothing less.

By the way, do I have to explain to anyone about my relationship with Yamakawa? Perhaps I do.

When and how did I first meet him? What mutual economic interests do we have? Or are there no such connections between us? Why did he get divorced? And did his divorce have any connection with me, past or present? What sort of life did he live and does he live now? Who is this Yamakawa guy anyway?

I can give almost complete answers to the above seven questions. To kick things off, the answer to the first question is "I've forgotten," or "I can't bring it to mind," and my answer to the second and third questions is "none at all." Now, to answer questions 4 to 7 I would have to stand on this bridge for at least another hour or so. Alas, the clock already shows six o'clock—precisely the time of our rendezvous. So we must conclude that unless he suffers an illusion like the one that afflicted me a month ago, there's no way I'm going to be standing here on this bridge for another hour or so. Of course one can't absolutely rule out the possibility of him falling prey to another illusion. After all, in the case of the Tiger Café incident, the very cause of the illusion was that I had confirmed the details clearly in advance.

Then again, could it possibly be that it is I, yet again, who is under some illusion? Surely not! Such a thing could hardly happen. Of course I cannot absolutely rule out the possibility, but unless that's the case, he really should put in an appearance very shortly, right here on this bridge. And in that case, it would be only natural for me not to start answering questions 4 to 7. Not only would I naturally not start answering the questions, I'd probably need to start adding extra questions too. After all, his habit of making frequent phone calls, so late at night that it's really a nuisance, is a sign that something is about to end, or begin.

"Well, I'll tell you the details when we meet up."

That was always his last line before hanging up. So, had something ended? Or started? Of course I would have to meet up with him to get the details. I did know that it had something to do with a woman. *Come hell or high water, I'm damn well going to get married again!* That's the gist of the details Yamakawa would provide, if

I may summarize them as briefly as possible in my own words. At least when it came to women, his eyes were focused on the future. I already knew of four women who might have some connection with that future. Four? It could even have been five. Whichever one it is, tonight I'll probably wind up going to her place with Yamakawa. For after all, it's been Yamakawa's custom to take me with him to the homes of women who may have some connection with his future, one after the other. Wherever we've been out drinking, that's been the final station on our journey, so to speak. And almost every time, we've had our last drinks there, sometimes carrying on right through to dawn.

So maybe he would have been far more suitable than I to be the hero of a novel. No reason he shouldn't have been. Why was it then, that despite all this, I had completely forgotten about Yamakawa while standing on this bridge? Probably it was because he was someone who was absolutely unconnected with me twenty years ago. I mean, unconnected to the reasons why I suddenly woke up early one morning and went dashing out of the house. Unconnected to the little country town in Chikuzen. Unconnected to the Early Bird Exam, Warabi, the Koga brothers, Kuga, the colonel's daughter, and Yoko san. Also unconnected, of course, to my old-style khaki infantryman's greatcoat. In short, absolutely unconnected to me as I was twenty years ago, and thus also unconnected with my daylong pilgrimage. Yes indeed, one day I was waiting on Ochanomizu Bridge for a particular man who was absolutely unconnected to me as I was twenty years ago, and unconnected with the one-day pilgrimage that had started with my sudden early rising. It was I who had gone wandering around looking for a lost coat. It was I who was waiting for Yamakawa. It was that sort of a day.

Beyond this bridge there's another bridge that looks like a dome. That bridge—what bridge is it? The blue and red neon that shone above it was, naturally enough, blurred in its reflection on the dark surface of the water. The sky above the bridge was already darkening, too. I put both hands in the pockets of my overcoat and stood there looking at the passersby walking to my left and right. However, nobody was wearing that khaki coat. And of course Yamakawa wouldn't be wearing it.